Isaiah Kumasi

By Chris Gray

A huge thanks to those people who have supported me with writing this book. Special appreciation is due to Malcy Dixon and Big Steve in Aberdeen for their continual encouragement and feedback, Shaun Taylor for his excellent artwork and my two best friends for nurturing the self-belief that such a project was possible.

This book is dedicated to the many young people that I have tried to help and support so that you might enjoy a brighter future. Your collective stories have inspired me to write just one tale.

I hope I've done it justice.

Part One

'Let parents bequeath to their children not riches, but the spirit of reverence.'
Plato

Chapter 1

Thursday October 2nd 2014.

I was impatiently leaning over the railings, outside of our flat. Being six floors up, I had a panoramic view of the nearby row of shops. I stared at their cheap, faded signs, mangled security shutters and multiple layers of graffiti that appeared to be fighting each other for prominence. In a few days the next group of naughty lads doing community service, would arrive and have to clean it up. They'd stand in their yellow hi-visibility vests, half-heartedly scrubbing away until the site was clean. By the next morning, there'd be a solitary, fresh spray-painted tag; a little 'fuck you' from the chair of the local graffiti artists.

The shops tended for all the luxury needs of the local population. There was the off-licence selling cheap, strong booze; a grocery store where the counter sat behind thick bulletproof security glass and, of course, the resident bookmaker where losing betting slips, torn-up in rage, would surround the entrance like a box of cheap confetti.

The names of the shops somehow represented the mediocrity of the local population. There was a store selling second-hand gear for toddlers called 'Baby Ga Ga'; an ink refill place for your printer named 'Alan Cartridge', and I even objected to the name of my favourite local kebab shop; 'Abra-kebabra'.

Below me, screaming and fighting over a discarded shopping trolley, were the four Critchlow kids. They should have been at school, but their Mum decided that they would benefit from a home education. She'd rather they did housework than homework, while she sat in her filthy armchair eating multi-packs of chocolate, smoking roll-ups, and devouring daytime television. I wasn't sure that's what she did, but I couldn't imagine her dilapidated front door was the gateway to a thriving home-based business empire.

Sharon was her name, a big, fat thing with manky teeth and dirty fingernails. Her outer layers of clothes cascaded, like a tent, over her considerable, undulating figure. She would always wear bobbly, stretched black leggings which appeared welded to her fat, cellulite ridden legs.

It was now a matter of time before her flat door was flung open and she would appear screaming the usual vile obscenities, prompting her flock of horrible kids to have to retreat to her lair.

The kids were all slightly different colours, and I suspected each had their own dad, but as no males entered their property, except of course the education welfare officer, my theory remained unconfirmed.

I flipped my hood up, not because it was cold but because it was a habit. It was something that I indiscriminately did when I was bored, which was most of the time. I reached into my front pocket and brought out a spliff - there was only half left. This initiated my first major decision of the day: Shall I, shan't I? I put it back for later.

I checked my mobile phone, again. I did this religiously, but more so when I was twitchy. It hadn't bleeped, so why did I think I'd received a message? It was like checking the front door every five minutes to see if there was anyone there, despite no one knocking. I had perfected a strange, almost military routine when I was edgy. It went something like: check your phone; put your hood up; take it down and then check your phone again. I was thinking of adding it to my CV under the heading; 'Hobbies and Interests.' It couldn't have been lamer than my current offering:

I enjoy playing computer games, watching football (provided it's not Manchester United) and socialising with me mates.

I couldn't think why I never got short-listed for job interviews; perhaps all employers were Manchester United fans? Or was it because, despite the bullshit I gave the Jobcentre, I didn't actually apply for any jobs?

What time was he going to get home? I'd been waiting for forty-five minutes, maybe an hour. I knew exactly how long it took to get from the prison to our east London flat as I'd made the trip on several occasions during his sentence. What I didn't know was what time he'd be released. Would it be first thing in the morning? Would the screws leave him hanging around just to piss him off, one last time? God knows. I checked my phone again, only on this occasion with a purpose. 11.48am. Surely, he'd be home soon.

I hadn't seen him for six months. Our meetings for the preceding two and a half years had been limited to visiting time at the prison. Those had been very confused and emotional exchanges. On my last trip, I detected things were not right as soon as he walked into the visitors' hall. He was starchy, twitchy, and confrontational. He'd refused to look me in the eye before announcing that I shouldn't visit him again. He described how everything was 'doing his head in'. The prison overcrowding meant he was banged up on 23-hour lockdown. He explained how his cellmate was driving him mad with his noisy wanking, heavy snoring, and the commentary he gave him every day on the consistency of his morning shit. When he spoke about him, I could sense his rage. The spit exploded out of his mouth as he described the intense hatred he'd developed. Most of this spittle appeared to be going over my face, but out of politeness, I wiped it off when I knew he wasn't looking.

He was a man on the edge, like a dodgy Chinese firework ready to go off in someone's face. I just needed to make sure it wasn't mine.

I obeyed his wish, and I didn't revisit him. My communication was limited to a poorly written monthly letter, which he ignored. Then a few weeks ago, I received a telephone call; he was to be released.

I was gripped with excitement in the days leading up to his return home. I'd spent hours organising how we were going to celebrate. It was probably the most planning I'd engaged in since unsuccessfully stealing the cake stand takings at a school summer fête. I had before us a cracking cultural agenda of activities involving drinks down the local; a couple of hours in the casino; a trip to the strip club to see his favourite Hungarian; and I'd even got us tickets for the West Ham game on Saturday. But as time ticked past and as I draped myself further over the railings, I started to get a familiar feeling, and one I'd had many times in my life, the deep sense of disappointment.

Would he even come straight home? I knew he'd be gagging for a beer, so perhaps he'd head straight into the nearest boozer. Devo was naturally ballsy, so walking into a strange pub in someone else's manor wouldn't bother him at all. Within the hour, he'd be talking to a few of the locals, regaling them with his stories and buying them rounds of shooters. Within three hours he'd have taken offence to something one of them had said and offered them out for a fight. He was a character and not everyone's cup of tea, but he was my big brother, and I wouldn't have a bad word said about him.

I was looking forward to seeing him out of his prison uniform and back into his designer gear. Devo and his designer gear, fucking hell! He never went out unless he looked immaculate and that would involve tending to his own clothes. He would rather donate his bollocks to science than have Mum do his washing. Instead, he'd head off every Saturday morning down to the launderette, then sit and stare at his clothes whizzing around the drum like he was their guardian angel. He'd always iron his shirts just before he went out and he'd spray them with his favourite Dior aftershave. 'Remember, it's the little touches that make the difference', he'd say to me. I'd try and copy him, but my Co-op body spray didn't quite have the same effect.

When he left school and started getting up to no good, he'd save money up under his bed. Then, every six months, we'd head off to the West End, and he'd buy something really smart. I used to marvel at how much money he'd spend on just one item of clothing. I'd proudly tell my mates; 'Seriously boys, three hundred nicker for a fucking jacket, just whipped out the cash he did, laid it on the fucking counter and didn't bat an eyelid.' I'd somehow claim a bit of credit for the story, with pride written all over my face. The lads would nod and listen because they knew what he was like; a top lad; a fella to look up to and more importantly, my big brother.

I just wanted to see him again. Watch his familiar gait as he walked around the corner and to see his smiling face. I needed to see him giving me that usual wink and feel the pat from his hand on my cheek. I couldn't wait to have him back at home with us.

Behind me, I heard the flat door open and the familiar waft of thick cigarette smoke and dragging of worn-out slippers on the floor.

"What are you doing out here?" She asked.

"Waiting for Devo," I replied.

"Devo?"

"He gets out this morning," I said.

"Does he?"

I sighed, "I told you the other day, Mum."

"Oh, that's right, I remember you saying you'd been stashing away your dole money so you could treat him." She stood and pulled out her fags and a lighter from her dirty nightgown and lit up. "So how much you saved up?"

"About fifty-quid."

"Fifty-quid is that all?! What's the plan then, a six-pack of beers down the park than an hour at Mecca Bingo?"

"No!"

"After spending a couple of hours with you, he'll wish he was back in prison."

She stood there sniggering to herself. She irritated me to death. I'd always resisted lashing out at her, unlike Devo, he would bite, and then they would go for it.

"What are you going do for him then, Mum? You couldn't even be bothered to visit him when he was inside. Your own son and you haven't seen him for two and a half years."

"He wouldn't have seen me if I'd gone. You know what he's like. Anyway, he'll be back inside in three months, you wait and see."

"No way, they won't get him again."

"Are you sure? You just make sure he doesn't take you down with him next time."

She turned around and walked back inside, never missing an opportunity to pollute the flat with more fag smoke.

Would he take me down with him? I'd thought about this a lot recently. Was my life heading for a term in prison, like my brother? I liked to think I ducked and dived a bit but the truth was I didn't. I was just feeding off the scraps that no one else could be bothered with; the odd item of nicked gear I'd sell on down the pub, or the occasional mobile phone I'd buy off a clucking skag-head for bottom dollar. I even got stopped by a copper the other day who found a carton of illegal cigarettes on me. He just laughed, 'Is that it? It isn't worth the paperwork!' He didn't even bother to confiscate the fags! No, prison wasn't something I had previously had to worry about. I was small-time; a little fish in a big East End pond, a fucking nobody. I knew it, and I hated it.

Not like Devo, he was smart, streetwise, a quick talker, the bloke that gets the laughs down the pub. He was involved in big-time stuff, proper ducking and diving. Jobs would go down, and people would say to me, 'was that your brother behind that score?' They would look at me with that cheeky grin of admiration. They knew what had gone on. They knew all about Devo.

He'd have never gone down unless that slag had grassed on him. I remember the knock on the door that morning from the Feds. Not the usual uniform lot, but big fuck off detectives in leather coats. They knew exactly where the gear was hidden, knew it had his prints on it, and more importantly, knew they had him bang to rights.

He'd been told last time by the judge that the next sentence was going to be years not months and they didn't let him down. Four of them, fucking hell, I nearly passed out.

'Now take him down!' The judge had demanded.

I remember his face like it was yesterday. It's the only time I've ever seen him look scared. Mum just stood up, looked at me in some smart-arsed way and said, 'There you go!' I deemed this a truly insightful piece of philosophy, at a time when her eldest son was heading off to serve a lengthy custodial sentence.

For as long as I can remember Devo used to ball-ache me about not going down the same road of crime as he had. He was always pestering me to get a job from the moment I left school. But I had no qualifications, no prospects, and no inclination to do some bullshit nine to five gig. I once saw him in prison, and I swore to him I'd have a job when he came out. I promised him I'd be off the dole and doing something useful. I was prepared to do anything to get his spirits up. I've always been interested in mechanics, I told him and explained that Roy, from the garage around the corner, was thinking of taking on an apprentice and that if ever he did he promised it would be me. Devo was made up, wished me luck he did, even patted my cheek as I departed.

But there was no job. The real story was I had bumped into Roy down the pub a few weeks earlier and, while two-thirds pissed, he loosely agreed that should he ever need an apprentice he would let me know. I hung on to it, not because I believed it would happen, but because a dole-boy, like me, needs some bullshit story to tell people when they ask why you aren't working. Me, a mechanic, really? I couldn't change a tyre on a fucking pushbike. It wasn't going to happen, and in any event, that wasn't what I wanted to do.

I wanted to be like my big brother.

When Devo used to go out on jobs, I used to beg him to take me. He'd always refuse saying that if he got nicked; I'd have to look after Mum. He used to come home buzzing after the job and would bung me a few quid. 'Here you go mate, treat yourself to some new Nikes.' But I hated it, hated it because I was never part of the action. I needed to be in the thick of it; to be there when it was being planned; to have my role defined; and then to experience the feeling, the buzz, the excitement after the job was done. I wanted to be on some detectives' whiteboard as a possible suspect, I wanted people to nudge each other when I entered the pub and to hear them whisper, 'there's that Boleyn Bates lad, he's proper naughty.'

I wanted to be someone.

But I knew that the only way to break-in was to bring him a plan; a plan that meant I could get involved, a plan that would make us both a pile of money.

Then, one night down the pub, a few weeks ago, I had an innocent chat with some geezer who owned a shop and bang! There it was, it just dropped in my lap. I could see straight away how it would work. I had my passport to partnering up with my brother, and I knew he wouldn't be able to resist it. I couldn't wait for his release so that I could tell him and we could get started.

Once he heard the plan, I knew I'd be in. I'd be part of his gang, ready for a slice of the action and finally, I'd achieve my ambition; I wouldn't be small-time anymore.

Chapter 2
Same Day

I'd spent hours walking around the flat, checking the front door and looking over the railings, but by mid-afternoon, I realised Devo wasn't coming home. I'd played Xbox for a few hours to kill time and I'd had it away with some geezer from Denmark on Call of Duty, who had turned out to be a Scandinavian fucking Rambo. I was convinced he would be back with us at home by now. I was gutted.

By ten o'clock at night I was sitting watching the telly with Mum. The news was on and, as usual, she was swigging strong beer out of a can while making ill-informed comments about every bulletin. Just as she was about to apply her political genius to the migrant situation in Calais, I heard a key in the front door.

"Who's that?" I questioned, with anticipation.

Mum didn't bother to look around, "Well, it's too fucking early for Santa."

I heard the door open and in he stumbled.

"Oi oi! Guess who's back, yes he's back, guess who's back, guess who's back, guess who's back, fucking back?"

I ran to greet him, "Alright, bro!"

"Hey up mate, how are you?"

As he wrapped his arms around me and kissed my cheek I could smell the strong aroma of booze on him.

"How's the mum of the year then, are you alright Rita?"

Mum just ignored him and carried on watching the telly.

"She's alright, bro. When did you get out?"

"This morning mate, I just needed a bit of 'me' time, you know what I mean?"

He winked and flicked his bollocks.

"I must say, Rita, I love what you've done to this place since I've been away, very moody. What a fucking shithole! Don't you two ever bother to tidy up?"

"Ask your brother, he's here all day," she snapped.

"I'll get it cleaned up in the morning, Dev."

"Don't tell me Rita, the reason you can't do it is that you're now putting in sixty-hours a week graft to provide for your family? Hmmm, maybe not then."

"Let it go, bro, let's have a nice night."

Devo then picked up a bulging plastic bag, "Look what I've got, three fucking doner kebabs, chips, chilli sauce and salad, salt and vinegar on the fries, now who's fucking having it?!"

"Do you want some, Mum? Devo's got the kebabs in." I asked, excited.

Again, she ignored us.

"Fuck her. Come on we'll have it all to ourselves. Go and get a couple of plates, will you mate?"

I walked into the kitchen where all the plates were piled up in the sink; they'd been there for days. Devo followed me in.

"Look at the fucking state of this place!"

He was right, it was a disgrace. The plates were covered in congealed food and used tea bags surrounded the soiled sink.

"Bollocks to it, let's eat out the wrapper," he said.

"I can wash up?" I asked.

"Fuck it, let's eat!"

We sat in the kitchen scoffing our food. He was eating like a scavenging beast, lashing chilli sauce all over his chops, and as he did, he was making a low-level humming noise. I watched as he was gently spinning around in his chair, the booze taking more and more of a grip on him. He stopped periodically to either burp or hiccup, before eventually polishing off his huge plate of grub. He sat back in his chair and did one last burp and then rubbed his slim stomach.

"Fucking beautiful!" he announced. He then looked across at me, "have you put weight on?"

I was embarrassed that he'd noticed. Months of bumming around the flat had taken their toll.

"I don't know," I replied, sheepishly.

"Fucking looks like it."

He paused as he cleaned the chilli sauce from around his mouth before licking his fingers.

"How's that bird you were seeing before I went inside, what's her name?"

"Ashlee."

"Ashlee, that's it. Great tits! Are you still seeing her?"

"No, we split up ages ago," I said, being coy.

Some secrets are best left buried.

"That's a shame. I might have a crack at it myself if I see her out. It's always best to keep it in the family."

He started to roll his finger across the chilli sauce that was left on the plate and then licked it off.

"Are you working yet?" he asked.

"There are no jobs around, bro. The eastern Europeans are taking them all."

"What are we going to do with you?"

I quickly wanted to change the subject, embarrassed at my lack of progress since his incarceration. Moreover, I was mindful of the promise I'd made him in prison that I would be working by the time he was released.

"I've saved up some money Dev; I thought we could have a few pints tomorrow down the Three Bells. Everyone's looking forward to seeing you; it'll be my treat as well, bro - the beers are on me!"

I felt like the fucking Milky Bar kid for released prisoners.

"A proper good knees-up down the boozer! I'll have some of that, son. Right, it's bedtime for me."

As he got out of his chair, he fell into the table taking the ketchup and cans of pop with him.

"Fucking hell!" He complained.

"Don't worry, bro, you get yourself off to bed, I'll clear up."

He grabbed the back of my head and stared into my eyes.

"Good boy, Bo, good boy."

He then kissed me on the cheek before lightly smacking my face. He got up and grabbed his bag before heading off to his bedroom.

"And remember you two, don't try getting a fucking cheap laugh tonight by locking my bedroom door and shouting 'lights out' now will you?"

I smiled; it was good to have him back.

I watched as he walked to his old bedroom and then saw him stop, turn around and stand there staring at Mum. She hadn't noticed him and just continued to watch the television, drawing from her cigarette. He then pointed at her, holding the pose for a few weird seconds. His face looked angry. I could see his bitterness; it was bordering on hatred and deep-rooted resentment. He shook his head before he turned and entered his bedroom, closing the door quietly behind him.

Chapter 3

Friday 3rd October 2014

I woke up to the familiar sweet smell of cannabis. I guessed that Mum must be having one of her medicinal joints. I rolled over and looked at the time on my phone: 12.41pm. I contemplated a couple more hours' sleep because, as usual, I felt knackered.

I couldn't ever get to sleep at nights; I would sit up gaming, messaging mates, or surfing the net on my phone until the small hours and, consequently, I was waking up later and later. Some days I would stay in bed all day. But with Devo home and given his hatred of laziness, I knew I had better get up.

I had a makeshift ashtray at the side of my bed, a chicken and mushroom Pot Noodle container that was three-quarters full of ash and butts. I spotted half a joint poking over the top, a leftover from a previous drunken night. What a result! I lit it up and sat on the edge of the bed pondering why it was a chicken and mushroom Pot Noodle container. The level of confusion was because I generally only have the chicken balti flavour.

I assessed my clothes which were, as ever, strewn across the bedroom floor. I tried to assemble some idea for an outfit that I was going to wear today down the pub. Devo would look sharp, and I wanted to be worthy of walking in his slipstream. However, given the state of the clothes on my floor, this was going to be fucking tricky.

I finished the joint, got dressed and walked into the lounge. Mum was sitting in her usual daytime attire of a grubby nightgown, and well-trodden slippers, and as usual was hooked to the cultural offering known to many as daytime television.

"Alright, Mum?"

As usual, she didn't acknowledge me; instead, she took the last drag from her joint before putting it out in her ashtray.

"Can you believe there's a couple on here that have just paid eighty quid for a fucking cigar cutter?" She said.

She was watching one of those antique programmes that she seemed to be obsessed with. I looked across at the television, the picture, as ever, was horrible and in every programme it appeared to be snowing thanks to the aerial which was no better than a fucking walkie-talkie antenna.

"Have they?" I said, attempting to feign interest.

"Eighty quid for something you can do with a pair of fucking scissors."

"I'm guessing they're antique though, Mum. Maybe, people collect shit like that."

"It's the auction in a minute, so we'll find out."

"Well, if that's the case, I'll put a hold to trading pork bellies on the stock market and see how this plays out."

I took a ringside seat.

"The fella with the hammer reckons they're worth between twenty-five and forty quid."

"What do you think?" I asked.

"I think he's spot on," she replied

I watched her take a deep gulp from her can of beer.

"And if he is, they're fucked!" she said.

"God, let's hope not. I once read of someone committing suicide on the back of losing money on a cigar cutter auction. By the way, where's Devo?" I asked.

"Hang on a minute", she replied.

We both suddenly became transfixed at the outcome of the most significant auction in the history of British antiques. I knew her pessimistic prediction was correct when the auctioneer decided only to raise each bid in two-pound increments.

They sold for twenty-four quid.

"Told you!"

That was her favourite phrase and she could never wait to say it. 'Told you', she fucking loves that saying. I'd decided it was her way of claiming righteousness along with a modicum of intelligence.

"You should apply to go on the programme," I said with a slightly devious level of sarcasm.

"I couldn't do any worse, I'll tell you that much. Eighty quid for a fucking cigar cutter, they must have been fucking bonkers."

"So where is Devo?"

"Gone out, he had to see his probation officer or something."

She then started to pick her nose.

"Did he say what time he was coming back?"

She assessed what she had retrieved from her nostril before rolling it in her fingers and flicking it on the already heavily soiled carpet.

"Didn't ask and I don't fucking care, to be honest," she replied.

I walked into the kitchen, which had, amazingly, been tidied up. The plates were washed up and packed away; the cereal boxes were back in the cupboards; even the crust of crumbs that lived on the floor and that crunched when you walked on them had been swept up. It was Devo's handiwork. I'd missed him. He somehow brought an element of order to an otherwise chaotic household.

I sat with my cup of tea dividing my thoughts between when I was going to tell Devo about my plan and sorting out this Pot Noodle conundrum. Finally, the front door opened and in he walked holding a shopping bag of goodies.

"Alright bro, how did you get on?" I asked.

"Ah you know, same shit, different smell. Have you just got up?"

"No, no, I've been up a few hours."

"Bollocks, you've just got up, haven't you?"

There was no point lying to him; he had a sixth sense as far as I was concerned.

"Sorry, bro."

"Don't worry mate; I appreciate that you've got a confirmed medical condition."

"Have I?" I said hopefully.

"It's called being a lazy cunt."

He then patted my face with his hand and winked.

"How does a bacon sandwich and cup of tea sound?" he asked.

"Nice one!" I replied, all excited at the prospect of a rare treat.

Devo had bought a pack of bacon, some fresh crusty bread, and real butter. After our well-worn frying pan had performed its magic, we sat and feasted, the butter melting and soaking into the bread. I noticed he was making that low-humming noise again as he was eating. Had he picked that habit up from prison or did he do it before? It was yet another issue, along with Pot Noodle-gate, that I was going to have to resolve. No wonder I didn't have time for a job.

Accompanying the bacon sandwich was a strong cup of tea with lots of sugar. We always used to have this on a Saturday before a West Ham home game. Devo used to say it brought us good luck, but given we lost as many games as we won I kind of doubted the superstition.

"Do you fancy an all-day drink down the Three Bells after?"

"Later mate, I've got to see a man about a dog."

"How about I meet you there about 5.30?" I asked.

"Sweet!"

"I'll call the lads and get them to meet us. I'll give Murray a shout as well and make sure he gets the fridge stocked up with cold beers."

I probably wouldn't do the latter. Murray was the landlord of the pub and asking him to get the beers in the fridge was a bit like reminding Simon Cowell to pick the best singer on 'The X-Factor'.

Murray had been the landlord of the Three Bells since I was born. He used to be a good friend of our dad's. Dad had long since gone AWOL. I don't remember him as I was only two when he left. The story was that he had a string of kids across London and the authorities were coming after him for big dollars. Apparently, he was seldom around anyway. Devo never mentioned him and neither, to any great extent, did Mum. I knew little about him, but I did know he was a big West Ham fan and used to go to games with Murray.

When Devo and I were old enough, Murray contacted Mum and offered to take us to the games. Murray used to get us programmes, burgers, the lot. He even used to take us to the midweek matches. They were the best, watching the games under the floodlights, the smell of the onions, the atmosphere, watching our fans lobbing coins at the away supporters. It was magical. I could seldom afford to go anymore, but I saw Murray when I could afford to drink down the pub.

Devo and I will never forget that he used to take us; it was something we would always appreciate. Every Christmas we'd club together to get him a West Ham souvenir. When we handed the present over to him, we'd both shout in unison, 'Murray Christmas!' He used to love it. After he'd unwrapped our gift, he'd parade it around the pub showing it off to all the punters, 'Look what the Bates boys have bought me for Christmas, lovely isn't it?"

Devo was checking himself in the mirror; he moved the zip down on his jacket about half a centimetre. He always had to look exactly right.

"Right adios, I'm out of here, catch you later."

I heard the front door slam. Where was he going? Was he heading off to meet someone to talk about a job they were planning? Would it be better than mine? I started to panic. I realised what was at stake. What if he didn't like my idea? What if he thought it was weak? I'd never get in with him then. But hang on a minute, maybe I could do the job myself? Maybe I didn't need him? Perhaps I could use some of his old crew to help me?

But there was a grave truth that I quickly had to face – I was a fuckwit. Moreover, a fuckwit who hadn't got a fucking clue how to plan, organise and execute a crime. No, it had to be with Devo. I realised that I had one crack at this; I had to tell him about the plan in a convincing way so that he wouldn't knock it back. I couldn't afford for it to sound like a bodge job.

The question that needed answering was when was I going to tell him? I decided it was going to be later tonight, that I'd strike while the iron is hot. He'd be full of lager and easier to persuade.

That was it then; the decision had been made. I'll present the plan to him this evening and then a new chapter in my, hitherto, under-achieving life, would begin.

Chapter 4
Same Day

The Three Bells is a traditional pub in London's East End. It's a twenty-five-minute walk from The Boleyn ground, home of my beloved West Ham United so, it's an ideal place to meet before the game.

The pub was pretty standard really; dartboard, a pool table and toilets that stank like a summer's days piss. It was a gathering of nothing but familiar faces and with that came a long-standing and established hierarchy. Those who'd had too much beer and would overdo it with the banter to the wrong people were abruptly reminded of their place.

I knew my place in the food chain, and it was right at the bottom. My only claim was to be the brother of a local lad who was known to be a bit tasty but was certainly not feared. Devo was top of the second division, whereas the premier league was for the real naughty lads; those fellas that ran the nightclub doors in the area, geezers who had boxed at a good standard or boys who had done long stretches for violent crimes. I was a back number, a nobody, a fella more often than not referred to simply as 'Devo's little brother'.

I arrived at the Three Bells about 5pm. The pub was filling up nicely with lads in work clothes who had finished for the day. Some of them had been on the juice since mid-afternoon and were loosening up nicely. I acknowledged a couple of fellas I knew before heading over to see Murray. He always gave me my first beer on the house.

"Here you go, fella," he said as he passed me a beer. "What time is McVicar getting here?"

"Who?"

"Your brother, what time's he arriving?"

"In about half an hour."

"God help us!" he joked.

"Here you go, bro, stick this behind the bar and let me know when it runs out," I said, handing Murray forty quid.

I knew full well that forty quid wouldn't last long with my thirsty brother catching up for lost time and necking lager like it was going out of fashion, but I banked on Murray helping me out a bit when it did.

Twenty minutes later and the pub door was flung opened and in walked Devo.

"Oi, oi! Dead man walking, stand aside!"

He was obviously several drinks in already. He walked around the bar shaking people's hands, getting hugs, sharing banter and having a crack with everyone. I ordered up two bottles of beer, and when Devo finally joined me, I passed him his bottle.

"Here you go, bro, good to have you back."

He grabbed me and kissed my head. I could smell the beer on him. I liked that smell; I felt it had a masculinity about it.

"You're a fucking top man," he said.

He then demanded everyone's attention, "Right you lot; shut up a minute I have an important announcement to make."

Everyone quietened down although we all knew what was coming.

Devo braced himself, "I'd like you to join me in a toast. Raise your glasses with me to the Queen of England!"

Everyone joined in. Devo loved his royal family toasts when he'd had a drink. The word was my Dad used to make them, and I reckoned that in his absence Devo had assumed responsibility and carried on the family tradition.

Devo then made his way over to his old partner in crime, the Brigadier. The Brigadier was the champion of the pub. He was the fella who used to chalk up odds during the live games that were being shown. He'd take in-play bets which ensured lively banter during the matches. You can imagine the reaction when someone put a tenner on the first scorer with the Brigadier at 33/1 only for him to pop up with a header.

He was a heavily built, ruddy-faced character, who'd buy all his designer clothes second-hand from various XXL geezers in the vicinity. He was a hilarious, quirky soul who would drink and drink until he fell over. The next day he would return to the pub fresh-faced and do it all again.

Devo loved him. It was well known that they would do naughty jobs together and afterwards they'd be in the pub flashing around their ill-gotten gains. I watched Devo laughing and joking with the Brigadier. I found myself drawn to them; I stared at their every reaction. It was a unique thing that they shared. I had to admit that I felt distant and just a tiny bit jealous. Here were two geezers that had done things together, that had memories to joke about when they were drunk. This is what I wanted; craved even. I felt on the outside of the action, I was in the cold, and I needed to come in. I wanted to be part of it.

That was why my plan was so important to me.

Devo returned, and we stood at the bar for the next few hours supping beers. Murray bought us some shooters while Devo put on some music. We had the greatest hits from The Jam, The Who and Madness belting out of the jukebox. He certainly loved his Mod and Ska music. He was getting more and more pissed and any old Tom, Dick or Harry who came up to the bar was getting a hug and a beer. Here he was, my brother, back in his manor, pissed up and on top form. I felt like a different bloke now he was back.

My mind drifted back to the plan. The mood, the timing, everything was falling into place. I was now looking for the right moment for me and him to be sat in the corner talking it over.

"Murray, are you going to the game tomorrow?" Devo asked.

"It's a Saturday, they're at home, and I've still got a hole in my arse, so what do you think?!"

"Bo's got us some tickets, so expect us in before the game for a few sherbets."

"Sounds good boys, it'll be like the good old days. Do you want me to take the pop crate down so Bo can stand on it and watch the game?"

Devo laughed, "Fucking hell, remember that big horrible fucking crate? How did you carry it all the way to the ground, Murray?"

"With great fucking difficulty! Ah well, it was worth it, the boy needed to see the match."

"I'm not sure he did given how shit he was at football," Devo said.

"No, I wasn't!"

There are certain rules in the East End, and one of them is questioning a man's prowess on the football pitch.

"You fucking were. Named after the Boleyn ground and you've got two left feet, and a first touch like a rapist."

Murray stuck up for me, as he often did, "Oh leave him alone, you weren't much better, Devo, if it weren't for the fact you were a dirty little fucker no one would have ever played you."

Devo then pointed behind the bar, "Look, Bo, there's that 1960's West Ham scarf we bought Murray for his Christmas present a few years ago."

The scarf was paraded neatly at the top of the liquor optics.

"I've got all my souvenirs you boys bought me, the programmes, the shirts, the badges, everything, they're all around here somewhere. I treasure them."

"It was our way of thanking you for taking us to the games, Murray. You didn't have to. We'll never forget it," said Devo.

He was drunkenly nostalgic, but he meant every word of it.

"My pleasure boys, we couldn't have you two going off to watch the Arsenal now, could we?!"

Devo turned to me, "What did you get Murray for Christmas presents while I've been inside?"

Murray laughed, "He'd forgotten all about me!"

Devo quickly turned stern, and the atmosphere instantly changed. "You did what?"

I suddenly felt my throat turn dry. "I didn't have any money, did I? I'm on the dole."

"And you couldn't have saved up just a bit and brought him something?"

Murray sensing this was getting tense, stepped in trying to calm things down, "Oh don't worry Dev, the boy's skint, I was only joking."

Devo ignored him and snarled at me. "Why didn't you get him anything?"

"Seriously Dev, I didn't have enough money."

"You didn't have enough money? The fucking flat smells like an Amsterdam fucking coffee shop, but you didn't have enough money?!"

I knew that look in his eyes, I had seen it many times before, and I was clutching at straws.

"Things have been hard, bro, I had to help Mum out."

"What do you mean things have been hard? How would you know what hard is? You sit on your fucking lazy arse all day; you bone idle cunt!"

"I'm sorry,"

I was desperate for this to pass; I knew his fuse had been lit.

"We've bought this fella a Christmas present for the last ten years, then the second I turn my back you can't be bothered to buy him anything."

"Leave it, Dev, don't worry about it, son, let's have a beer." Murray was pedalling hard to diffuse the situation.

"I'm sorry Dev," I said, desperate to calm him down.

"Why are you apologising to me, you fucking useless cunt? It's Murray you should be apologising to. I'm going outside for a smoke."

He then stormed off, shaking his head.

"Let him calm now, Bo. Here you go, have another drink," Murray passed me another bottle of beer.

"Murray, sorry, bro, he's right. I should have bought you something." I said meekly.

"Don't worry son," he replied, generously.

Half an hour later and Devo was nowhere to be seen. I was feeling rotten. I knew I should have bought Murray a Christmas present. I had thought about it, but selfishness had always got the better of me. Getting a quarter of an ounce was preferable to having to buy someone a present.

I had let Devo down and the evening had turned into a disaster with my designs of getting him to buy into my plan in tatters. I decided to nip to the toilet then go home.

I walked in and stood at the urinal while making small-talk to a geezer I knew. Chatting with someone while you're both having a piss always seemed a bit odd to me for some reason. I think it's the moment when one of you has to start shaking your cock that makes me feel awkward. Anyway, he shook his first then left, so I just stood there alone.

Suddenly I was struck hard in the ribs; I fell to my knees and turned to see who it was - Devo. The firework had ignited. He furiously grabbed me.

"You fucking useless, little cunt!"

He smashed me hard on the side of the face, I could feel the skin on my eye open, and blood was suddenly pouring me.

"How could you fucking do it? How could you? He took us to every fucking home game!"

He then started to kick me, repeatedly in the stomach. I just curled up, screaming.

I heard him slam the door of the toilet as he left. I eventually got to my feet, only to fall over again as I slipped on my piss that had saturated the floor. I managed to get to my feet a second time, before staggering out of the pub's fire exit.

Chapter 5
Saturday 5th October 2014

I was lying in bed physically and emotionally wounded. My head was throbbing, and as I slowly turned over, I felt the soreness in my ribs. I did a double sniff of the air as there was an odd smell. This would usually have been my rancid trainers at the side of my bed; however, this aroma had a more acidic pungency to it. I raised my hands to my nose. Piss! Perhaps washing my hands when I arrived home, given I was flailing around on the pub toilet floor like a stranded fucking seal, might have been a good idea.

What would have been an even better idea would have been to buy Murray Christmas presents when Devo was in prison. I had let them both down, but right now it was my failings towards Devo that were causing me the most angst. My brother, my hero and the closest thing I had to a father figure, and I had sold him short. Maybe he had over-reacted - did I deserve a beating for what amounted to little more than an oversight? I lay in bed shaking my moral compass, for once a refreshing change from my cock, to see which direction it would come up with.

My mind drifted back to the summer of 2004. I was due back at school after the long break, and after months of hard wear and tear my trainers had finally given up and the sole had fallen off. For the last three days of the holidays, I had been playing football in my flip-flops. Mum had been promising to buy me a new pair of trainers, but now she didn't have a choice as I had no shoes to go back to school in. I had given her specific instructions about which ones to buy. I knew she didn't have much money, but the pair of Adidas trainers I wanted were in her price range, so she had agreed to get them for me.

One afternoon, she arrived back at the flat, pissed and barely able to stand up. Sure enough, she was holding a box of trainers, but these were not the Adidas ones I had asked for. In fact, these pumps weren't even fucking branded. What she had bought me was the worst pair of trainers in the world. They were a pair of fucking horrible black plastic things with silly fucking arrow stripes on them. I was horrified. She kept telling me they were fine and that they were expensive. Despair filled me as I envisaged the unrelenting ridicule I would get at school the next day. All the other lads would be returning with their pukka Nike Air pumps of different colours, and I would walk in wearing these fuckers. It was a schoolboy nightmare.

When Dev saw the trainers, he turned and asked Mum whether she had enjoyed spending the money that was due for her son's trainers on booze. She defended herself by saying it was her money and she could spend it on what she liked. Maybe she was right.

The dreaded piss taking started as soon as I arrived in the playground when some lad opened with 'Alright, Bo, didn't know you'd clinched a trainer sponsorship with Tesco?' After that, it just got worse and worse. Eventually, after school, a group of four lads thought it a touching end to a horrible day to wait for me at the gates then jump me so they could take my trainers off. The road was full of school kids who had finished for the day, and the biggest of the four lads got everyone's attention as he put on my trainers and started prancing around pretending to ask out girls. 'Do you fancy coming on a date with me, babes? I'll promise to wear these trainers if you do.' Everyone was laughing while I just sat on the pavement wanting to die and hoping and praying that no one would notice that I was wearing an old pair of Bart Simpson socks.

Then I spotted Devo walking towards the school gates. I watched as he stood there staring at this lad. It was like every second he carried out his act of pantomime Dev's aggression would go up another notch. Within thirty seconds or so the notches ran out, and he proceeded to hand out a beating, the like of which, you don't usually see at the gates of a school. I remember blood cascading down this lads face. I watched as the girls looked on either screaming or with their hands over their mouths. He then announced to everyone that should he find out that his little brother had received one more comment about his trainers then they would get the same treatment.

No one ever mentioned them again.

One Friday at school, three weeks later, it was announced that someone had stolen the tuck shop takings for the week. The day after this, Devo had surprised me by buying me a pair of top of the range Nikes. He never told me where he got the money from, but I knew. When I returned to school I was as proud as punch, showing off my new trainers. The teachers were that suspicious that I was even told to report to the Headmaster. When he asked me who had bought me the trainers, I explained, as Devo had told me, that Mum had won at bingo and had treated me. He'd been around the block a few times though and wasn't buying the story. When I left his office he shouted to me, 'Boleyn, you tell your brother that I'm getting the police involved in this.'

When I arrived home, I told Devo about his threat. He did nothing more than piss himself laughing. I remember him saying, 'The next time you see the Headmaster, Bo, ask him what day they're filming the Crimewatch reconstruction?!"

That was Devo; he'd always look out for me despite the times when I would pull up short. I realised I wasn't going to make a big deal about what happened last night. I had let him down, and I should have known better. In any event, I still had my plan to tell him about, so I needed him on my side.

I lay in bed for at least an hour replaying last night's regretful incident and staring at the Pot Noodle container. I don't even like chicken and mushroom flavour, why would I have bought this? Something was amiss.

Then there was a knock on the door.

"Yeah?" I responded.

"You're not having a wank, are you?" asked Devo.

"No."

He then walked into the bedroom holding a mug.

"Here you go mate; I've brought you a nice cup of tea."

He placed it on the side of my bed and sat on the edge of the mattress.

"Sorry about last night, Bo, I was out of order," he said, humbly.

"No, I'm sorry," I replied.

"I shouldn't have beaten you like that. It won't happen again, mate, I promise."

"Okay, bro."

I sensed an opportunity here. Even though I was planning to apologise to him and smooth it over it was evident that he felt guilty. I could make this work for me. He'd probably stay in a forgiving mood all day, and then, later on, I could talk to him about the job I'd planned. He might agree to do it out of sympathy, even if he didn't think it was up to much.

I needed to lay it on, but not too thick. I wasn't dealing with a mug here.

"What does my eye look like?" I asked.

"You've got a proper shiner, mate."

"Have I?"

I was quite pleased about this. It would give me a combative look ahead of today's match.

"Look, I don't want it getting around that I gave you a slap, so would you mind saying that a couple of geezers jumped you on the way home?"

"Yeah, of course, Dev."

"No one saw what happened, so the story won't get questioned."

"Yeah, yeah, no problem."

"Thanks, mate. Right, here's the drill, its match day at West Ham, so you know what that means, don't you?"

"Bacon sangers and strong tea?"

"Exactly!"

Now, this may sound like a re-run of yesterday, but you can't have enough of a good thing.

"So, get yourself up and showered, I'll iron you a shirt then get the frying pan on. After that, I'll get you a pint down the pub." he said.

"Nice one!"

He held his hand out, "Mates?"

I shook it, "Mates!"

This was all working out beautifully. Today would be the day that Devo would buy into the plan, and I'd take the first step onto the ladder that I so craved.

Chapter 6
Same Day

We were down the pub, and predictably, I was getting a bit of light-hearted stick about my black eye which, if I'm going to be honest, I quite enjoyed. Suffice it to say I beefed up the story just a tad. According to the revised version, during the beating, I handed a few decent punches out myself. It seemed a shame not to grab a bit of street cred out of a tense situation.

It was well received by the lads, who were buying me beers. By 1.30pm the pub was alive with West Ham songs. Devo continued to be in an apologetic mood, putting his arm around me and holding my hands up when we were singing. It was great.

West Ham won the game 2-0, and we were back in the Three Bells by 5.20pm. As usual, the beers were flowing and so were the football songs. The evening game was on the telly, and the Brigadier was holding court and chalking up odds for the match on the darts blackboard. I popped a fiver on a 66/1 first goal scorer bet, just to watch him squirm for a while before the bet went down.

By 9.30pm as the local curry houses and kebab shops were filling up, the pub was thinning out, and Devo was well and truly tanked up. We were sat together chilling out, and I decided it was time to seize my opportunity.

"Hey Dev, I know about a job we can do together."

"What you on about?"

"A job that is going to be easy and worth at least ten large," I said, trying to sound as convincing as I could.

"What sort of job?" He asked.

"I know a geezer, Ricky Santini, who's got a little shop down the Old Kent Road. Every couple of months he gets contacted by some fella off the continent who brings in a load of bent fags and booze. All branded stuff like, but knocks it off to him cheap."

"And?"

"Apparently, the driver only makes two drops, one to Ricky and the other to an old Polish geezer. Now Ricky only has about a third of the stock, and he pays about five large for it. That means this old Polish geezer must be having the rest."

"Okay."

"So, I asked him to find out exactly where this Polish geezer's shop was. It's down the Stratford Road. It's a big fucking place called the European Store. It sells all the stuff to the Europeans that they used to get back at home. When the driver turns up at Ricky's gaff, he's always moaning because the Polish geezer is always alone when he makes the drop, and it takes them fucking ages to unload all the gear into his shop."

I paused and took a swig of my beer.

"Anyway, I found out when the last delivery was being made, and I waited outside the shop. Sure enough, the old man rocked up about 6.30 in the morning, opened up and then the delivery guy turned up about an hour later."

"What, so we are nicking a load of fags and fucking booze?"

"No, the delivery driver only deals in cash. I even saw the Polish geezer giving him the dosh on the street. He didn't think anyone was around; it was a huge fucking wad of fifties!"

"You're telling me we turn up at just after 6.30 in the morning, stick a gun in an old man's face and walk away with ten large?"

"Easy peasy Japanesey."

I could feel the pendulum swinging in my direction.

"This is an excellent plan, mate."

"Yeah?!"

"Only there's one big fucking hole in it."

"What's that?"

"I'm not doing it."

"What?"

"Retired, finished, out of the game."

"You what!" I said incredulously.

"You heard!"

"But this will be like taking candy from a baby, Dev."

"I'm not bothered if it involves nicking Charlie's golden fucking ticket, I'm not doing it."

"Fucking hell!"

"I've just done two and half years, so have you got any idea what they would give me if I got caught sticking a fucking pistol in some old fella's mush?"

"What are you going to do for dosh then?"

"What you should be doing mate; working. That fella I popped out to see the other day was a lad I'd met inside. His dad's got a warehouse. I start there on Monday."

"You're fucking joking?!"

"Straight up, I've finished with the criminal life."

"Why?"

"Because I woke up every morning for two and half years and had some fat cunt watching me take a fucking shit, that's why!"

"Oh come on Dev!" I was getting desperate.

"I'm not doing it, and neither are you, so do me a big fucking favour will you and drop it!"

Fuck me! I didn't see this coming at all. I anticipated him perhaps finding a hole in my plan; laughing at it; telling me I wasn't the person to do it with him, but throwing the towel in and going straight? No, I hadn't seen that coming at all.

Bollocks! Back to square fucking one, as usual.

Chapter 7
Monday 7th October 2014.

I woke up and checked the time, 11.28am. I was gutted. Plan 'A' was in the wheelie bin, and the reality was 'plan B' didn't exist. It never did. In fact, it was rare for me to even have a 'plan A', let alone a 'plan B' as well.

I lay in my stinking bed, with my filthy quilt wrapped around me hoping that Devo hadn't bothered to go to work. I needed him to be awoken by his alarm, and give it the, 'fuck this for a game of soldiers' routine, before rolling over and going back to sleep. Maybe then he'd give my plan a second look.

However, as the flat was deathly quiet that outcome wasn't looking good; there wasn't even the usual high volume racket of some bullshit daytime TV programme coming from the lounge.

I got up and went for a nose around. There was no one in, so that could only mean one thing; Devo must have turned up for his new warehouse job. Shit!

I ambled into the kitchen, lit up a spliff and made a cup of tea. The flat was fucking Baltic, but for some reason I sat at the table wearing just my boxer shorts. I was freezing my bollocks off, and it quickly became one of those ridiculous situations where you need to change the circumstances of what you are doing, but you just can't be fucking arsed.

My ears pricked up with a modicum of hope as the front door was opened, but in walked Mum. She headed straight into the kitchen, as no doubt the smell of my spliff had sent her 'Free Soft Drugs Available' light flashing.

"Alright, Mum?"

"Fucking wankers!" she replied, fiercely.

Oh dear, wrong question, now stand-by for take-off.

"What's up?" I asked, bracing myself.

"I've just been down the Jobcentre, that's what's up. Can you believe that they're questioning whether I've got depression? I've only got to go and see some independent fucking doctor so he can check me out."

"So? Tell him what's up, and he'll sign you off."

"Are you fucking stupid or what? These doctors are on their fucking payroll. He'll be getting a bonus to tell them I'm fit for work. Before you know it they'll have me back on fucking job seekers allowance, and I can't manage on that."

"Play up when you go and see him. Tell him you hear weird voices in your head, blokes persuading you to try and buy antiques at sky-high prices."

"This isn't a fucking joke! I can't go back to work just look at the fucking state of me."

I did look at the state of her and to be fair she had a good point.

"Come and sit down, here, have a bang on this,"

I passed her my spliff, which she gleefully accepted and took a couple of massive drags.

"Did Devo start his new job?" I asked.

"Fuck knows, when I woke up, he'd gone."

"He must have done then."

"Fucking mug, the amount they will take off him in tax he may as well not bother," she snarled.

I contemplated this for a second. The amount of tax someone pays was not something I had a working knowledge of, having never been in the receipt of a single pay packet in my entire life. A point recently made by a perceptive, if slightly cheeky, Jobcentre work coach.

"Do you fancy a cup of tea?" I asked.

"Tea? No, fuck that; I'm going to have a tinny."

She then opened the fridge and brought out a can of 9% lager, with some eastern European branding on it. I had tried one once, and it was fucking horrible, it was like a cocktail of beer, sherry and treacle. She loved it though, and I watched as she gulped it down.

"Fuck me, that's better!" she said joyfully.

She went straight back for more, only this time it dripped down her face onto her already grubby sweatshirt. Hang on, that was my fucking sweatshirt! Cheeky fucker, she's stealing her son's clothes.

"It's fucking freezing in here, why are you sitting around in your underpants like fucking Tarzan?!" She asked.

I didn't have an answer for that.

She then looked at her watch, "Christ, look at the time!"

"Don't tell me; the financial markets have opened in south-east Asia?"

"Don't be fucking stupid; Bargain Hunt has just started."

"Of course it has," I replied.

While Mum pitted her wits against the elite of the United Kingdom's budding antique dealers, I decided to opt for my soon to be warm again bed. A busy afternoon doing fuck all was in the offing.

17.52pm. I was still in bed surfing the net on my mobile phone. This was thanks to the Bangladeshi fella next door who, three months ago, was struggling after SKY delivered his new Wi-Fi hub. He couldn't read the instructions so, having received a knock on the door from his anguished missus, I went to his flat to discover he was trying to wedge the phone plug into his bathroom razor socket. Anyway, I was able to rig it up for him and get him and his family online so they could spend evenings dancing around to films on the Bollywood channel. He offered me a fiver for my trouble, which I politely declined. Of course, I needed a fiver, but the jewel in the crown of this particular act of kindness was nicking his Wi-Fi password. It was no big deal for him, but it did mean that I could get myself online whenever I was at home, and do all manner of things.

In this instance, I was on a dating site called Plenty of Fish. The real fun of this meat market was that I had set up a bogus account and was masquerading as a very muscular black fella whose image I had found on Google. My source of entertainment was swapping saucy messages with desperate fat woman. Fucking hell, the pictures that they would send were unbelievable! They would stick all sorts of things up their snatches and arses and then take a snap, which wasn't something I suspect that the inventor of the 'selfie' had in mind when the product was in development.

Unfortunately for 'Lloyd's' harem of woman, when it came to him returning the favour with a promised picture of his enormous hard cock, the trail would go cold. You see, I had a slight problem in that I didn't have an enormous cock to take a picture of and, in any event, mine was white. Anyway, I was swapping messages with Angie120290 from Bermondsey who promised me a picture of her massive, wobbly tits, just as soon as her husband took the kids out.

I then heard the front door open and assumed it was Devo. I quickly got dressed as I needed to assess the lie of the land. With any luck, he fucking hated his new job and wouldn't go back again.

He was sat in the kitchen reading the paper.

"Alright Devo, how did you get on?"

"It was alright mate, hard work but it feels good to be doing something."

"Nice one," I said, struggling to hide my disappointment.

"I bet you were dying for me to say it was shit and I'd quit, weren't you?"

Not for the first time he had read my very predictable emotions. I then did what all people do in such situations like this; deny it.

"No of course not, I'm pleased for you. Is there any nice skirt working there?"

"It's a warehouse, Bo, not the fucking Playboy mansion."

"Fancy going for a pint later?"

He dropped the paper onto the table and sighed.

"No, I fucking don't. It's a Monday night, and I've got to be up in the morning to go to work." Then he just flipped, "you don't fucking get it, do you mate? You bum around here all fucking week, without the slightest idea what a day's work feels like. What are you going to do with yourself, Bo? You're twenty fucking two, and you haven't worked a day in your life."

"Do you think you can get me a job at your place?" I asked.

"You fucking would as well wouldn't you? Forget using your initiative to find a job; you would happily have someone else do it for you while you sat around here tossing it off. No, fuck off! Get your own fucking job, you useless little cunt."

I turned and walked back into my bedroom, dragging my feet in the process. The reality is I hadn't got a clue how to go about getting a job. Who the fuck would employ me? And even if they did, I'd fuck everything up on day one, and then they'd get shot of me. Devo was right; I was a useless little cunt, at best.

I sloped back to my bedroom and turned to face myself in the mirror. I stared for a few seconds then did that snarling face I had seen rugby players do just before kick-off. It was time to act, time to come out fighting; it was time for Boleyn Bates to roll the dice.

Chapter 8
Tuesday 8th October

13.18pm and I had just got up and was once again sitting in just my boxer shorts, in the kitchen, finishing off the only thing we had in the flat to eat; Coco Pops. I'm not sure that eating them with water rather than milk added anything to the culinary experience, but the semi-skimmed in the fridge had turned to cottage cheese.

I was feeling pretty pleased with myself having achieved two things since I'd woken up. Firstly, in the absence of another Pot Noodle container, I'd managed to compress the ash and butts that were in the existing container to just below the 'Add boiling water' line. I'd have a further two weeks use out of that fucker. More importantly, I'd established a very clear plan of action for how I was going to start making a few quid. Now I admit that it wasn't exactly 'The Dam Busters', in terms of its technical details, but I had a feeling that there may be some profit in this little venture.

The plan was this: on our estate; the local naughty drug dealer was trading exclusively in hard gear; heroin, crack, coke, meth etc. For some reason, he wasn't interested in trading weed. Perhaps there just wasn't the profit in it, or maybe he couldn't be bothered with the soft drug clients and preferred the clucking demands of the hardened crack cocaine addict. I didn't know for sure the reason, but I did know the outcome. Soft drugs were like rocking horse shit on this estate. I'd given up trying to buy it in the immediate vicinity, and I ended up hooking up with some geezer called Enzo, from down the Three Bells, who became my dealer.

I'd noticed that quite a few people from the estate would see me smoking a spliff and ask me if I'd got any to sell. Occasionally, I would have more than I needed, so I would flog some of it ensuring that there was a little profit for yours truly.

On the back of this critical market analysis, I decided that I'd buy a larger than usual consignment of gear from Enzo. This would enable me to negotiate a decent discount; then I'd let it be known gently around the estate that I was the bloke to come to for your soft drugs. I was sure it wouldn't tread on the toes of our resident Class A dealer, and if it did, then I would stop and resort to plan B, with the usual plan B caveat applying.

I had set up the meeting with Enzo by sending him the usual text. Now, of course, this avoided the obvious rhetoric like, 'Alright Enzo, can I buy some drugs from you?' That was way too risky. What he had in place was a code to ensure the nosey Feds wouldn't bother us over an insecure telephone network. The code was, 'I'm interested in buying one of your kittens for….' You would enter the cash amount, and Enzo would know how much gear to bring with him. If you fancied another drug, say coke, you changed kittens to puppies, heroin was goldfish, I think. Now I realise it wasn't exactly the Enigma code, but it seemed to be effective.

I only ever used to buy kittens. I never liked the idea of snorting puppies up my nose. I knew given my track record for fucking things up, that it would probably get blocked in my nostril and I'd end up in the infirmary and then on some fucking Channel 4 programme about embarrassing hospital visits, along with some fella who liked to have hamsters nibbling at his arse.

I usually just bought the gear from Enzo on the street but, as this was to be a proper business meeting, I'd moved the venue to the trading and commerce hub of the East End - the Three Bells pub.

Now, Enzo was a decent enough fella, although I suspect, as with any drug dealer, that he would have his nasty side. As such, I needed to respect that I was jumping over to the other side of the fence and with that came a whole raft of unknown and frankly unforeseen factors.

Enzo was in his early thirties, well dressed and, as appeared the tradition with naughty Italians, good looking. Despite his name, there was no sign of a soft, romantic Italian twang. This fella had been schooled in the East End and spoke with a proper cockney accent.

Regarding getting my venture off the ground, I did have a slight problem, well quite a big fucking problem actually; the issue of collateral - I didn't fucking have any. Well, I say that, I had sixty quid left over from my dole money, but it was obvious I needed a little bit more. Having kicked this problem around for some time, I realised there was only one thing for it; I'd have to bite the bullet and sell my precious Xbox console and games. I had loads of games, football ones, driving ones, even the ones where you bum around Los Angeles torturing police for points. They had mostly been purchased from the local burglars who drank down the pub, in fact, come to think of it, so was the actual Xbox…and the extra controller….and the steering wheel. I reckoned that with the console, a stack of games and the other bits and bobs I'd get about two hundred and fifty quid. That would give me a credible three hundred smackers to get the party started.

I'd bagged up the Xbox and the rest of the stuff and was ready to head off to Big Frank's.

Big Frank's was a popular, local second-hand trade-in shop in the heart of the East End. Frank, the owner, and a big fucker at that, would buy any old shit off you. However, if he knew it was hot, you'd get an offer that was commensurate with how desperate you were to off-load it. The nicked gear he bought would then just disappear out of London in a puff of smoke. It would probably next see the light of day in some faraway town or city being flogged in a shop owned by one of the dodgy pals from his network. However, if the gear was kosher, he'd trade it in his shop, and for that, you'd get a slightly better price.

Despite his operation being as bent as an MP's expensive claim, the Feds had long since given up trying to nick him. A few years ago, they even tried to get him with a sting operation. They had recruited a desperate informant to try to sell him some dodgy gear, dirt cheap. But Big Frank could smell a rat from a mile off even if it had enjoyed a day pampering itself at a spa, quickly told the informant to fuck off. This was particularly bad news for the geezer in question because snitches last as long around here as a skinny dipper in the Antarctic.

I planned to head off to Big Frank's then onwards to meet Enzo at 3pm. I would buy wholesale drugs to the value of three hundred nicker and, in effect, start my new life as a Class B drug dealer. It hardly made me Pablo fucking Escobar but out of small acorns and all that.

But, there was one thing I had to avoid at all costs; I had to make sure that Devo didn't find out, because if he did, well, think Chernobyl, doused with napalm sprinkled with anabolic fucking steroids!

Chapter 9
Same Day

Bollocks! Big Frank knew the Xbox and the games were bent. He took one look at them and laughed. I hadn't noticed the fucking console had a sticker on the back with some kid's name and address on it. I had never met 'Adam Martin, 23 Robert Peel Road, Whitechapel,' but I had immediately taken a dislike to the horrible little cunt.

Big Frank offered me fifty quid for the lot. I then had to undertake some hardball negotiation with him, proving that when Boleyn Bates puts his mind to it, he can haggle with the very best.

Well, nearly very best. I got fifty-five quid.

With the other sixty quid, I had in dole money, which would soon become fifty after I'd bought Enzo and me a pint; I'd got just over a ton. Maybe this wasn't going to be quite so straightforward, after all.

It was 14.52pm, and I was frog-marching down to the pub, consciously thinking about the need to put my game face on, whichever fucking face that was. I walked in, nodded to a few of geezers, bought a couple of lagers and headed to a table far away from prying eyes. When Enzo arrived, I'd make out we hadn't had a chat for a few months and that this was just a friendly meet, before I slowly edged the conversation to the issue of me buying drugs from him at a wholesale cost. I knew exactly how to play this.

Within a couple of minutes, Enzo walked in and was looking around for me. I waved him over.

"Alright Enzo, how's it going then?"

"Do I look like a cunt to you?"

Not a great start.

"What?"

"I said, do I look like a cunt to you?"

He obviously wasn't happy.

"No, why?"

"You've invited me into a pub, bought me a pint and you're sitting me at the table furthest away from the fucking bar. Now either you're wearing a wire, and you're trying to get me nicked, or you're going to ask me for some bullshit favour."

"Well, put it this way," I said blushingly, "I'm not wearing a wire."

He slowly sighed, "What do you want, Bo?"

I hushed my voice, "I reckon there's market around my estate for weed, Enzo. Nothing big and nothing for you to waste your time on, but for someone like me there's a few quid to be had."

"I know where you live, that's Cazley's manor. What makes you think he's going to let you move in on his patch?"

"Because he doesn't bother dealing weed, bro. He's strictly class A narcs. I've tried to get it off his boy's dozens of times, but nothing, bro, zero, nada."

"What do you want from me then?"

"I usually pay you thirty sniffs for a quarter of an ounce. How about I start to buy it off you in bulk, for say fifteen?"

"Fifteen?! Fucking hell! You do know how this works, don't you? Fifteen is only just above what I'm paying for it."

"Twenty then, I can go to twenty. Come on Enzo, you know we can make this work!"

"How much do you want to buy off me?"

"Well, there's the problem."

"I thought so. Listen, mate, why don't you go back to flogging nicked phones and piss smelling perfume rather than wasting my time?"

I hadn't seen Enzo like this before; he's usually a pleasant fella. If I was honest, I was finding his change of mood a little unsettling.

"Alright, listen I'll give you a hundred quid for one and a quarter ounces, if you'd be prepared to lend me another two ounces, I'll give a further two hundred quid when I've sold it on. By then I'll have another dole cheque, and we'll be off and running."

"And what do you think happens if you don't pay me my two hundred quid back?"

"I will pay it back, Enzo."

"Do you promise?"

"I promise!"

"Cross your heart?"

"Cross my fucking heart."

I even crossed my heart with my hand before realising that he was taking the piss.

"Fucking hell, okay, never let it be said that I don't encourage new business start-ups. Come on; you'd better follow me to the car."

"You do realise that you're stepping into a dark and dangerous world? This isn't a job at fucking Argos; this is drugs, money and people and generally speaking when those three get together the party can turn a little nasty."

"I know, Enzo. I'm ready for it."

"I hope you are, and remember, any comebacks on selling this gear on Cazley's patch and you keep my name out of it, comprendes?"

"Yeah, mate, I've got it."

As we walked to Enzo's car the full meaning of his warning hit home. But I also spared a thought to the awfulness of a job at Argos, and with Christmas around the corner as well – I could only imagine how fucking busy it would get!

I sat in Enzo's motor with him, and the deal was done. He even threw in a consignment of little plastic bags for the gear to go in when I sold it. To be honest, I'd forgotten all about those little fuckers. I might have to have an 'Introduction to drug dealing' brainstorming session to make sure I didn't forget anything else.

I headed home with a bag of weed that had cost me three hundred quid. I reckoned that by the time I had been a little economic with dividing up quarter of an ounce consignments I'd get around five hundred notes for it. The deal was that in a fortnight Enzo was to be paid back his two hundred quid; otherwise, it would magically become three hundred and counting. I'd love to know what APR that put the loan at, but the Bank of Enzo was certainly not your usual high street lender.

The only thing I had to do now was to find a bunch of people that I could sell it to; oh, and to keep this operation away from Devo. For this to succeed I was going to have to achieve something that I didn't have a great track record of; I was going to have to work smart.

Chapter 10
Wednesday 9th October

I had my own stash of weed, which I was to sell for money, and it felt good; I felt like I was somebody. I lay in my bed looking at it whilst nodding. I'd treat myself to just one roll-up, but that would be it. I was determined to be disciplined. Today was all about kick-starting my business; sourcing new customers, getting my face out there, pressing flesh and networking.

I also knew exactly who my first client would be, as I could hear her coughing her guts up in the bathroom. But there would be no mate's rates, not even for Mum. Everybody would have to pay the same price. This situation required self-restraint and fortitude - whatever the fuck they were.

I picked my clothes up off the floor and got dressed. I had bagged up a load of quarter of an ounce consignments last night, but I wasn't taking the entire stash out with me. You see, I was even starting to think like a drug dealer now; you shouldn't take too much gear out with you just in case you get nicked or mugged, and be assured, both scenarios around here were very likely.

So, with a small consignment ready to be taken out with me, I needed a cunning hiding place for the remainder of the stash that I was to leave here. It had to be somewhere the Feds wouldn't look if I got raided.

After a full two minutes of careful, strategic thinking I shoved it under my bed.

Hang on a minute, was I not forgetting something? I quickly got down on my knees and feverishly looked around. The reason for the sudden panic was because about six months ago I had heard a strange squeaking sound coming from underneath my mattress. I'd assumed it was my bed springs finally giving up after months of high velocity shagging with my ex, however, I was to find out later that I had a family of fucking mice sharing my bedroom with me.

This prompted me to have to borrow the neighbour's cat; a fucking vicious thing called Terry. (That's the cat, not the neighbour, although, I suspect he could be a fucking handful as well.) Thankfully, the cat was a pro-baller when it came to hunting down mice, he was like a fucking feline Special Forces operative, and after a couple of minutes in the bedroom, Terry got shot of them all. We stood and watched in admiration as he went about his business, whilst his owner, Ace, provided me with a commentary of Terry's hunting strategy. Terry relished the challenge as he chased them around before biting his ferocious fangs through their little necks.

My worry in this instance was whether another family of mice had moved in. I surveyed under the bed, but there was thankfully no sign. The last thing I wanted was to return home later to discover that my weed had vanished and to have a family of fucking mice, high as kites, lying on my bed with the munchies, eating packets of cheese.

Okay, with the main bag of weed safely stashed away it was time to engage my first client. I walked into the living room where Mum was watching one of her antique programmes.

I needed to get the sales rapport rolling with a confident introduction.

"Alright, Mum?"

"Can you believe these twats on here have just paid forty-five quid for a fucking snuff-box?"

I decided that the ensuing conversation was likely to be tortuous and that it might be worth delaying signing her up as my first customer. Anyway, even if I got her to swear to never tell Devo, she would inevitably end up getting pissed and spilling the beans. Therein was a good lesson I had learnt in life: never tell an alcoholic a secret.

It was time to leave the flat and commence trading. As I opened the door, I took in a sharp intake of breath. Life felt good. I was about to start my journey as an apprentice drug-dealer, and I couldn't have felt prouder.

Chapter 11
Same Day

After exiting the flat, the feeling of immense optimism lasted only ten short steps. I stopped suddenly in my tracks as I realised I'd left my stash of weed on the cistern of the toilet. Last's night's kebab was far too heavily doused in hot chilli sauce and had prompted an emergency shit. Without thinking, I took the gear out of my trousers so as not to compress it. Bollocks! If Mum decides to nip for a piss during that meaningless bit of the antique programme when the presenter kills a bit of time by nosing around some fucking stately home, she'll discover the stash and be clawing her horrible yellow tipped fingers through it.

I anxiously opened the door and sprinted to the loo. It was a false alarm! Thankfully the auction was in full swing, and she hadn't moved. I grabbed the stash from the toilet, and I was back on track. As I was closing the door, I am sure I heard the faint murmurings of 'Told you'. Fucking hell, she even says it to herself!

I had thought long and hard about where to set up my stall and had decided to position myself near one of the main doorways to the biggest blocks of flats. I was only going to speak to those people I had seen around and knew. My pitch was that I had bought some gear but had to lay off it because of a chest infection; I'd got a bit left and was looking to off-load it. This exercise was all about establishing a new client base. Once I had, I intended not to be hanging around anywhere except my mobile phone, which would become the hotline for anyone wishing to indulge in a soft drugs only recreational diet.

Four hours in and I had spoken to dozens of unemployed fellas, haggard looking birds and a couple of disabled people where my angle on the weed was medicinal. I had handed out my number loads of times, made some warm contacts, established myself as a friendly face, but alas, there had been no sales. I was hungry and needed a piss, so I headed back to the flat.

Mum was fast asleep on the settee. There were eight empty cans of loopy juice on the coffee table despite it being barely five o'clock. The cupboards were pretty much bare, so I toasted the last stale crust of bread, and in the absence of butter, I spread brown sauce on to it.

Re-energised, I hit the streets again for my second stint. I was determined to be back in for eight o'clock to make sure I didn't run into the naughty lads, and more importantly not to alert Devo.

The second session was much the same as the first; plenty of chitchat with geezers who looked like they'd enjoy a puff, but no fucking sales. Shit! I was flat. I thought I'd be off and running by now and that I'd have a few quid in my pocket. I was skint and hungry, and with only a tin of ravioli in the cupboard, the chance of a decent dinner was looking slim. My only hope was Devo finishing work and bringing back fish and chips for us all.

It's fair to say that this scenario didn't play out.

"So, you had dinner at the Three Bells tonight then, Devo?"

"Fucking lovely it was, Bo, two nice pints after work and then a big plate of gammon, chips peas, bread and butter. Murray did us proud. You ought to try it mate."

"Nice one, bro," I said, as I nearly ripped my fucking fingers off trying to open the ravioli tin with this blunt, fucking tin opener. Oh, fuck it! I put it back in the cupboard and had another bowl of Coco Pops with water.

After that, I just lay on my bed. The thought of playing on my Xbox crossed my mind until I remembered that robbing cunt Big Frank had bought it off me and had no doubt flogged it on for a fourfold profit. I bet that fat bastard hadn't had Coco Pops for his tea.

Then, out of the blue, a text arrived:

Alright, m8, any chance of a kitten for £30?

Okay, so I had shamelessly nicked Enzo's code, but why not? And who cares, I was in business! By the time we had met up and done the deal I had received another text, then another one. Then the first geezer came back to me for more gear. Apparently, his brother wanted some, fucking hell - here we go!

By lunchtime the following day I was back on the blower to Enzo with a text:

'Gear sold, replenishment needed!'

Within minutes he had replied:

'Have you forgotten the code, you thick cunt?'

In my excitement, unfortunately, I had. Anyway, I set up the buy and smiled as I noticed a slightly admiring look on his cheeky Italian face because he knew it, Bo fucking Bates had arrived!

Back at the flat and I decided to do another four hours seeking more new clients around the estate, then I would use the last four hours servicing my new-found customers. It was like I was writing a start-up business manual for the aspiring drugs dealer. But this drug dealer was smart, and he had established hard and fast rules.

The rules were dead simple, well actually, it was the singular; the *rule* was dead simple: Do not come to my flat; I will come to you. It was only three or four minutes' walk maximum between flats around here, so it was neither here nor there for me, and given the extra fat I had put on it recently, the exercise was welcome. I suppose there would have been other rules, like, please don't tell the Feds, or Cazley, or my semi-psychotic brother, but under the circumstances, simplicity was key.

For the next six days, and with a lot of networking and pristine customer service, the hare was very much running at Walthamstow. I was doing alright, nothing heavy, but I reckon I was making about eighty quid a day. Good money for a fella who was used to just over a hundred quid a fortnight on job seekers allowance.

For the first time in my somewhat underachieving life, Boleyn Bates was pointing in the right direction.

Chapter 12
Monday 1st December 2014

I'd been up and running for eight weeks, and it's fair to say that business had ballooned big time. I had roughly three times more demand than I had gear. The problem was I couldn't generate the capital to get what I needed.

I made my regular trip to see Enzo, but this time there was a major problem; the well was dry, meaning his supplier had run out of weed. He could see that I was desperate; I was a drug dealer without drugs, which was like Ronald fucking McDonald announcing he was out of burgers. Thankfully, Enzo had another solution. Out of kindness, and very much on the basis that this would be a onetime gig, he gave me the number for an associate of his. He described the geezer as 'a fucking massive black fella, who you don't want to fuck about with, called Troy.' Now I won't lie, this description got me a little jittery, but business was business.

I left the meeting with Enzo and had sent Troy a message. Within minutes he had replied, and within two hours I was meeting the geezer in his big, fuck off black BMW. We sat in the back of his car, which was a proper pimp wagon, leather seats, cool music and gold teeth everywhere.

This guy was a player; different class. He had his own driver, and there were two other geezers stood around the car, on the look-out while we chatted. I told him I needed a small stash of weed, but Troy offered me the world. I gave him the six hundred pounds I had on me, and he gave me a grand's worth of gear, which I agreed to give him back within the week. If I pulled my finger out, I could shift this within six days, maybe even five given my ever expanding client list. Shit, I even had a teacher from a local college on my books now who was buying it for all the kids in his design class.

I couldn't deny that Enzo was a good contact, but Troy was different gravy. This guy had the gear, and he understood how the market worked. A dealer needs his stuff quickly, and Troy could get what you needed, when you needed it.

Back at home and I needed to keep a careful lid on things, but it was difficult. I was excited, and deep down I was dying to tell Devo. But I knew he would fucking hate it and go mad as there was something about drugs that he despised.

I decided to maintain a morose look around him like I was still struggling. The extra time that I was spending out of the flat, I had put down to seeing some bird from the estate, but I knew that time was running out. Sooner or later, he would find out; it was a certainty.

I also decided on no flash purchases. I remember Robert De Niro in Goodfellas going fucking ballistic at his crew after they had pulled a massive robbery. They were rocking up to a bar in flash cars and with their birds in fur coats. Admittedly, I didn't have a bird, neither had I passed my driving test, but that wasn't the point, the onus was on being sensible, well at least for the time being.

I had sixteen hundred pounds worth of weed, and in five days I could be holding three and a half grand! There was no doubt that a lot had changed in the last two months.

I lay in bed admiring my massive stash of weed. My storage area had been upgraded from under my bed to inside my old sports bag at the bottom of the wardrobe. It had crossed my mind that even the thickest of East End coppers would probably find it should the flat be searched, but with the exception of putting it amongst the remaining Coco Pops, I was struggling to think where to hide it.

I kicked back, my mind quickly drifted to the riches that were lying ahead. My trusted makeshift Pot Noodle ashtray would shortly be upgraded to a gold fucker with personalised cigarette butts in it. 'Boleyn Bates – Winner' would be the tips insignia. Some of them would have rich red lipstick around them from some gorgeous blonde that was hanging around me for my money. I'd also have that nice red lipstick every night around my cock.

It was all just around the corner now, within touching distance. I lay back on my bed and smiled and then nodded to myself, again.

Chapter 13
Sunday 7th December 2014

The gear was sold, and I had made three thousand one hundred pounds. During the previous six days, I had treated myself to a couple of nights out and flashed a bit of cash around some strippers in a lap dancing bar. Why not? I had earned the fucker.

I had dropped a text to my man Troy and told him I had his cash. I wanted to make sure this geezer got paid up before anything else happens. I was lying on my bed when his reply came through.

> **Gud lad. Petrol station on mile end rd @7pm.**
> **I'll send my boys to pick u up.**
> **It's time we had a drink.**

Fucking hell, Troy wanted to have a drink with me! He must be impressed with the speed in which I'd moved the gear. I envisaged the scene; we'd be at a fancy bar, me, Troy and his crew. They would all be looking sharp in swanky designer togs, but what about me – what would I be wearing? I looked at my bedroom floor where pretty much the contents of my wardrobe were on show. It was a pathetic array of dirty old hoodies and t-shirts. This won't do; this wouldn't do at all. I can't go turning up for a drink with a geezer like Troy dressed like a fucking street urchin. I'd got money in my pocket, so it was time to get myself some nice gear. It was time to roll the wheel of fortune and do it the Devo way.

With that thought, I got dressed, caught the tube and headed to the West End. I was buzzing. For the first time in my life, I had money in my pocket, a kick in my step and was dining at the top table. I walked around the West End feeling like a Prince. I was visiting the world-famous shops on Bond Street, Knightsbridge, and Covent Garden. I flashed my cash around like some fucking big-time pimp, and I was getting cups of coffee, free aftershave tasters, the fucking lot. I bought myself a wicked Armani jacket, a pair of Stone Island jeans, a pair of cool Adidas pumps and a CP Company t-shirt. There was small change leftover from seven hundred quid. I was so thrilled that I visited the toilet in Harrods and got changed into my new togs, having to painfully cut through the labels with my teeth. I was going to meet up with Troy looking like a proper geezer, not a fucking mug.

The recurring problem I had was Devo. He knew his brands, and he knew his prices. I kicked this around my head while having a seven-pound pint in a bar in Leicester Square. Bollocks to it; I'll tell him, come clean; explain the money; let him know that this estate was a fucking goldmine; full of people looking for weed. I had a full range of ages, races and religions now on my database of customers (my phone) from fourteen-year-olds making their way in the world of drugs to old age pensioners having one last bash at getting high before they kicked the bucket. I may well have been the only drug dealer in London who was compliant with the Equality and Diversity Act.

I'd even offer Devo in on a partnership if he wanted. But there was no way he could talk me out of doing this, not now. I had taken the brave steps to set this up. It was mine, my own little business. I finally had something I could be proud of.

Chapter 14

Same Day

Just after 7pm and I was standing at the petrol station, as instructed. I had Troy's money safely tucked away in the pocket of my Armani jacket. There was a twinge of nervousness though, I mean, I was being picked up by a big-time drug dealer, and I didn't have the faintest idea where I was going. But he had no beef with me, I had borrowed some gear from him, and he was getting paid back before the deadline. Surely, even within the slightly skewed moral code of the drug dealer, this wasn't a crime?

I then received a notification on my phone alerting me to yet another message from one of Lloyd's fans on Plenty of Fish. This wasn't unusual given the volume of traffic this fella generated, only this time the picture of the woman with her legs open was Sharon Critchlow, the fat, manky toothed bird with a hundred kids who lived in our block. I took a closer look at the picture, Jesus; she needs to get that looked at, it was like a badly packed kebab.

Suddenly I heard the thunderous bass of some grime tune coming from an approaching car. The black BMW pulled in, the window was lowered, and a face appeared.

"Are you Blow?" The face said.

"It's Bo," I replied.

"Get in."

The rear passenger door opened and I got in with more than a tad of trepidation. There were three black fellas in the car, two in the front and one sat next to me. Fucking hell, these boys looked proper naughty. The fella next to me nodded his head.

"Where are we going?" I asked slightly awkwardly.

I was ignored, and the music was blasted back on. I sat back pretending to look relaxed but secretly wondering what the fuck I had let myself into. I was massively out of my league, think Leyton Orient v Barcelona, with Leyton Orient suffering from a crippling injury list and a suspended top-scorer. Still, there was no point making a cunt of myself now. I was in the car and what was done, was done.

After about twenty minutes we pulled up at a nightclub in Lewisham. The club was not open, but we got out of the car and walked in. It was a posh place inside, just as I had envisaged, all chrome and mirrors; proper swanky. As we walked past a table, one of the fellas gestured for me to take a seat. A minute later, Troy appeared with some geezer behind him with a bucket full of ice, a bottle of champagne and a couple of glasses.

Troy came over, smiling and shook my hand.

"How are you, geezer? Welcome to my club."

"Thanks, it's well smart."

"It's how we like to do things, geezer, you know what I mean?"

"Yeah," I replied, not being entirely sure how to act.

"I understand you've done some good business."

He started to pour out the champagne and pass me a glass.

"It's been good, very good. In case you were wondering, I've got your money." I said nervously.

I went into my pocket to give it to him, but he reached out and stopped me.

"Good lad. Give it to Big D on the way out, will you?"

I looked at the door where there was a fella about the size of a chest freezer. I was guessing this was Big D.

"Now then geezer, you'll need some more gear, won't you?" he asked.

"I do, but shouldn't I contact Enzo first to see if he has any?"

"Fuck Enzo! You're my boy now. You buy from me. He let you down last time, geezer; he'd run out of gear, which could have fucked your operation."

"I suppose."

"I suppose?" he repeated, he then edged closer to me and lowered his voice.

"Dealers are like vultures, geezer, they circle above you waiting for a time to pounce, and when the time's right, they go straight in. By the time you'd got your hands on a fresh load of gear from Enzo, your customers would have been shopping at a different supermarket."

"I get you."

"But, that would never happen if you're buying from me. I've always got the gear, my friend and loads of it. You want it, and you come and see me."

"But won't Enzo get upset if I stop buying from him?"

"Maybe, and if he does, you let me know. I'll square it with him; everything will be sweet, geezer. Now how much are you after?"

"The same amount again would be good."

"But you're shifting it in a matter of days; there's no point you coming here every week, it's bad for productivity. I tell you what; let me give you a decent sized stash to keep you going. At the end of the month you bring me four grand, the rest you can keep, how does that sound?"

Troy winked and chinked my glass. He then gestured over to one of his crew who came over with what looked like a full shopping bag of fucking weed. Blimey, I'm not sure my sports bag in the wardrobe would be big enough to store it.

"Okay, that sounds fine," I said trying to act cool.

By my rough calculations, I could be on to make three or four grand in a month!

Fucking hell, I might even consider not bothering to sign-on anymore.

"I've got to crack on," said Troy.

He stood up and took another small swig from his champagne glass. I suspected that would not be the last drop he would have this evening.

"You finish your drink, and then one of my lads will take you home. You look after that bag, geezer; there's a few quid in there."

I looked down at it; he wasn't lying. I sat back and enjoyed the champagne. There was no rush. I had royally fucking arrived on the scene, and I was going to enjoy it. I even picked the bottle out of the bucket and poured myself another glass, and as the barman looked over, I winked at him. That's it, Bo, you let them know you aren't a fucking mug.

Suddenly the music came on in the club as the DJ for the evening was testing the sound system. I suddenly got a warm glow, maybe it was from the champagne, or maybe it was the feeling of success.

I took another swig from my glass and nodded my head, this time to the beat of the music. Life, for the first time, felt fucking beautiful!

Chapter 15
Thursday 11th December 2014

Should I ever be invited to write the dummies guide to starting up your own business as a drug-dealer, then I am pretty sure that the opening chapter would detail the importance of providing a customer focused and friendly service in the backdrop of a competitive and somewhat aggressive market.

This was fast becoming my unique selling point, giving me a healthy market advantage. I had established critical customer service levels, which I worked hard to adhere to.

Having received a text from a client, my Service Level Agreement was that they would have their gear within fifteen minutes' maximum, provided they had the cash. Oh, and plenty didn't, 'can I give it to you tomorrow?' No, fuck off! 'Can I swap a quarter of weed for some old DVD's I've got?' No, fuck off! I even got offered a blow job in lieu of payment on one occasion, which I wouldn't have minded so much about, but it was from a fucking fella.

'No pay, no play', that was my motto. I hadn't associated how the 'no play' element of that phrase related to getting your drugs, but it was a message that was certainly being understood from my demographically diverse customer base.

18.48pm and I was on the move between flats dropping off goods like an on-foot pizza delivery man. Five calls, four cash payments with the non-payment visit being the offer of a fucking fifteen-year-old microwave in lieu of a quarter of an ounce. That cunt was officially on his last warning.

I decided to put in a bit of face time around one of the block entrances when out of the shadows Enzo appeared. Bollocks! I had, since seamlessly transferring my wholesale drug purchasing to Troy, received three missed calls from him and four texts, all of which I'd ignored. I was hoping that the penny would drop and he'd work out that two plus two equalled Troy being my supplier and that he wouldn't think about unsettling this arrangement, especially given Troy's propensity to extreme violence.

"Alright, Bo, I'm assuming you're not stood here selling tickets for a fucking charity raffle?"

"Alright?" I replied.

I became nervous, but I knew I would have to act cool and hold my own.

"Have you changed your mobile number?"

"No."

"Didn't think so, so what's the deal, have you fucking skanked me?"

"What do you mean?"

"You know what I mean, you were buying your gear from me, and now you're not. Have you fucking skanked me, or what?"

"Look Enzo; you put me on to Troy, I got some gear from him then after that he just dumped a load more on me. What could I say? I couldn't fuck him off, could I?"

"Of course you could. You could have paid him back the money you owed him and walked away. Only you didn't."

"I know you're pissed off, but can you take this up with Troy?" I said, desperately trying to deflect any further confrontation.

"That makes it sound like I've got a billing complaint with the fucking council," he said.

"What?"

"This has got fuck all to do with Troy. It's between you and me."

"I'm in the business of selling gear, Enzo. You didn't have any, so I went somewhere else."

"I put you on to him as a favour, you ungrateful cunt, and this is how you pay me back?"

I decided that it was time to roll the dice.

"Well, here's the deal, how about I tell Troy that you came around here giving it fucking large - is that what you want?"

"This isn't about Troy and me, it's about me, and you and I just wanted to let you know that you've made an enemy."

"Oh, big fucking deal!" I was coming out fighting.

"You're a fucking novice who is already rubbing people up the wrong way. In my book, that's a really bad fucking move!"

"Fuck yourself, Enzo, who are you anyway? I'm Troy's boy now; you're no one. You're a fucking one-man band, a small-time Charlie. So why don't you do yourself a favour and fuck off!"

"Listen to you."

"No, listen to you. You ride solo, bro. I don't. I've got a fucking army behind me, and they are all tooled up and ready to attack and all I've got to do is to click my fingers."

Enzo just stood there, stared at me and smiled.

"You're a fucking schoolboy swimming in the wrong pond. Oh dear, Bo, I do wish I hadn't helped you start-up now. When you come unstuck, I might end up feeling responsible."

"Whatever."

He walked off. With any luck, I'd seen the last of that cunt, and I also had, for the first time in my life, called someone else 'small-time'.

I decided at that point that should I ever write my dummies guide to starting your own business as a drug dealer, then 'Small-time' would be the title of chapter two.

Chapter 16
Same day.

I arrived home after 11pm, the flat lights were on, but it was deadly quiet. I assumed Dev was bedded as usual. He had certainly gained a new-found discipline since he left prison. He was taking this job seriously, and I got the distinct impression this one was a keeper.

I sat at the kitchen table reflecting on my new life and the challenges it was presenting me. I had acted ballsy around Enzo earlier, but it wasn't something that came naturally to me. Despite living in a tough area, I was still quite a sensitive individual, which seemed a little odd given my less than orthodox childhood. Still, I did have a good track record of brushing things off quickly, and this was something I was going to need to do from now on.

I then ran various scenarios in my head of what might have happened if Enzo had started to get aggressive with me. I stood up, and air punched little moves, two rights and a left, 'have that you, cunt!' After I had delivered the punches, I stood bouncing up and down on my toes, ready to hand out more. Who was I trying to kid? I was no street fighter. The scraps I'd had with kids at school were low-level wrestling matches, which by the way, I had invariably lost. Mike Tyson, I was not, and I needed a reality check.

But I knew that trouble was lurking, it was probably just around the corner. There's no doubt that the money I was making now, while not a king's ransom, was worth having. Someone would come sniffing along soon; it was simply a matter of time.

The front door opened and in walked Devo - bollocks! The evening was going from bad to worse. I only needed Mum to come through and begin a lecture on the prominence of Japanese porcelain in the current antique market, and that would put the icing on the cake.

I wasn't ready for him; I was totally off my guard. I had all my new togs on, and unless he went straight to bed the shit was just about to royally hit the fucking fan.

"Guess what I've got us, Bo? A couple of quarter pounder cheeseburgers!"
He walked with his takeaway bag and dropped it on the table, before turning to me.

"Fucking hell, if they're handing out Armani jackets at the Jobcentre then I'm going to sign on myself!"

"Do you like it, bro?"

"Like, it? I fucking love it! Stone Island fucking jeans, as well?! Did you get lucky on the scratch cards?"

"Not exactly."

"Didn't think so; come on then, what's the story, or should I guess?"

"You aren't going to like it, bro."

"Ah, that one; got you! What are you fucking playing at?"

"I'm making a mint Dev; I'm just selling a bit of weed around the estate. No one else is doing it."

"'No one else is doing it,'" he shook his head. "How long have you been doing this for?"

"A couple of months."

"And the local dealer's happy with you trading on his manor?"

"I haven't heard shit from him, bro. The fella I get my gear off is a right horrible cunt; I think he knows that and he's leaving me well alone."

"Oh that's okay then," he said sarcastically, "it sounds like you've got it all sorted."

"There's room for two though, Dev, you can join me, if you want?"

"Now that's an honourable offer, but given my sudden affinity to freedom and not wanting to spend Christmas on 23-hour lockdown in a shoe-boxed sized cell, I'll pass, if that's okay with you?"

"I was making sure you didn't miss out, Dev that's all."

Devo then just sat down at the table and looked at me for a few long seconds before he sighed.

"Fucking hell, Bo, just look at you, all dressed up in your new flashy gear, making money selling drugs, you're even acting differently."

"I'm moving up in the world, Dev," I said proudly.

"'Moving up in the world,' you've been watching too much fucking Scarface. Where do you think this is all going to end?"

"Does it have to end?"

"Every story has an ending, mate. What's your ending going to be; Prison? Stabbed down an alley? Shot in the back of a car?"

"I told you, I've got someone watching my back. I've got nothing to worry about, bro."

"Can I tell you how I think this will play out?"

"Fucking hell, can you leave it out? If I wanted some advice, I would have rung the Samaritans!"

"Listen to me for a minute; this is how I think this is going to play out. I might be wrong, but this is where I'd put my money. I reckon in the next few weeks a couple of local geezers are going to see you swanning around in your new flash clothes and say to themselves, 'I want a piece of that.' Then they'll make a move on you."

"I am in a crew, though." I interrupted, desperate to prove to him that I could make this work.

"Just fucking shut up and listen! They'll make a move for you to see what your reaction is. To see whether you're someone that kicks back, whether you're a fella with a mob behind him. Now, if what you say is true, then your cavalry will come running in, and you'll be fine. But if they don't, then it's you against them."

"And then I'll have to let them know what I'm about."

"But you're no tough guy, mate, and they will suss you out in a second. You'll get slapped around a bit, and that will be the end of your little business venture. They'll take your patch, take your customers, they might even take your brand new fucking Armani jacket."

"I knew you'd try and throw cold water on this. It's a bit of weed, bro and I'm making some money for once!"

"It's drugs; it's fucking toxic, I'm telling you, mate."
The conversation suddenly became heated.

"It's fine isn't it when you're going out nicking stuff off people, holding up post offices, pinching cars, but that's okay because Devo fucking Bates says so."

"I don't want this life for you; you're my little brother."

"So, it's okay for good old Dev, but not for me because I'm your brother?"

"Do you think I ever looked at myself in the mirror, when I was doing those things and felt proud?"

"You used to love it, don't fucking pull that one with me."

"It was a front. I was fucking ashamed of myself. I would have much rather had an honest job and been pulling cash in for you and Mum."

"Well, that's alright then Dev, because you've got your fucking straight job now. Bully for you! Forty hours a fucking week, you fucking mug!"

"Fucking mug?! I've been out celebrating tonight because I've just been made warehouse manager today!"

"Warehouse manager, oh big fucking deal! I'll earn more in one fucking day than you'll earn in a week."

"It's taken me less than three months to get this job so don't you take the piss out of me, you cocky little cunt."

"Go and lecture someone else, bro, because I'm through with listening. For the first time in my life, I'm making something of myself, and you want to spoil it."

"You're selling weed on a high-rise fucking council estate, you fucking knob. You're talking like you're Lord Sugar's next apprentice!"

"Can't you be pleased for me just for once in your life? Can't you just let go of this need to protect me, because frankly, bro, I'm finding it suffocating."

"It wasn't suffocating when you used to come home from school, and the bullies were having a pop at you, though was it?"

"That was fucking yonks ago!"

"You've got a fucking short memory. How many times did my little brother come crawling up to me, 'Alright Dev, someone's giving me some stick, could you sort him out?'"

"Well, those days are over!"

"They are, are they? Right, then you remember the time and place where you said that. Right in this fucking room, right fucking now! From now on, tough guy, you fight your own battles, because I've retired from doing it."

"I've got tougher people than you on my side now. I'm in bed with proper naughty lads. I mean, not being funny, bro, but when it comes to being hard, you're not exactly fucking premier league."

"Good, glad to hear it. Now do me a fucking favour will you, your former bodyguard's hungry and wants to eat his burger, so fuck off!"

I left and went to my bedroom.

I lay on my bed. Fuck him! Fuck Devo and fuck his fucking code. It was time to do it my way. My rules, my game, my fucking result. For the first time in my life, I was in total control, and I had edged out in front of him, and the truth was he didn't fucking like it.

Well, fuck him!

Chapter 17
Friday 12th December

I woke up with that very distinct feeling, the feeling you only get when you have argued with someone you care about. It's like a horrible dull pain in your guts. Any stubbornness you might have demonstrated afterwards, where you've convinced yourself that you're right, starts to wear off, leaving only hurt. Last night's row with Devo was the first time I'd ever snapped back at him. Generally speaking, when he told me to stop doing something, I did. Was I right to challenge him? If I was honest, the real reason I was so prickly about him confronting me was that I knew he was right.

I had become a drug dealer, and you can sugar-coat it as much as you like with the 'it's only a bit of weed,' sort of shit, but a dealer of drugs was what I had become. I had taken the soft option and made a few quid the easy way. It's not that I felt any great social responsibility not to become a drug dealer, but somewhere deep inside me, it did not feel right. Maybe it was Devo's influence and his aversion to drugs and everything they stand for. But what is the difference between selling someone drugs and nicking their car off them? I lay pondering this, but couldn't draw any conclusions. No wonder I didn't choose to study philosophy at university.

For the first time in my life, I was making some dosh, and that gave me a reason to carry on. I mean, what else was I going to do? If I took Dev's advice and agreed that he was right, then what - saunter back to the fucking Jobcentre; tell them the drug dealing trade wasn't for me and ask them if I could sign back on? Of course, I couldn't. Any risks I was taking now had to outweigh the downward spiral of being a dole-boy again.

I glanced at my bedroom floor; it was good to see that my expensive new clothes were dispersed all over the place. The week after I had brought them I'd hung them up in my wardrobe, which, while falling to pieces and only having one door, did somehow perform the function of keeping them hanging straight. But this temporary sense of discipline quickly dissipated back to the piss-poor level that I always operated at.

I was once again in that sort of mood where you indiscriminately shake your head throughout the day. Where you think about your life and shake your head, think back to the argument you had with someone that means something to you and shake your head, look at a hundred-pound t-shirt screwed up on your floor and shake your fucking head.

I rolled up a big, fuck off spliff. I needed to relax and get my act together. My phone then bleeped. My mobile drugs store was a 24/7 gig and the first order of the day had been received. Sixty quid's worth was needed as soon as possible in flat 24, block B. This was a regular customer who always had the cash ready, so I needed to get my shit together, and I needed to stop shaking my fucking head.

Despite me feeling emotionally fragile, it had to be business as usual.

Chapter 18
Same day

It was evening, and the estate was getting busy. There were plenty of punters around who were dying to supplement their Friday night with a nice little bag of low risk, high gain narcotics. The scene was set to make a decent buck.

I was standing in my usual position, which was a useful vantage point to eye-up a buyer who was seeking a dealer. People were coming and going, some going home from work, some coming home from the pub but it was then that I saw the silhouette of three youths walking with a swagger and heading in my direction. The time had arrived, and the cavalry was on its way. I saw one of them nod his head as if to acknowledge confirmation of their target.

I took a gulp.

This was the moment that I had dreaded.

I knew this was going to happen sooner rather than later, but sod's law dictated it would be the day after the lecture from Dev.

Enter three fellas, roughly my age, in various items of cool street wear, making a beeline for me. They looked serious, and they meant business.

Despite being very clear in my head what I was going to say when this moment arrived; I still felt the urge to run. But I knew I couldn't. I had Troy as my trump card in my back pocket. I would flash his name around, and I knew this would keep the wolves from the door because they wouldn't dare fuck about with him.

I just needed to keep my powder dry.

"Cazley wants to see you," opened the tasty looking black fella.

"Let's do it then," I said and followed them out of the estate.

We walked to the nearby subway where a black Mercedes had been driven onto the grass verge. As we approached, the door opened and a toned, muscular mixed race fella got out of the vehicle, he had tattoos all over his neck and creeping up to his face.

It was Cazley.

I approached him slowly.

I noticed the tears that were tattooed down his face, although I suspected this fella hadn't cried for a while.

"Six weeks ago, the eyes and ears tell me about some new face selling off a bit of spare weed on my patch. 'A bit of spare weed', I said. 'Let him do it, let's be generous and give him a free lunch'. A couple of weeks later, and the eyes and ears are telling me that this spare weed seems to be lasting the new face quite a long time.

'Find out who he is', I tell them. 'We might need to teach this little cunt a lesson'. 'He's doing well for himself', say the eyes and ears, 'maybe you missed a trick, Cazley, maybe you should have bothered yourself by selling weed after all'? 'Maybe I should', I said. 'Let's keep watching him, who knows; he might be good enough to find all the customers that we need to make this operation worth our while'. A couple of days ago, the eyes and ears are now telling me that our new friend is spotted walking through the estate, bold as fucking brass, carrying a big fucking shopping bag which we are pretty sure is not full of delicious fruit and veg. 'Now it's time that we had a chat' I said, 'go and get him for me', I told them. So, we meet at last."

"I never meant to tread on your toes; I'm only selling weed."

"Only selling weed?"

"You've never bothered with it; I tried to buy some from your boys loads of times, so we decided to give it a go."

"We decided, did we? So, who's we?"

"Me and Troy."

"You and Troy?" He looked fucking narked. "What's the arrangement with you and fucking Troy?"

"I get my gear off him."

"And?"

"And what?"

"Do you just buy it from him, or did he tell you to sell it here?"

"Just buy it from him, but he knows I sell it here."

Cazley, lowered his voice, "So we are clear, did the dentist tell you to sell it here, or not? It's a yes or fucking no question."

The dentist? I assume he meant Troy.

"No, but I'm in his crew. I'm one of his boys."

"In his crew?" He repeated. The other lads laughed. "Did you hear that fellas, he's in his crew!" They continued to laugh.

Cazley shook his head then took a big sigh before he clicked his fingers. A fella then got out of the Mercedes and pulled from his pocket a gold bladed knife, which he passed to Cazley.

Fucking hell, I was in big trouble now.

I then felt my arms forced behind my back. The three fellas then grabbed me as I struggled and dragged me to the car pushing me against the door. One of them wedged his massive forearm under my chin holding my head in position. Cazley then pulled the knife and put the tip literally on my fucking eyeball. I was hyperventilating with fear, shit, was he about to blind me?

"Here's what's going to happen. Sylvester and the lads are going to go back to your flat with you, and you're going to give them three things. The shopping bag of weed you picked up the other day, your stash of money and your mobile phone. Now, I'm a very busy fella, and I don't like being fucked around, so unless Sylvester is back here in twenty minutes with weed, cash and your phone then I'm going to have my boys drag you over my car, and I'm going to pop one of your eyeballs with the tip of my knife. Do you hear me?"

"Yes."

"And should I ever see you even selling so much as a packet of Rizla around here and I'll pop the other eye out as well, you got it?"

"Yes."

"Good, then fuck off."

Bollocks, I was snookered.

I trudged back to the flat with my four new guardian angels. Sylvester had his big right hand grasped around my forearm on the off-chance that I was fucking daft enough to try and do a runner. I walked into the flat, and thankfully Devo wasn't in. Mum, predictably, was pissed and asleep on the settee. I decided to play this with a straight bat, no drama, no tricks, just give them what they came for and then let Troy deal with them afterwards.

They followed me into the bedroom and waited. I got the money and the gear out and handed it over along with my mobile phone. The cheeky cunts even whipped my phone charger out of the socket as well.

There was a pause as Sylvester acknowledged to the others that they had got what they came for. Then one of them then grabbed me aggressively around the collar, and they led me out of the flat.

I knew what was coming next. There was no way Cazley was going to let me off without a shoeing and looking at these fellas this beating was going to get rough. I was led outside the flat, and that's when fear took a grip on me. I tried not to let them know that I was scared, but I couldn't hide it. I began to tremble and indiscriminately plead for mercy. Devo had framed it perfectly the other day, I wasn't a tough guy, far from it, and this was going to be a timely reminder.

They led me to the stairwell and threw me down the cold, grey concrete stairs. As I tried to get up, I felt a hard punch on the side of my face; it was to be the first of many.

Chapter 19
Saturday 13th December

I woke in a right state and gingerly limped out of bed, wincing in agony as I tried to walk. Being thrown down the stairs had properly fucked up my left ankle. I looked in the mirror and my heart sunk. It was worse than I thought; a black eye, a massive cut on my nose, split lip, the full nine yards. They had properly gone to work on me.

I had already established my play; I would go and see Troy and tell him what had gone down and let him deal with it. That cunt Cazley had nicked our gear, and a fella like Troy wouldn't take that lying down. I may well have started a gang war, but so be it, Cazley had to be taught a lesson.

I did have one slight problem; I didn't have Troy's mobile number. That was sitting on my mobile phone SIM card, which was sitting in my mobile phone which I'm guessing would now be sitting in the pocket of a Nike hoodie, which alas, did not belong to me.

I limped around the bedroom eventually managing to put my clothes on before I ventured slowly out. Mum, as usual, was watching Saturday Morning Kitchen, which for someone who never cooked, seemed a very odd choice of programme. It was 10.51am so Devo would be down at the launderette, regular as clockwork. I needed to get my shit together and get over to Troy's place. It would be a trek on the tube over to Lewisham and a torturous walk to the underground with this fucking ankle, but it had to be done. My objective for the day was clear; I needed to get Troy involved in this dispute and get my fucking patch back.

I hobbled out of the flat, went down on the lift and exited out of the main door. As I did, who was stood there, clear as fucking day? Enzo.

"Alright, Bo? Fucking hell mate, you don't look too clever!"

"Leave it out, Enzo."

"There's good news and bad news on the territory front. The bad news is you've lost your patch. I mean, don't be too cut up about it; you fucking gate-crashed it anyway. The good news is, guess who Cazley has given it to?"

Fuck me; I was broken.

"Congratulations, I'm thrilled for you."

"And, hey – thanks, buddy. You've worked up all the weed smokers on the estate who will now, very happily, transfer over to buy gear from yours truly. Cazley didn't think there was much of a market for it, but good old Bo Bates proved him wrong. It's like Dragons Den but with soft drugs."

"Look Enzo, no hard feelings mate? You win. I need to go over and tell Troy that I've lost this patch. I haven't got his number mate; you couldn't give it to me, could you?"

"Of course I can, anything for an old mate, have you got a pen?"

I did as it happened, one of those funny little blue pens you get from your local bookmakers. Enzo got his phone out, and I scribbled the number on my hand.

"Nice one," I said, through gritted teeth.

"Give Troy our love, won't you?" he said with a smug grin.

I walked off. Fuck him. I would get straight on the blower to Troy, and I'd make it my business to ensure that this cocky prick would be the first head to roll. I made my way to one of the few telephone boxes in the area, chucked in a quid and dialled the number. It was the first step to a full declaration of war.

The phone rang a few times before, "Good morning, how can I help?"

"Is Troy there please?" I asked.

"Troy, there's no Troy working here, I'm afraid."

Had Enzo given me the wrong number?

"This is an advice line for schoolboy's who swim in the wrong pond," the voice said.

"What?"

I then got uncontrollable laughter down the phone. Bollocks, it was Enzo. The cheeky cunt had given me my own number, which of course I hadn't recognised. Cazley had obviously given him my phone so that when my clients wanted drugs, he could now service the sale.

"Do you remember what I said? You're a fucking schoolboy swimming in the wrong pond, oh and in case you were wondering I was sat in the car watching you when Cazley held that knife against you. You see, I've become his 'eyes and ears'."

Chapter 20
Same day

My painful journey across the City was finally at an end as I arrived at Troy's club. I knocked on the door several times before some geezer finally answered. I explained the situation and that I needed to urgently speak to Troy. Reluctantly he let me in. The fella sat me down while he called him. I could hear muffled conversation before he finished the call and told me that Troy was on his way.

I don't know which fucking way he was coming from because he turned up a full three hours later. He walked over to my table and greeted me with a handshake.

"How's it going, geezer? I wasn't expecting to see you for another few weeks. Ouch! It looks like you've had a spot of bother." He said scanning my wounds.

"You could say that. Cazley's mob kicked the shit out of me. He's taken all our fucking gear and money."

"Naughty, naughty!"

"It's gone Troy, all of it."

"What cash and weed?"

"Cash, weed, my mobile phone with all of my contacts on, everything we had, gone!"

"That's a shame," he said, sitting down and looking at me.

"Yeah, it is," I said.

Troy shrugged his shoulders, "So?"

"So, what are we going to do about it?" I asked

"What are we going to do about it? Sorry, I don't think I understand?"

"He's taken liberties, bro; he's properly taken the piss out of us. We've got to hit him back, haven't we?"

"Have you?"

I could see where this was heading.

"I can't do this on my own, Troy."

"Who do you work with?"

"I thought I worked with you?"

"No, I mean away from here, how many lads have you got in your firm?"

"What firm?"

"Oh dear, so it's just you?"

"Yeah, me and….I thought I had your backing, bro?"

"Did you?"

"I thought I was 'your boy', part of your team, that's what you told me!"

"Now hang on a minute, geezer, you come here, I give you weed, you sell it, then you bring me money back, and then we repeat the cycle, that's a business relationship. I'm not sure it means we are sharing a double bed, does it?"

"Aren't you going to do anything then?"

"Let me get this straight geezer; you decided to start selling weed on Cazley's patch?"

"But I only-"

"Did you or did you not start selling weed on Cazley's patch?"

"Yeah."

"And he found out about it and gave you a good hiding and nicked your gear?"

"Yeah, that's right."

Troy then shrugged his shoulders, "That's why this has got nothing to do with me. Look, if someone came muscling onto my patch, selling gear, nicking my trade, I'd kick the shit out of them. Whoever he was buying his gear off, is neither here nor there. You started selling on Cazley's patch, and he did the same to you; fair play to him."

"So it doesn't bother you that they've nicked your gear?"

"It was your gear geezer. The second you agreed to pay me for it, it became your gear."

"You're not going to do anything about it then?"

He shook his head. "What you need to understand is that if I go into battle with another crew, it has to be over a serious fucking problem, because it will cost me men, money and the heat from the Old Bill will be unbearable. Nobody wants that if it can be avoided."

"Bollocks! What am I going to do now?"

"Find another patch, only if you want a word of advice make sure it's not an area where you'd be stepping on someone else's toes. There are plenty of them about."

"Is there?"

"You've just got to look hard for them."

"And if I found somewhere, would you be able to get me started with some more gear?"

"Absolutely geezer, I'll help you," he said with a friendly smile.

"Okay, nice one. I'll get to it. I'll have a scout around and be back in a few days with a couple of suggestions if you don't mind helping me?"

"Of course not, you just let me know which area you have in mind, and I'll give you the lowdown on what I know about it."

"Great!" I signed with relief "Thanks, Troy, I appreciate it mate."

"Think nothing of it."

I got up to leave, and he grabbed my arm.

"You haven't forgotten about the four grand you owe me though, have you?"

"What?! I told you, I haven't got it, they nicked it."

"That's not my problem. You've got three weeks until it's due."

"I'm not going to be able to get my hands on that sort of money; I'm skint."

"Four grand geezer; three weeks today; otherwise, I'm afraid I'll have to initiate my debt recovery procedure."

"What do you mean?"

"Unless I see my green on this table in three weeks' time I'm going to find you, and then I'm going to snap off half a dozen of your teeth, and that's just for starters. Now you have a good think about it."

I felt the blood drain from my head and a sat in a lightheaded trance of fear. Cazley, Enzo, the dentist. What fucking world had I entered?

"Dwayne, get this geezer a beer on the house, will you? Goodbye, Bo, I'll be seeing you in three weeks."

Troy got up and left.

Three weeks to get a sum of money together that was more than I had owned in my entire life. I just wouldn't be able to do it; it was impossible. I was in desperate trouble.

The barman then brought a beer over to me and poured it slowly into the glass before placing it on a coaster, I thanked him, and our eyes met.

"A little bit of advice my friend, find that four grand; do whatever it takes but make sure you pay him. I've seen him do some terrible things to people."

Chapter 21
Same day

When Cazley's boys had escorted me back to the flat, the thick cunts took everything, everything except the cash I had made on the night. That was safely tucked away in my jacket pocket. I had traded just under three hundred pounds of weed that day, and I still had the dosh. It was better than nothing and maybe my passport out of this. Talking of passports, this was one of the only official documents I owned. Devo had bought it for my 18th birthday. The plan was that we were going to watch West Ham play in Europe and we very nearly did until Devo got in a fight with some of the locals in Marseille and we ended up spending the night in a foul-smelling French nick before getting deported home first thing in the morning. Still, the passport could still be a useful commodity, as I now had an option - I could fuck off out of Dodge and escape this mess. The only issue was I wouldn't have a fucking clue where to go. My German was a little rusty having only ever been to three lessons while at school; I was probably banned from re-entering France because of the aforementioned aggro in Marseille, and to be honest, I wasn't entirely sure where Spain was.

I sat on the edge of my bed weighing up my options, which appeared to have one thing in common; they were shit. But there was one thing I could do; maybe there was just one way out of this?

After a couple of hours of hard thinking I had decided that this was my only tangible option, but it was equivalent to me attempting a bungee jump attached to a cobweb, such was the danger associated with it. However, I knew that only by paying Troy off would I be free, free of some geezer who would be happy to offer me a competitive dental plan and released from the horrors of this shit-stinking industry that I now so regretted becoming entangled in.

I needed to be able to escape and start again. I'm not entirely sure what 'start again' meant, but I was committed to answering this question, assuming this little life-threatening predicament gets resolved.

It was a risk, but bollocks to it; it was the only plan I could think of.

Later that day, I'd visited Ricky Santini, who had provided me with information about the delivery driver from eastern Europe, and in the process, I'd had my only stroke of luck in the last, miserable 48-hours. The driver was due to make a drop four days before my deadline with Troy. That would make sense; it would be just before New Year's Eve and exactly when a delivery would be required. He explained that the schedule was the same as usual. That had to mean the lorry driver would deliver the lion's share of the goods at the European Store. If he did then all of the chess pieces were in position for me to do the robbery. But the horrible reality was that I was going to have to become an armed criminal, and in doing so I'd risk a lengthy spell in prison should I be caught. My palms started to perspire just contemplating it. I recalled vividly the inside of the prisons from back when I visited Devo, that distinct smell; the uniforms; the broken look he had as a consequence of being incarcerated - fucking hell did I have the bollocks to do this?

I wasn't sure if I was thinking straight, but at least I was thinking; seeking solutions and making decisions. If this all went to shit, then years in a prison cell would give me ample time to reflect back and pick the bones out of what I should have done differently. But right here, right now, there appeared to be only one way out of this. To do the robbery would surely provide me with enough money to pay my debt? I ran my tongue over the edge of my front teeth and decided that I quite liked them being attached to my mouth. This had to be worth the risk.

I was committed to robbing the store, to scare an old man and steal his money, I had to. I also decided I would neither invite, nor tell Devo about it. If I invited him, I was certain, even despite my dilemma that he'd refuse, but then he would be drawn into the equation, and it would get messy. Moreover, as soon as he became involved, I would lose the last bit of control I had of the situation No, I had to keep Devo out of it. I would tell him that my current bumps and bruises were nothing more than an occupational hazard, and I was still on track, selling drugs and making a pile of dosh.

But that still left me with one big motherfucker of a problem; I couldn't do the job on my own, it was way too risky for a one-man job, and in any event, I was a total novice and didn't have a clue where to start.

I needed a wingman, someone with form, someone to guide me through the dangers and pitfalls of a gig like this, I needed a fella with a cool head who could keep calm under intense pressure.

There was only one man for it, and I was limping down the road to have a pint with him.

I was off to the Three Bells to see the Brigadier.

Chapter 22
Same Day

When I arrived at the Three Bells at 5.05pm on this Saturday afternoon the only reason in the world that the Brigadier would not be in here drinking was that he was either hospitalised, dead or on holiday. Now, given he believed holidays were for wankers, as was, according to him, washing your hands after a piss and taking fruit to work, the latter was highly unlikely. The Brigadier being in the Three Bells at this time on a Saturday was a mathematical certainty because drinking is what he did and the Three Bells is where he did it.

He always seemed to have money for a beer, I wasn't sure how he generated his regular income, but he always had money for beer, gambling and the odd second-hand piece of designer clothing.

I walked into the pub, and sure enough there he was alive and kicking and propping up the bar, scratching his ruddy little fat face and reading his copy of the Racing Post.

The Brigadier spoke in a strangely soft and gentlemanly way and therefore, so did everyone who conversed with him.

"Evening Brigadier."

He peered over his paper, "Good evening, old son."

"Have you got a minute, I've got something you might be interested in?"

"I hope it's a tip for the 6.05 at Leopardstown?" He joked.

"I think you'll find this is more of a certainty."

"A certainty? I'm not sure there is such a thing, but it's a fucking good way to get my attention."

I ordered us a couple of pints and found us a table far away from the boisterous Saturday afternoon crowd.

I explained the job to him in as much details as I could. Poker-faced, the Brigadier, just stared back at me. When I finished, he sat back in his chair and scratched the underside of his chin.

"Why haven't you asked your brother to do this?"

"He's out the game, bro, retired. I reckon that last spell in the nick has put him off."

"Why do you want to go down this road, this isn't your sort of thing?"

"Honestly? I've got myself into some serious shit, bro, see my fucking face for details."

He stared at me for a few seconds pondering before he announced, "Okay, count me in!"

"Good lad!"

I was mightily relieved. Maybe a chink of light had finally appeared, albeit a big fucking risky one.

"Have you got a tool we can use to scare the old man?" I asked.

"A tool? Oh no brother, we'll need a 'piece' for this job. That shopkeeper will guard his money like the crown jewels; if we take a tool, we'll end up having to hit the poor old sod. No, a piece will have him handing it straight over."

"Right great, and have you a got a 'piece'?"

"Has David Beckham got a tattoo?" he said with a smirk.

"Gotcha! Okay, let's hook up nearer the time to go through the details."

"Sounds like a plan old son."

"Hey, Brigadier, thanks, bro, thanks a lot," I said.

The relief was oozing out of the pores of my skin.

"Now let's have a fucking good old drink," he said.

Chapter 22
Sunday 14th December 2014

I was lying in bed looking at my new piece of shit mobile phone that I had purchased the day before. It was a 'pay-as-you-go' fucking walkie-talkie, sold by Tesco and made by slave kids in Indo-fucking-China. The little luxuries were limited to phone calls and text messages. Surfing the net for porn would have to be temporarily put on hold, as would swapping messages with Lloyd's army of cock-hungry fans.

I looked across at my new makeshift ashtray. I'd retained the Pot Noodle brand as that was pretty much a family tradition, but I had now thankfully reverted to chicken balti flavour, and with that, I had achieved a simmering level of psychological comfort.

I lay back on my virtually plump-free, twelve-year-old pillow and reflected on the last few weeks. Barring the last couple of days, I got a faint tinge of optimism. Bo Bates had single-handily established a very nice little earner. So much so, that the big boys felt compelled to come and take it from me. That only goes to prove that it was worth taking, and I had achieved this myself and not with the usual help of my brother. Perhaps I'd been under-estimating myself? Sure, I was a fuck-up merchant at school, but that was years ago. Maybe the corner had been turned; maybe I could pull this job off after all?

As if my life as a soft drugs dealer had not been precarious enough, I was now upgrading to being an armed robber. I was all too aware, assuming I went through with the robbery, of the two distinct routes that my life would take based on the outcome. Outcome one was that I successfully carried out the crime and paid Troy off. Outcome two was rather more sinister; either I didn't get the money, or I got the money and then got nicked. Hang on, was that three outcomes? The dread of this third outcome then swept over me. What if I did the job and got nicked before I'd paid off Troy? Fucking hell, I'd be serving time in prison with the only thing to look forward to when I was released was having that mad bastard going medieval on my teeth. Outcome two and three were both a calamity, and as I contemplated the awfulness of them, I again ran my tongue along the edge of my front teeth and briefly wondered what tool Troy would use to extract them.

Realising that I had my whole life riding on the outcome of this robbery, I needed to have it all sorted out. The planning and execution of this had to be undertaken with military-style precision. I would have to have everything very carefully organised and scheduled right down to the second. The time we met; the clothes we wore; who would do what; how we would enter the shop; how we would exit; where we would go afterwards; whether we'd split up or not; where we meet after that. The full works, everything. It would be tight, and it would be polished because I could not afford for this to go wrong. The mere thought of this made by bowels wobble; either that or it was the zealous portion of chilli sauce that Mario at the kebab shop had administered on my small doner last night.

I assessed my cuts and bruises in the mirror; there didn't seem to be a great deal of change since yesterday. Fucking hell, they had given me a real kick-in.

I heard Mum walk through the front door. Given her predictable drinking habits, she would have been down to the shop to replenish her stash of high alcohol loopy juice having used up the supplies during her usual thirsty Saturday.

I knew her routine; she would feverishly enter the flat, stack the fridge up with eleven cans taking the twelfth for herself to drink immediately as a 'settler'.

'Settler' was a word that she'd invented, and it had somehow entered in the Bates' family vernacular. Dev and I would describe the first beer on a hangover in the same way. A fried breakfast, after a drinking session, was a 'settler', as was a hot dog before an important West Ham match. No one could accuse the Bates family of a lack of linguistic innovation.

I decided to challenge myself to get Mum to say the word 'settler' in the first ten minutes of our conversation. (Although come to think of it, having ten minutes' conversation with her was in itself a challenge.)

I walked into the lounge, which as ever, was pretty much blackened out, compliments of the permanently drawn curtains. I nearly gagged on the thick cigarette infused air; there ought to be one of those warning signs that they put on fag packets about getting cancer above our fucking television.

Mum sat there watching the said television, devouring that first can like she had just served a ten year stretch in Holloway prison. However, given my circumstances, I reminded myself that custodial analogies might not be a good idea.

"Looks like you're enjoying that, Mum?"

"I fucking needed it, I tell you."

"I bet. How would you describe it?"

"What do you mean?"

As ever, she was holding a conversation with me, without taking her eyes off the television.

"You, know, what's the purpose of the first drink of the day?"

I was handing it to her on a plate.

"What?"

"What does that drink do to you in terms of getting you back on track?"

She then turned to look at me, "What are you fucking on about?"

Shit, she wasn't taking the bait. In fact, she wasn't even sniffing the bait.

"Oh, don't worry about it."

I sat down deciding to have another go in a minute or so. She then stopped watching her television programme and turned to me.

"Fucking hell, look at the state of your boat race!"

"Good, isn't it?"

"How did that happen?"

"Aw, you know."

She turned back to continue watching the television. I decided to check on how much attention she was paying.

"I got dragged down our stairwell by three black fellas who kicked the shit out of me."

"Oh right."

Ah nice, she appeared to drift back to the TV programme and was giving me her vacant look, but to satisfy my curiosity, I would check.

"Yeah, I'm pretty sure it was three members of the Jackson 5. The Old Bill said there's a fair chance of an arrest, which would apparently fuck-up their plans for a reunion tour."

"Hmm."

As I thought, zero interest.

"Have you seen Dev?"

"No."

"I'm going to have a cup of tea; do you want one?" I asked.

"No, but you can get me another can, this settler has gone down a treat."

And therein was a lesson in life; good and bad things happen when you least expect them to.

I went to the fridge and got Mum another can, as I passed it to her she remarked that it wasn't very cold like it was my fault. Luckily, I had long since learnt to ignore her and her fuzzy logic.

I sat in the kitchen having a cup of tea. Sunday brunch was going to be a toss-up between a Fray Bentos pie and a Scotch egg. However, given that the latter looked like it was on the turn and liable to kill me if I was to even remove it from its packet, I decided to take the safe option of a tinned pie with a best before date of 2018. How do they do that – I mean, how can you put meat into a tin and it's still okay to eat three years later? I decided to put that question to the back of my mind. I needed to be focused on the robbery, and I couldn't afford to let the long-term preservation of tinned meat distract me.

Pie in the oven and cup of tea number two on the spin and in walked Devo. I hadn't seen him since our altercation. He walked into the kitchen and took one look at me.

"Oi oi, looks like you fucked up the stuntman audition," he said.

I smiled, and so did he.

"Something like that," I replied.

He playfully pretended to punch my face and winked.

"Sorry, Dev," I said.

"What for?"

"Everything."

"Are you going to be alright?"

In the one question, I knew what he was asking. Was this kick-in the end of it, or was there another beating in the offing? I decided to give him half the truth. I couldn't bear to drag him into the Troy saga.

"It's over now, bro. I'm out of the game, lesson learnt."

"You sure?"

"A hundred percent."

"Good boy. What's that cooking?"

"A Fray Bentos pie."

"Oh fuck that, let's go down and see Murray. I'll treat you to a pint and a Sunday roast."

"Nice one!"

Devo had that unique knack to make me feel special, loved and wanted. He was the only person who could provide that. I adored the fella; worshipped the ground he walked on; idolised everything about him.

I went into my bedroom to get changed and felt my bottom lip wobbling. Pull yourself together, for fuck sake, but I couldn't. I just had to lie down on my bed to cry. I sobbed my heart out in one vast outpouring of emotion, the horror of my beating, the debt with Troy and perhaps, most importantly, my falling out with Devo. It all came out.

I got myself together and got changed, and then realised one primary truth; I knew that unless this robbery went to plan, my life would be pretty much over before it had ever really begun.

Chapter 24
Monday 29th December 2014

Twenty-four hours until the robbery.

The thought of it turned my stomach. I would say that it had ruined my festive period, but Christmas in our house has always been shit. Mum had stopped buying presents yonks ago and in fact, doing pretty much anything to celebrate. Devo and I had eaten a fry-up for Christmas dinner before heading over to the Three Bells for a piss-up with the other lost souls in the area.

However, much more positively, the planning of the robbery had gone well. I'd met the Brigadier, and we had gone through the job in microscopic detail. He was to bring a handgun to the robbery, which he was to wave around, but was on strict instructions not to use. We had loosely agreed that if the old Polish fella was overly stubborn, then we'd bail out.

We'd agreed to do the job on foot, as there were a series of nearby alleyways and exit points which meant if we got pursued by the Feds then we'd stand a greater chance of giving them the slip. I had spent hours in the vicinity assessing the twists and turns, the back gates we could run through, and the garden sheds we could hide in.

On the day of the robbery, I was to meet the Brigadier outside a strip club at 6am. From there we would have a short walk to the European Store where there was a bus stop opposite the shop so we could pretend to be waiting for the number 54 until the arrival of the old man.

I was as nervous as hell and tried to stop thinking about all the things that could go wrong. I daren't ask anyone how long a sentence I would expect to receive if I got nicked, but I knew, even for someone with a clean criminal record, that it would be years, not months.

Devo had gone back to work after the Christmas break, and I felt desperately lonely. What a fuck-up, what a total fucking fuck-up this had all been. I had dreamt of doing this job with Devo to get myself onto the ladder. I was badly regretting it all now. I was forced to do this robbery but would do anything to get out of it.

The good news was I had the Brigadier on my side; an experienced cool head; a lad who had been there and done it; a trusted sidekick of Devo. We had a chance; I know we did. We could do this. Come on; it was time to believe in yourself. By this time tomorrow, I'll be paying that bastard, Troy, off and I'll be free. The thought of it was like a distant glow of sunshine, I could see the light, but I couldn't yet feel the warmth.

I was due to meet up with the Brigadier later at the Three Bells, just to go over the last-minute details. He didn't think it was necessary, but I insisted. I agreed to meet him at 8pm, and I would have no more than a quick half a pint. I needed to have a clear head and be on top of my game.

I just spent the day in my bed, my stomach was churning, my head felt light, and my mouth was as dry as camel shit in a desert.

I then made myself a promise that if I got through this episode I would make sure that my life would take a different direction and I would get myself a regular job. I would never again turn to crime. I would become a hardworking, law-abiding person and contribute something to society. I had realised that there are no shortcuts in life. There is no fast-track to riches. It's about commitment and graft and if I got through this I would turn the corner and embrace these elements.

I would be able to look back on these few months and put it all down as a learning curve. In twenty years' time, I would have a great story to tell down the pub. People would look at me and wonder how I had ever got caught up in a gig like this.

It was just before eight o'clock and I entered the Three Bells, where, stood right in front of me, was a walking, human fucking train wreck.

The Brigadier was legless.

Murray was warning him about his behaviour as he was spilling his pint everywhere, randomly unzipping his top and showing off his belly to the locals, while singing Glasgow Rangers songs.

I pulled him to one side, I was livid, but had to keep my cool.

"Bo, how the fuck are you old son?" he asked.

He put his arm around me and was spitting beer all over my face.

I lowered my voice and dropped my head towards his ear. "We're doing the job tomorrow morning, bro, are you going to be okay?"

"Yeah mate, I'm just having a couple of ales, are you having one?"

"Brigadier, are you going to be okay?" I asked, sternly.

My future was riding on this job getting done, and this clown looked far from up for it.

"Of course I fucking am, are you suggesting I'll bottle it?"

He immediately started to get aggressive. I needed to diffuse the situation. I had to keep him on-side.

"No, no, not at all, okay, so I'll see you at 6 in the morning?"

"Nice one mate. Where're we meeting again?"

Fucking hell, he'd forgotten where we were meeting. What fucking chance did we have? I didn't need this the night before the fucking job. If he turned up in no fit state he'd be liable to do anything, the plan would go to rat shit, and then we would be fucked.

As I trudged home I decided that I had to think positively, the Brigadier was a drinker, that's what he does, he'll be okay in the morning, he's used to it. I convinced myself everything would be alright. It had better be. I had no time to play with, if he let me down, I was fucked, and I knew it.

I decided that I would ring him at 5am to check if he was up, maybe send him a text as well.

I was somehow even more nervous and tense than when I arrived at the pub. I shouldn't have gone. We both knew the plan. I should have stayed at home and assumed he was alright.

I felt more alone than ever as the rain started to come down. East London seemed a very dark, lonely place right now. As I walked through the cold, quiet estate, I had an empty, aching feeling.

I then made a life-changing decision and one that could come back to haunt me: If the Brigadier did not show up in the morning, I would do the robbery alone.

Chapter 25

Tuesday 30th December

D-Day – and there could be no turning back. It was 4.55am, and I'd had no sleep. The churning in my stomach had become so intense that it was causing me to double over in pain.

I had sent a text message to the Brigadier ten minutes ago and had received no response.

I decided to ring him; my hands were shaking as I tried to find his number on my phone. I hit the call button, after several rings, my call diverted to an automated voice mail service.

Shit!

I was panicking. I rang him again, then again, then again. You fucking wanker! I was stomping around my bedroom; my mind was all over the place. I rang him again, nothing. I then went into the kitchen; my worst fears from the previous evening had been realised; he was obviously going to bail out on me meaning I'd have to do the robbery on my own.

As the blood drained from my brain I quickly ran over the variables, but I had no other option. I then took a carving knife out of the drawer, gave it the once over and then decided that this was to be my weapon.

But what the fuck was I going to do with this?

Surely it would scare the old man wouldn't it? I mean I was a totally stranger dressed head to foot in black brandishing a big fucking blade.

But what if it didn't? What if he could sense the fear in my eyes; could see my arm trembling as I held out the knife, then what?

Fuck! I called him again, but still nothing. You fucking let-down cunt! I could feel myself perspiring despite it being just above freezing in the flat. I clomped around some more, tightness now creeping across my chest.

It was 5.21am; I had to make my mind up soon. Maybe he would be at the meeting place, and his phone was on silent? Or perhaps he was that pissed last night that he was fast asleep?

My stomach contorted, I sat on my bed with my head in my hands writhing in agony. I couldn't do this alone, and I knew it.

There was only one thing for it.

I opened the door and crept into Devo's bedroom where I started to whisper his name.

"Devo, Devo, Devo!"

Suddenly his bedside light came on.

"Fucking hell, what do you want?" he asked.

His squinting eyes adjusted to the light. I knelt down at the side of his bed.

"I'm in big fucking trouble, bro."

"What?"

"I've got a dealer after me for four grand. I've got to pay him by Saturday otherwise he's going to kick the shit out of me."

"Fucking hell, Bo!"

"There's a way out, Dev. Do you remember that job I told you about?"

"With the old fella and the shop?"

"That's it. The drop's this morning."

"This morning!"

"I wasn't going to tell you; I was going to pull the job with The Brigadier, only he's gone and let me down."

"What?"

"He was pissed out of his head last night, and now he's not answering his phone. If I'm going to do this job I've got to leave in the next five minutes."

"And you want me to do it with you?"

"If you don't, I'll have to do it on my own, and I don't know if I've got it in my locker."

"Forget it, Bo. Let's see if there is another way of getting that four grand."

"We won't be able to do it, Dev. I'm nearly out of time. This is my only chance. I need your help, bro, please?"

"For fuck sake, you know what I've got riding on this!"

"I know, I know, I know, Christ, Dev, I'm only here because I've run out of options; you're my only hope."

He rubbed his face, "Fucking hell, okay, fuck it, let's do it."

He noticed I was holding a kitchen knife. "What the fuck's that? Are you going to nick this fellas money or carve him a joint of meat?!"

He got up and dipped deep into his wardrobe before bringing out a handgun.

"Fucking hell, bro!" I said, shocked.

"Never turn up to a gunfight with a knife. Balaclavas?"

"In my bedroom."

"Gloves?"

"Same."

"Okay, let's fucking do it. We can discuss the plan on the way there. What time does the old man arrive?"

"About 6.30."

He looked at the time on his alarm clock.

"Let's get a move on; send a text to The Brigadier, tell him the drop has been cancelled and the gig's off, just in case he wakes up."

I went back into my bedroom and gathered the balaclavas and gloves. The smart money was now on us to complete this job, but the stakes had moved up several notches. The fact remained that if we got nicked, Devo would be going away for a very, very long time.

And it would have been all my fault.

Chapter 26
Same Day

As we were marching to the European Store we were going over the plan in detail. Devo was barking the orders, and I listened attentively. I was getting nervous, and I detected a definite shift in his mood as well. We weren't playing games now; this was the real deal, and the stakes for each of us could not have been any higher.

The usually busy streets of the East End were dead. Most people were still on their extended Christmas holidays, and this had to work in our favour regarding nosey on-lookers.

Our plan was clear, and phase one was in operation as we stood at the bus stop, pretty much toe to toe in black with the balaclavas acting as hats for the time being. If anyone passed us they would not bat an eyelid; we just looked like a couple of fellas on their way to an early shift.

I explained to Devo that the old man had an alleyway at the side of the shop and this is where he parked his car. His usual arrival time of 6.30am came and went. I found myself checking the time on my mobile phone every thirty seconds. It didn't take Devo long to snap and to tell me to stop doing it.

After a couple more minutes a car drove down the road and slowed down. It was the old man's Mercedes.

"Here he is, Dev." I took a big gulp; this was it. There's was no backing out now.

"Okay, Bo, show time. Stick to the plan and follow my lead."

I'd told Devo that there was no side entrance to the shop. So, having parked up, the old man would walk around to the front and unlock the entrance door. The alarm then activates, and he walks to the alarm panel, which is just inside his storeroom and turns it off leaving the front door temporarily unlocked in the process. He then returns to the front door and locks it before he potters around the shop waiting for the delivery to turn up. Our window of opportunity was after he had de-activated the alarm and on his return to the front door. This is when and how we would get in.

Sure enough, he walked out of the alleyway, opened the front door and walked into the shop, as he would have done every morning. This was our cue to walk across the road and the point at which we pulled down our balaclavas. We then waited for him to head back towards the door, knowing the alarm was deactivated.

With the lights now on in the shop, sure enough, the old man, no doubt in a very long-standing routine, headed back to the front door. In we went with Devo leading the way brandishing the gun. The old man saw us and panicked. Devo was in charge of issuing the instructions. He started to shout at the old man.

"Right, you cunt, we know you've got a bundle of cash, now you've got thirty seconds to give us the fucker, or I'll shatter one of your fucking knee caps."

We had an unknown factor that worried us both. We didn't know whether he had the money on his person or whether he had it stashed in the safe. The latter would cause us a headache because then we would have to convince him to open it.

We weren't to be lucky.

"It's in the safe." He said. Bollocks! "I don't have the keys; my son has them."

He was lying.

Devo grabbed him and slapped him lightly in the face.

"Listen, I know you're lying, and if you lie again, I'm going to put you in a fucking wheelchair. We know your delivery man comes in the next hour and you pay him cash. Now you either give us this dosh or I'm going to pop a cap in your fucking spleen. It's your choice?"

Blimey, Dev was good at this, very convincing.

"Okay, I'll take you to the safe."

We then walked to the back storeroom where there was a makeshift office in the corner with the safe under the desk. The old man took out his safe key opened it and handed us a pile of money. There was no more than five hundred quid.

"What the fuck's this?" Screamed Devo, "now give us the rest of the fucking money, you old cunt, or I'm going to fucking kill you!"

"There is no more money," he replied.

I could see Devo losing his patience.

"We know there is, now give it to us or this will be your last fucking warning."

"It's all I have got. That's it. Please take it."

"You pay the driver, it's thousands in cash, now I mean it, I am going to count to three, and then I'm going to blow your fucking head off."

Devo then placed the muzzle of the pistol on his head. He looked fucking livid.

"One-"

"Fuck you!" said the ballsy shopkeeper.

"Two"

"For fuck sake, he's going to kill you, just give us the fucking money," I screamed.

The old man was having none of it; talk about bottle!

"Three! It's your last chance," roared Devo.

Devo then smacked him around the head with the gun. He stumbled over and then collapsed; he appeared to be out cold.

"Quick, check him!" demanded Devo.

I started rifling through his pockets; he was wearing a suit jacket and trousers. I found his wallet with thirty quid in it, nothing in his suit pockets, and nothing in the other trousers; bollocks! We both looked at each other, knowing we were running out of time and options.

"Check the cash till, I'll keep my eye on him," ordered Devo.

I ran through to the shop and around the counter. The till was locked, I picked it up and threw it to the floor, upon impact the cash drawer partially opened, but there was no money in it.

This was turning into a nightmare. I was panicking like shit and looked under the counter feverishly pulling out the contents. There was nothing there. I returned to the back store.

"Fuck all, bro - nothing. Let's go!"

The old man started to come around, and as he did he appeared to be having a fit.

"Fucking hell, prop him up," yelled Devo.

We then grabbed an arm each and sat him on a pallet of canned food and as I did I felt something weighty in his suit.

"He's got something in the lining!" I said.

"Get the fucker off him," said Devo.

So we removed his suit jacket, and sure enough, the cunning old bastard had a zip stitched into the back lining. I opened it up - boom! A stash of notes evenly distributed along the bottom lining of his suit. I grabbed it then showed it to Dev.

"Ring the bell; we've just hit the fucking jackpot!" I said.

"Bag it up and let's get the fuck out of here," Devo said coolly.

I removed a plastic bag from my pocket and filled it with cash. I even got a faint waft of the kebab that had been transported in the bag just the day before.

We then left the shop via the front door. Someone was twenty yards away but walking in the other direction; a good start. We ran to the first corner then turned down it. We were out of view of the main streets CCTV at this point, so we took the balaclavas off. We walked very fast but had agreed not to run. By the look of the old man, he would not be phoning the police for at least the next ten minutes. At the next corner, we split, Devo put on a red baseball cap, and I took off my black sweatshirt and wrapped it around my waist, revealing a blue t-shirt.

"See you in Piccadilly," said Dev.

I smiled back at him.

Our routes were equidistant so we would both arrive back at the flat in about fifteen minutes.

When I arrived, Devo was already there. I walked into the kitchen, and we high fived each other and hugged.

"Fucking get in there, bro!" I shouted.

"Well done mate, you did fucking well. How much have we got?" I opened the bag where there was a serious stash of money.

"Fucking loads of money, that's how much!"

We hugged again.

Devo was so hyper that he got me to ring him in sick; he was in no mood for work after what we had just pulled. I emptied the bag on the kitchen table and counted it. Just shy of £13,000! Plus the five hundred odd quid the old boy had tried to fob us off with. Not a bad morning's work.

We then sat down and went through what we had done and how we had done it. If the Feds were going to find out it was us then how? Had we given them any evidence? We didn't think so. It was a clean job. Fucking great! We had earned nearly seven grand each. I could pay Troy off and still have some dosh leftover. It just couldn't have gone any better.

My plan from this point was simple, head over to Lewisham for noon, pay the four grand out and that way if the Feds did pinch us at least I wouldn't spend my sentence in prison watching my back, worried about taking a shank from one of his boys.

I went into my bedroom and lay down on the bed. My heart was still racing. Mission accomplished! I had got myself out of the quicksand, a little bit bruised and a little bit guilty, but I had survived, and it felt fucking good.

I was over the worst of it now, and I was pretty sure that nothing, from this point forth, could go wrong.

Chapter 27
Same Day

By just after 1.30pm two things had happened; firstly, Devo and I had taken a trip over to Lewisham and visited Troy. I paid him his four grand and, despite a very kind offer to take another bag of drugs to sell, I politely declined. He looked far more convivial than he did the other day when he was threatening to extract my perfectly good, albeit not particularly well-maintained teeth.

If I never see that cunt again, it will be too soon.

The second thing was that we were in the Three Bells necking lager. Devo didn't have the burden of Troy's debt, so he was the arse end of seven large up on the day. No wonder he was in a celebratory mood. I decided that I was going to be careful with the balance of my money. I had no income around the corner, and I was facing the dreaded prospect, once this pot of cash started to run dry, of having to sign back on the dole.

Devo was enjoying the moment and was ordering up shooters for me, him and Murray. Murray knew the score.

"You boys had a good morning then?" he asked deviously.

"Ah, you know Murray, some days the whole world smiles with you!" I said.

"Have you got the boy involved this time, Dev?"

"Got him involved? It was his fucking gig!"

"Was it now," remarked Murray.

"Call it a coming of age," I said.

I was feeling as proud as punch, despite realising that it was going to be my first and last crusade into the world of serious crime.

Murray raised his glass. He knew better than to ask any details. See no evil; hear no evil and all that. As the landlord of a naughty East End pub, it was pretty much written into his job description.

"Here Murray, do us a favour will you mate?" asked Devo. "Should the Brigadier ever ask you, then this job never went down, alright?" he winked at Murray.

"Whatever," replied Murray.

That flippant acknowledgement was as a good as a cast iron promise. That's the way it worked.

"To be fair he was invited in on it, but he fucked up," Devo said. "Still, what's done is done, and his loss is my gain."

"Are you back in business now, Devo?" Murray asked.

"No, but you can never rule out the odd comeback gig, can you?!" he said with a naughty smile, the raising of his glass and the purchase of another round of shooters.

This afternoon was going to be fun.

By 5.30pm we were fucking shit-faced and the shine on the day diminished, just a little, with the arrival of the Brigadier. He didn't waste any time in walking up to me at the bar. I needed to pull my shit together.

"Alright, Bo, what happened to the job then?" he asked with a threatening seriousness.

"The delivery driver bailed out," I said, without being able to make eye contact with him.

"Oh right. You and Devo don't seem too bothered about it though; look at the state of you?"

"He's had a promotion at work, that's why we are celebrating."

"Has he?"

"And anyway, what happened to you, I was ringing and texting you first thing?"

"I live ten minutes' walk from the meet point; I was getting ready when you contacted me."

"Anyway, it doesn't matter now."

"Out of interest, if the job was off, why were you so insistent on talking to me?"

"Erm, the job was on until I got a text from my mate just before I text you."

I wasn't very convincing, and he knew it.

"Right, well, I hope you boys enjoy your night. What are you celebrating again?"

Don't try and catch me out, you fat cunt.

"Devo's promotion," I replied.

"Ah, that's it, Devo's promotion."

He then gave me a long, hard stare before heading off to the fruit machine.

Devo and I continued drinking for the next few hours. The Brigadier refused to come over and speak to us. It was clear that he had copped the right arse. Devo, however, most certainly had not and he must have bought the whole pub a drink, except the Brigadier who kept on refusing. Bollocks to the fat twat.

Back at the flat and it was kebabs and chips to round off the evening. We sat at the kitchen table laughing and joking about the day we'd had; re-enacting parts of the robbery, taking the piss out of each other in the process.

As we got up to go to bed, I grabbed Devo and held him tight.

"I don't know what to say, bro?"

"You're alright mate. You would have done the same for me."

"You've saved my life."

"Then one day you can save my fucker!"

We hugged, and I held him tight in my arms. When I was in the shit, he had, yet again, come through for me. Devo, my brother and my hero - I didn't know what I would ever do without him.

Chapter 28
Wednesday 31st December 2014

Oh my God, my fucking head was killing me! I felt like I had an arrow, brandishing the Stella Artois motif, piercing through one of my eyes. I lay there for a while allowing myself to drift back into a cocoon of calm acknowledging that life was not all bad. Then I sighed, that sort of sigh you do when you've narrowly missed getting your front teeth pulled out by a mad bastard. I had dodged a bullet, or in this instance a pair of pliers. I had learnt a tough lesson, and now it was time to move on.

I contemplated the rest of the day and had a wave of optimism; it was going to be a good New Year's Eve. For once I had a few quid in my pocket, and there's no doubt that the events of yesterday were worthy of another night's celebration.

After ten minutes I finally had to succumb to the need for paracetamol, so I dragged myself into the kitchen, barely able to raise my head and knocked back a couple of tablets. I wondered if Devo had gone to work or whether he had pulled another sick day? Surely he couldn't put a day's graft in if he felt like me?

I walked into the lounge where Mum was sitting pondering the last clue on The Times cryptic crossword. Well, okay this wasn't entirely true, she was, as usual, necking a can of mental juice, while watching her favourite afternoon programme. Yes, it involved antiques, only this time the presenter isn't that posh ponce with a dickie bow, but some geezer who looks like he's been baked in a tandoori oven. For some reason, they appear to refer to him as the 'Duke', which I find a bit odd given he's no more royalty than I was a member of the Eggheads.

"Alright, Mum?"

"This twat on here is trying to flog a set of postcards; I mean fucking postcards! He reckons they're worth two hundred quid, but the dealer's only offered him forty. He looks fucking livid."

"What sort of postcards?"

"Those cartoon ones with fat birds at the seaside."

"What do you think they will go for?"

"Eighty quid tops, then he gets the choice to either take the money or take them to auction."

"Then what happens?" I asked.

As it happens, I knew, but I was finding the conversation strangely engaging.

"If he goes for the auction then he only gets what they sell for, less the auctioneer's commission which is around 15%."

This was a strangely articulate answer, maybe completion of The Times cryptic crossword was only around the corner.

We sat there and watched as the dealer maxed out his offer at eighty quid.

"Told you," she said.

She had, but I simply never tire of her saying it.

The owner of the postcards was having none of it and decided to go to auction.

"Told you," she said, again.

Did you though? I'm not sure you did on this occasion. I might have got an extra 'told you' for no reason. The day was already getting better.

The auction was a total disaster; think fat cartoon birds on a postcard meets 9/11. They sold for forty-five pounds. The fake-tanned fella then wrapped his arm around the geezer and made some impassioned speech about that being the luck of the draw. Can you imagine how gutted he must have been? He'd brought in his prized postcards, which he thought were worth two hundred notes, and had sold them for a measly forty-five quid. If only Mum had been there to guide him through this entire predicament.

"Forty-five quid, Mum, that's shit!"

"Less the commission," she added.

She then turned, looked at me with a smile, like she had solved some tricky murder case. She held her grin long enough for me to appreciate the shocking condition of her teeth.

"Oh yeah," I said. I wasn't sure what else to say to that. "Any sign of Devo?"

"I've not seen him."

I then went back to bed hoping the tablets would get shot of this bastard headache. As I lay there my no thrills mobile phone rang. It was Devo, and he gave me a short, sharp instruction:

"Get the fuck down to the Three Bells, now!"

He hung up.

Something had gone badly wrong.

Chapter 29
Same Day

It's amazing how quickly a hangover subsides when the possibility of a lengthy prison sentence pops its head over the horizon. This was sure to be a game changer, and it had to involve the Old Bill being on to us. Any jubilation that I had after we had completed the job had just vanished. My throat was dry, and I felt light-headed.

This fucking robbery; what had I gone and done?

I walked into the pub and spotted Devo who was sat at a table with Murray, no drinks, no smiles, just worried looks. I walked over.

"What's happened?" I asked, anxiously.

"Come and sit down mate," said Devo in a hushed voice.

Murray was looking pensive. Something was badly amiss. "Tell him, Murray."

"Did you know that the local Old Bill operate something called a 'network'?" Murray asked.

"A 'network', what the fuck's that?"

"It's the Old Bill's way of getting a message out into the criminal community, without having to go to the press. They generally do it to serve their own purposes."

Devo then chipped in, "They go around to all of the local boozers, where they know that naughty fellas drink, and they drop things into conversations with landlords, bar staff and the locals."

"I had two detectives in here earlier for a couple of oranges juices and some chit-chat, I knew straight away that they wanted to network something. They told me about a robbery on the Stratford road yesterday."

I looked at Devo.

"It's all right; I've told him, Bo."

Murray continued, "Now it turns out that during the robbery, the fella that owns the store died."

"What?" I said.

"He had a heart attack," continued Murray, "the Old Bill ended up knocking the door down about midday when it was obvious he was in, but the shop wasn't open."

"Fucking hell, Dev, what have we gone and done?!"

"That isn't the worst of it, Bo" replied Devo, "it turns out the old man wasn't Polish; he was Russian."

"How does that change anything?" I asked.

"That doesn't change anything, but what does change everything is that he was the favourite uncle of the head of the London Russian Mafia," he added.

I thought I was going to be sick; "Oh fucking hell, Dev!"

"Now it's alright, Bo," Devo said, just having a glance around to see if anyone was around, "there's no reason for us to suspect anyone knows we pulled the job."

"You're going to need to tell him the rest though, Devo," said Murray.

"Tell him what?" I said.

Fucking hell, what was coming down the track next?

"The Old Bill who spoke to Murray, said this Russian geezer, what's his name again?"

"Zorkov," said Murray.

"That Zorkov has gone ballistic, and he's sent the cavalry out looking for the robbers. He's got his men swarming around the area on strict instructions to find who did it."

Murray continued, "Apparently this Zorkov fella is a fucking psychopath, an old-school Russian who has done a stretch in one of those fucking horrible Siberian prisons. He's got the full Ivan the Terrible CV; he's into drugs, people smuggling, guns, the fucking lot. The Old Bill made it clear that whoever has done this should turn themselves in immediately for their own safety."

I ran my fingers through my hair. Fucking hell we were in deep, deep shit. "What are we going to do fellas?"

"Nothing, Bo. Let's hang tight. We didn't kill the geezer; he'll realise that in a few days and if they don't turn anything up then he might lose interest."

"Bear in mind, Bo, that this geezer has got his fucking fingers in all sorts of pies. If he doesn't turn up who did it in a few days, he'll have picked another fight with another geezer, and he'll turn his attention to that," said Murray.

"But what if he doesn't? What if he doesn't, Dev; then what? We can't spend the rest of our lives wondering if today's the day that he finds out it was us."

"I don't know mate. We'll have to cross that bridge when we come to it, but if we play this with a straight bat then he'll never find out, and we'll be in the clear."

"Look, for what it's worth, I've put the word out to a few trusted mates to keep their ear to the ground. Now don't worry, I haven't told them it's you two who pulled the job, but they will know to tell me if anyone says anything."

Well, it's fair to say that this news has taken the shine off the New Year's celebrations. Fucking hell, I've traded in being days away from potentially having my teeth extracted to being hunted down by the Russian Mafia.

Just when I thought I had climbed out of the pressure cooker I had been dropped back in it, only now the dial had been turned up several notches.

I had to accept that should the Russians find out it was us who pulled the robbery which led to the death of the shopkeeper then there would be only one outcome.

My brother and I would be killed.

Chapter 30
Thursday January 1st 2015

I had endured some pretty chronic New Year's Eves, compliments of being brought up in a poor family, mothered by an alcoholic and living in a deprived area, but last night was, by some way, the worst. I'd had little sleep and had spent the entire evening in my bedroom contemplating the position we were in.

I left my bedroom and went into the kitchen where Devo was sat at the table, cup of tea in his hand and deep in thought.

"Alright, Dev?"

"Alright?"

His tone was right off. I made a cup of tea then joined him at the table.

"Have you heard from Murray?"

"Nope."

He was staring into space, seemingly unable to look me in the eye.

"I was just wondering if he heard anything last night, with the pub being busy and all."

"Fuck knows."

"What are you thinking?"

"You don't want to know."

"Why?"

"Nothing, leave it."

"No, tell me."

"To be honest, I'm just wondering how the fuck you got me dragged into this mess."

Bollocks, I had dreaded him turning this on me.

"You didn't have to get involved," I said.

This was right up there with the most fucking stupid things I have ever said.

"'Didn't have to get involved,' oh fuck off! You came into my bedroom grovelling like a little fucking pussy, what was I going to do?"

"Come on Dev; I had no idea this was going to happen."

"Fucking Polish bloke, you stupid cunt!" he said shaking his head.

"How was I to know?"

His mood then started to become aggressive, "Because this is the East End of fucking London, you fucking mug! You always find out about the people who you're nicking off."

"What difference would it have made?"

"What difference?! What difference?! He was a Russian, Bo. That's Russian, like Armenian, like Albanian, countries with deep gangster connections. If you had told me he was Russian, I would have insisted that we postpone the gig until I'd done some research on the geezer."

"I couldn't postpone it! I had three days to get the dosh together before some fucking psycho was going to start pulling my teeth out!"

He sat there shaking his head, "You fuck everything up though, don't you? I should have fucking known."

At that point, Mum walked in, "What's all this noise about then?"

Devo snapped straight back, "Oh why don't you fuck off and go and watch one of your stupid fucking daytime programmes, you useless cunt!"

"That's not very nice," she replied.

However, she could see things were getting tense and rightly decided to retreat to her antique consultation office.

I decided it was time to have my say, "I fuck everything up? You can fucking talk, who was the one, only a few hours after the job went down, spraying his money around the boozer? Buying every man and his dog a fucking drink? 'Oh you don't want a pint, come on have a short with us?' Could you have made it any more fucking obvious?"

"I can pass that off as celebrating my promotion, Bo; you said it yourself to the Brigadier."

"You got promoted fucking weeks ago, how long do you think it's going to take the Russian mob to find that fucker out?"

"Alright, alright, calm down, this isn't helping anyone."

"What are we going to do, Dev, I'm fucking scared, bro?"

"Nothing, we are going to do nothing. We are going to act like we've got nothing to hide. So, it's back in the boozer today having a laugh and a joke, acting like we've got nothing to worry about. Come on get yourself ready; it's time to get going. Oh and don't wear that fucking Armani jacket, stick one of your shithole fucking sweatshirts on."

"Are you sure about this?"

"We can't stay here all day. I feel like I am out of control. At least we'll be in the thick of it if the shit kicks off and we'll hear it before anyone else. Now go and get changed."

I traipsed back to my bedroom and got dressed, very slowly. I was shitting myself, and there was no point denying it. I walked into Devo's bedroom to tell him

I was ready and it was then that I saw him sticking his gun in the back of his trousers.

"Jesus, what the fuck are you going to do with that?" I asked.

"We're not playing with boy scouts here mate, and if they find out that it was us who pulled the job, then my little friend might give us a few hours to get the fuck out of London."

Chapter 31
Same Day

It was just after 2pm when we entered the Three Bells, and I could not have felt more downbeat. It was New Year's Day, so the pub was quiet as the locals slept off their hangovers.

We walked to the bar where the barman grabbed Murray's attention and Murray, in turn, ushered us out to the back of the pub.

"It's not good news. Zorkov is throwing his men and his money at this. He's determined to find you," Murray explained.

Fuck me; I wish Murray hadn't said, 'find you,' it only underlined the deep shit we were in.

He continued, "He's got a team going around the pubs, cafés, snooker halls, nightclubs the fucking lot. They are all wearing these fucking 'GoPro' cameras so they can film as they are going around. The word on the street is that he's got a couple of the Old Bill on a grand a day getting the footage streamed to PC's and then telling his fellas who they should be talking to."

"Fucking hell!" I said.

"It doesn't get any better. He's flashing his money around trying to get bits of information. My mate reckons it's a matter of days before he starts to hand out hidings to the usual suspects, just to loosen a few tongues. It's going to get fucking ugly boys, you need to know that."

Devo had heard enough, "Okay, but let's stick to the plan, no one knows it was us, so he can be handing out fucking Milky Bars for all I care, but if no fucker knows anything, then we're going to be fine."

"Has anyone given you the impression they're on to anything?" I asked.

"No mate; nothing. Look, sorry boys, I wish I had some better news, but at the moment the heat is about gas mark fucking ten."

"Alright, mate, let us know if you have any further updates," said Devo, he patted Murray on the shoulder, and we re-entered the bar.

As we did, we both instantly spotted a massive fucking geezer entering the pub. He must have been nearly seven fucking foot and about twenty stone. He was wearing an earpiece and was not bothered by anyone seeing it either. He had a shaved head with a horrific scar running down his face, probably done with a knife. What sort of mad bastard would have done that to him? I nudged Devo lightly, and he tapped me back to acknowledge that he had spotted him.

The massive geezer was with another decent sized fella, and they were flanking a smartly dressed bloke, with a stone cut face, leather jacket and hair that was immaculately greased back with shaved sides. They were obviously, very obviously just nosing around, taking a look at people. I suspect one, maybe all of them were wearing cameras, and all of our faces were being recorded. Our heads were well and truly above the parapet now.

If they did have any evidence of our involvement, then this untimely visit would surely seal our fate.

The pub went deathly quiet as the locals knew exactly what was going on.

"Alright, boys?" yelled over Murray, "can I get you a drink?"

The three of them walked over to the bar. The fella with the leather jacket did all the talking.

"Three glasses of tap water please."

He spoke excellent English, but it was clear he was either Russian or from another eastern European country. Murray filled up three glasses from the sink.

"Are you the landlord?" he asked.

"Yes, I am," replied Murray, defensively.

"You must be Murray, then?"

"And who are you?"

"Petrov. I assume you know why we are here?"

"No."

"Are you sure? The European Store on Stratford Road, does that ring any bells?"

"I heard about it. The shopkeeper died in the raid, didn't he? Very sad."

"Wasn't it? His nephew is grieving, badly."

"Give him my condolences."

"Why, you have never met him?"

"It's our tradition, my friend."

Murray placed the glasses on the bar, and Petrov handed two of the glasses to his bodyguards.

"So what brings you to my pub today?" Murray asked.

"We are in town for the funeral."

"Are you related to the deceased?"

"You could say that," replied Petrov.

The three men then took a seat. Fucking hell, it was like a scene from a western. Nobody dared move. My guts dropped, this whole affair had turned me to jelly. I quickly marched off to the toilet and straight into the cubicle where I locked the door. About a minute later, someone walked in.

"You alright, Bo?" It was Devo.

"Dev, we're in fucking trouble mate!"

"Now stick to the fucking plan, and stop talking like this because it isn't helping."

"Do you think we should hand ourselves in?"

"Are you fucking mad, you heard what Murray was saying, they've got Old Bill on the fucking payroll, how long do you think we'd last in the nick?"

I then heard the door open.

"Devo Bates, I understand?" Fuck me, it was Petrov, and he knew who Devo was.

"Yeah, that's right."

"Nice to meet you, I'm Petrov. I'm assuming you've heard about the robbery on Stratford Road?"

"Heard about it, but I don't know the details."

"Two men broke into the store and stole some money and scared the owner to the extent that he had a heart attack and died."

"Sorry to hear that."

"I understand you're no stranger to crime, Mister Bates?"

"This has got nothing to do with me mate?" Devo said, very slightly irritated.

"I didn't say it had; I'm just asking you a straightforward question, are you or aren't you a stranger to crime?"

"I've done a bit, in my time."

"'Done a bit,' that's a nice way of putting it. I understand you have recently been released from prison?"

"Fucking hell, what's this about? Yes, I was released a few months ago, and now I am going straight, and I've got a job in a warehouse."

"Wow, congratulations!" Petrov said sarcastically, "I need to find out who did the robbery, Mister Bates."

"I don't know mate, I'm sorry."

"I understand that you English have a saying about there being honour amongst criminals."

"Thieves, the saying is; honour amongst thieves."

"Ah yes, my apologies. Well, whatever the saying is, I am going to test whether it is true or not. I'm offering ten thousand pounds cash to anyone with any information that can help us. If we catch them, I'm going to pay another ten thousand. Let's see whether twenty thousand pounds tempts the loyalty of the cockney criminal."

"Well, let's see."

"Here's my card Mister Bates. You will call me should you hear anything? Remember, twenty thousand pounds cash. I'm guessing that might seem a lot of money to a young man who works in a warehouse."

There was a pause of several seconds, I assumed Petrov had left, but then he spoke again.

"Mister Bates, do tell your friend, The Brigadier, that I would like to speak to him, urgently."

That was it. The Brigadier would find out that we skanked him and pulled the job ourselves. Once he gets a sniff of the generosity of the Red Square gang, he'll take the twenty grand and live happily ever after.

The game was nearly up.

Chapter 32
Same Day

We left the pub immediately and went straight home. I sat solemn-faced in the kitchen, despair filling me. I needed to find some inspiration; some words that might make me feel better.

"Fucking hell, we're fucked," I said.

Devo grimaced, "Will you stop fucking doing that?!"

"Doing what?"

"You keep randomly saying 'fucking hell' then sighing. Jesus, Bo, I'm trying to think here!"

"What about, what is there to think about, Dev? Isn't it all so obvious? The Russians will find the Brigadier, who will then know that we lied to him and pulled the job ourselves and for the sake of twenty fucking grand, he'll shop us in."

"He wouldn't do that mate, not the Brigadier."

"It's twenty grand, bro, and we skanked him on the job. Why wouldn't he?"

"Not the Brigadier. He wouldn't do it."

"How can you be so sure?"

"Because he was on the job that I got nicked for and I didn't grass him up!"

"I didn't know that."

"Well, you do now. I could have grassed him up and got a year off my sentence, but I didn't. He knows that. He won't shop us. He owes me big-time and anyway, whatever has gone on between us he would never take us down."

"So, what are we going to do?"

Devo turned to me very stern-faced, "I fucking mean it, if you keep asking me the same fucking question over and over again you won't have to worry about the Russians because I'll fucking throw you off the balcony myself."

"Okay, just tell me the plan."

"We do nothing. That's the plan. We do nothing until I say otherwise".

Mum then walked in to get another can of beer out of the fridge.

"You two are in trouble aren't you, I can tell?" She asked, perceptively.

"Oh, there's nothing to worry about, Rita, we've only got the Russian Mafia trying to track us down so they can kill us," spat out Devo.

"Don't bring them back here then, will you?" she said before going back to the lounge.

Devo looked incredulous. "Did I hear that right? 'Don't bring them back here,' that's what you say about a stray dog, not the fucking Russian Mafia. Anyway, what the fuck would they want to come back here for? Christ, I'm surrounded by wankers. I'll have that put on my fucking headstone. Devo Bates. RIP. Killed because he was related to clueless fucking idiots."

Shaking his head, Devo headed off to his bedroom and slammed the door.

I sat and pondered. Okay, Bo, listen to your big brother, he's never let you down. We can get out of this, we can and we will.

I'd spent most of my life doing exactly what Devo had told me, and if I had listened to him about the drugs business and all the shit that went with it, then we would not be in this position now.

Never more did I need to listen to him and do exactly what he said because otherwise, we would both end up getting killed.

Chapter 33
Monday 5th January 2015

I'd spent the past 72-hours petrified and holed up in the flat, incarcerated like some caged animal. My only freedom was to nervously look out from the balcony railings to see if the grim Russian reaper was arriving. I knew they would come, it would be anytime now, and when they did, I knew it would be the massive geezer with the scar. I just had this premonition that he would do for me. I could envisage his face standing over my dying body with the grin of a killer.

Maybe I'd be lucky enough to see them coming, and if I did, then I would run for it, run to my brother and then we could escape together, escape from this place and hide, conceal ourselves from these bastards, escape this life, and never set foot back in this shithole ever again.

But I won't see them coming will I? Their business was to find people who had stepped out of line and a thick fucker like me wasn't going to outwit them.

I hadn't had any more than a couple of hours sleep in the last three days, and it was taking its toll. My head felt fuzzy, and I couldn't think straight. I kept nodding off for a few seconds at the balcony then suddenly waking up, startled and scared.

As the darkness descended, I was hanging over the balcony, and that's when I spotted Devo making his way home from work. As he walked towards the entrance to the block, I noticed two menacing looking geezers following him. Shit! I panicked, should I call out? They were homing in on him, walking quickly, fucking run Dev, run for fuck's sake! I watched open-mouthed; was I about to watch my brother get slaughtered?

But the geezers walked past him, no doubt off to settle another score elsewhere.

I sighed. I was a nervous wreck, broken and weak. I knew I didn't have much left in the tank.

As I sat at the kitchen table, a worried looking Devo walked in. He threw down a copy of the local evening paper onto the table.

"Turn to page four," he instructed.

As I turned the pages I looked in horror as I saw the CCTV picture taken from the shop's security camera of Devo and me with the headline:

SHOPKEEPER DIES AFTER RAID

I read the article, and as I did, I realised that my life had become this surreal nightmare. I read a line and then read it again out loud.

"'Police have put forward a reward of £5000 for information leading to the arrest of the robbers.' A fucking reward!"

"Murray reckons they're only doing this to wash us out for our own safety. They want someone to grass on us so that they can take us in."

I wiped my face with my hands. I was starting to believe that handing ourselves in was our only option. I couldn't stand any more of this.

"It changes nothing, Bo. It's a picture of two fellas dressed in black with balaclavas on. It could be anyone."

"Have you talked to the Brigadier?"

"What about?"

"'What about?!' About the fact that he's the only one who could grass us up for it, that's what about!"

"I told you he would never do that. He's solid, and he owes me. Now don't ask me about it again."

"Do you think we should hand ourselves in, Dev?"

"You what?!"

"We're sitting ducks here, and it's a matter of time until they find out that it was us who pulled the job then they'll come for us. At least if we hand ourselves in we can try and enter some sort of witness relocation programme."

"'Witness relocation programme!' You've been watching too much CSI fucking Miami! We aren't even witnesses, you fucking dummy, we're the criminals. Do you think the Old Bill would give two fucks if a couple of scumbags like us got shanked in prison?"

"I think this is the only angle out of this, Dev. I can't think of another way."

"Then stop fucking thinking because it's not helping," he yelled, "now let me repeat the fucking plan one last time for you because it's dead simple, read my fucking lips: we…..are……going……to…..do…….nothing! Now shut the fuck up about it."

He then headed off to his bedroom.

I had always been fascinated by the videos I had watched online where someone's life had radically changed in the blink of an eye. The free climber who loses his grip on a ledge and breaks his back; the car driver driving innocently down the road only to get mangled up by an oncoming lorry; or scenes of a bomb going off leaving people badly injured. It wasn't an unhealthy fascination where I would enjoy watching these types of videos; no, it was more my curiosity about how the course of a person's life can radically change in just a few moments.

My life was about to drastically change. I don't know whether you could quantify it as in the blink of an eye, or a few seconds and I don't suppose it really matters because, in the end, the result is still the same. That thing, whatever it is, happens and you then have to deal with the life-changing consequences.

The *thing* that happened to me, whilst sat in this fucking miserable, cold kitchen was the exchange of tense, unpleasant words with my brother.

Made all the more unpleasant because it would be the last time we would ever speak to one another.

Chapter 34
Tuesday 6th January 2015

As I opened my eyes the first thing I saw was Mum standing over my bed shaking me to wake up.

"Fucking hell Mum, what're you doing?!"

"The police are in the kitchen; they want to talk to you, urgently."

The police – shit was I going to prison? I hurriedly got dressed, and as I did, I thought back to when they came to arrest Devo. It had been a big fucking drama; they'd knocked down the front door; made loads of noise, used riot gear; the lot. No, they hadn't come to nick me. It seemed that this issue would not be settled in a manner quite as straightforward as that.

I walked into the kitchen where two plainclothes detectives were sat. One of them was familiar to me, as he was one of Feds who was here the last time Devo got nicked.

"Alright?" I said, trying to act casually.

"Boleyn Bates, DI Harry Cornell and this is DS Simon Brotherstone from the Met. Do you know where your brother Devo is?"

"He's at work, why, what's up?"

"He's in a lot of trouble."

"Trouble, why what's he gone and done now?"

DS Brotherstone got involved in the conversation. "I assume you know there was a robbery some days ago, close to here, on the Stratford Road?"

"I heard something about it," I said trying to be cagey.

"The perps threatened an old man with a gun causing him to have a heart attack," said Brotherstone.

"We know your brother and one other man did the job," Cornell said.

"Okay," I said.

I was desperately trying to remain evasive and not give away the ramifications of what I had just been told.

DI Cornell continued. "After the robbery, your brother and his sidekick left the premises with the money and then turned down Northcott Avenue, a quiet little street, and a perfect exit from the scene of the crime. What they didn't realise was that about fifty yards down this road lives a fella who's had two expensive motorbikes nicked from his garage about six months ago. After the last theft, being a bit pissed off, as you would be, he had security cameras installed, and one of them points straight out onto the pavement."

Oh, bollocks! We had removed our balaclavas at this point, I was sure of it. But hang on, before I started throwing my hands up, they didn't know it was me with Devo. Otherwise, I'd now be in handcuffs.

"Now the fella with the CCTV pictures contacted us this morning to tell us that he had found another image on his system that we might be interested in," Cornell said.

DS Brotherstone then re-joined the conversation, "That's when we got confused because we hadn't received the first lot of images that he said he'd given to us."

"What do you mean?"

"Last night the fella with the CCTV got a visit from two detectives. These detectives had spotted the cameras outside of his house and had knocked him up asking him whether he had any footage from the morning of the robbery. Of course, being the law-abiding citizen that he is, he was only too happy to help them and retrieved the images from his system. Only these detectives weren't detectives. We are pretty sure they were either members of, or on the payroll of the Russian Mob."

DI Cornell then pulled out a couple of pictures. They were a little grainy, but for some reason, Devo had turned his face to the camera. As clear as day it was him. I, however, was partially concealed and you could not see my face.

"Turns out your brother has gone and shoved a gun in the face of the wrong fella this time and now he's in the sort of trouble that you can only have nightmares about," added a stern-faced Cornell.

I gulped for air. "He's at work mate; can we go and get him?"

Cornell lowered his voice, "We've been there, Boleyn."

I was shaking and panicking, "No, no, you haven't, since he got out of prison he's got a new job in a warehouse, he's not at the old place anymore, he's at a new place, and there's no way you can know this." I was beginning to wobble.

"We do know this, Boleyn. We called his probation officer first thing this morning, and he gave us all the details, the name of the company, how long he's worked there, we even know about the promotion he's recently had."

"Let's go there now and check. He'll be there." I said, in a state of panic.

"We've been there," said Cornell.

"You haven't; he's there. He'll be at work. We need to go there now!" I was raising my voice in desperation.

"You need to calm down, mate," said Brotherstone, "he's not there. We called around earlier. He didn't show up for work this morning, and no one has called in for him."

"Fucking hell! Fucking hell, Devo, no!"

"Now, if you know where he is you need to tell us now. We're his only chance," said Cornell.

"I don't know; I swear I don't know. What a fuck up!"

"'What's a fuck up'?" Asked Cornell, "what do you know, Boleyn? Now is the time to tell us."

"I knew he was planning to do the robbery. I tried to talk him out of it." My survival instinct had kicked in. I wasn't ready to roll over just yet.

"Did he say who he was doing the robbery with?" Brotherstone asked.

"No, he'd never tell me shit like that."

It was obvious that they had not even considered that it was me who was with him.

"Look, we need to get to your brother and fast. If we don't then things are going to get really bad for him. We also need to know who the other person in the picture is. If you know anything, absolutely anything, you need to call me."

DI Harry Cornell placed his card on the kitchen table.

"He's dead isn't he?" I asked.

"I don't know mate. It's too early to say," said Cornell.

I looked at his face. He had that resigned looked.

"You know he's dead, don't you? They've got to him and killed him."

"As I say, if you can think of anything that might help us give me a call."

Chapter 35
Same Day

I was in a delirious state. What should I do next, tell Mum? What was she going to do? Anyway, I didn't know for sure that they had got to Devo. He might have spotted them and ran, or maybe they had got him, and he had fought them off somehow. But he would have called me to warn me of the threat. My phone, check your fucking phone! I ran into my bedroom and grabbed it; the network was down – fuck!

I decided to run to the only person left that I could trust. I legged it out of the flat over to the Three Bells. Murray was my last chance.

As I was running, I was playing out the scenarios in my head; if he'd evaded them then what would he have done next? Maybe he would go and hide and then contact me when the dust had settled. From what the police had said it was clear that the Brigadier had not shopped us, so he might have contacted him, wanting to keep me out of it. When I had watched TV detective programmes set in America the bad boys never liked to talk on 'cell phones' it must be because the Feds can somehow listen in on calls. Maybe that's why Devo hadn't contacted me.

Or maybe it was because he was dead.

I suddenly stopped running, and it felt like the blood had drained from my head and that my legs were going to buckle. I rested against a fence, gasping for breath. The cold winter air swept over me, and as I looked across the vast estate, there was a grey, grim look to the sky. My eyes then became drawn to a large black man in the distance who was sitting on a bench and appeared to be staring at me. I couldn't make out his face, but I could see the whites of his eyes. As I stared back at him I had to accept the truth; they had got him, and they had killed him. That's what they did, and that's how they worked. I stood up straight, desperately trying to regain some composure. Then a second sledgehammer hit me; I could see the full picture now, it had all played out in my head. They knew it was Devo, but they didn't know who the other person in the picture was. They had caught him, and they would torture him until he gave me up. He would hold out because he was tough, but every man has his breaking point, and they would eventually find his, and he would have to tell them.

I threw my head back and looked at the sky, oh Devo! I hope they didn't hurt you, bro. You could have just told them at the start; I wouldn't have minded. I got you into this shit in the first place; you didn't need to suffer for a waste of fucking space like me. What have I done? Oh God, I hope it was quickly over for him. I hope they didn't make my big brother suffer.

I looked across at the bench. The black man had disappeared, as had my hopes of ever seeing my brother alive.

I ambled the rest of the way to the pub; I was beaten, I had no fight left in me, and I'd thrown the towel in.

You can come and get me now you fuckers; I've surrendered.

I got to the pub, and the door was locked. It wasn't even opening time yet. I knocked on it, and Murray answered.

"Fucking hell, I've been calling your phone non-stop." he said flustered.

"I know what's gone on, the Feds have been round to the flat. He's dead, Murray."

Saying it out loud was like stabbing myself in the heart.

"You'd better come in," he said, peering apprehensively behind me and checking the coast was clear.

"What have you heard, Murray?"

"One of the lads has been in; the Old Bill has made it known that Devo is missing and he's being hunted down. It's likely the Russian's have caught him, and now they are after the Brigadier."

"What?!"

"Apparently the Russians have got a CCTV picture, and they are sure the other fella is the Brigadier."

Devo - that's what he would have done, he could never give me up because we're family. He knew someone had to take the fall for it and he had told them it was the Brigadier. They would never question that as they were old partners in crime.

"Do you think they will have got the Brigadier as well?" I asked.

"No."

"How can you be sure?"

"Because he's hiding upstairs."

I knew the implications of this instantly. "But no Devo?" I asked, in desperation.

"Sorry, mate."

"What's his plan?" I asked.

"What do you mean?"

"Is he thinking of doing a runner?" I asked.

"He has no plan. This place is his home. It's all he knows; he wouldn't know where to run to if he did."

"What's going to happen, Murray?"

Murray sighed and pulled out a bottle of scotch and two glasses. He poured two generous doubles then passed one to me.

"There may come a point in a man's life when he has to face a grave truth, and I'm afraid your time is now, fella." Murray put his arm on my shoulder. "The Brigadier didn't do that job, Bo, you did. If we're both going to honest with each other, we know that Devo is dead and in all probability he told them it was the Brigadier who pulled the job with him because he thought he had a better chance than you of escaping. But it's not him who needs to escape, is it?"

I shook my head.

"What should I do, Murray?"

"Okay, listen up. The Russians think it was the Brigadier who pulled the job with Devo, so they are looking for him and not you. That buys you a bit of time. So go home, grab your passport, chuck a few clothes in a bag and take the rest of that money from the job and anything Devo might have knocking around his room. From there get yourself down to Heathrow. There's a flight out at just after 3pm today to Alicante. It lands local time just after 6.30pm. I've got a mate of mine who owns a bar out there in Benidorm. He'll pick you up from the airport. He'll be holding a sign up with 'West Ham' on it. If the sign says anything else then fucking run for it. He'll text me from Spain when he collects you. Then I'm going to tell the Old Bill, the Russians and anyone else that needs to know, that it was you who did the job with Devo, not the Brigadier. The fact that you've fucked off will confirm the story to be true."

"What will happen then, will they come after me?"

"Assume they will. Assume the worst. Assume every day is your last. Keep your wits about you, boy, and go and hide. Spain is a big fucking country, so go deep and keep away from the beaches, where someone might spot you."

"Okay."

"You're clear about the plan?"

"Yes."

My throat was so dry I could hardly talk, I drank some Scotch.

"You have to go. Don't think for one second you've got a chance of surviving around here, son because you haven't; you have to leave."

"I know. I get it. Can you thank the Brigadier for me please, Murray, and if he ever finds out that it was Devo that told the Russians it was him, can you apologise for him? Devo would do anything to protect his family."

"You're wrong, Bo. Devo would do anything to protect you."

"What have I gone and done?"

"Come here."

Murray hugged me tightly, and I knew that everything in that moment changed.

My life as an East Ender had died. I would leave to travel to Spain this afternoon, and I wouldn't look back, but I doubted that I would make it. I didn't have it in me. I wasn't built for this sort of gig.

I left the pub and walked home, alone. I was scared. I wanted Devo; I wanted my brother. I wanted him with me and to tell me it was going to be alright. I cried out for him. I cried out for the mistake I had made and the life I had chosen.

This fucking life I had chosen.

Chapter 36
Same Day

I arrived home and sat on my bed. My world in one morning had been turned upside-down and it's heart had been ripped out. I had lost my brother to a group of men, who, within a couple of hours, would hunt me down and kill me. My only option was to go on the run and escape to a land where I knew no one and to face never returning to London ever again. I would have to leave Mum all alone, a vulnerable woman in a dangerous city.

What would Devo do? Yes, that's how I needed to think. It didn't take a genius to work out that I couldn't stay here. Remaining in London was a death sentence. Could I stay in this country and relocate somewhere else? No, at least if I were in a foreign land, I might stand a better chance of evading them. In any event, Murray had arranged a pick-up for me from the airport so I would be disrespecting him if I didn't show up.

I pulled my trusted sports bag out of the wardrobe. The same sports bag that I stored my weed in. If only I could go back to this point in time, I could have avoided all of this unfolding. My brother would still be with me; in fact, he would be at work, fuck me, that's all he wanted to do, to go straight, to get a regular job, to be a normal person, but along came his little brother to ruin it all for him.

The guilt was starting to cut deep, and I knew it wasn't going to get any better.

I looked at my phone; 11.42am; it was nearly time. I hurriedly packed my sports bag with a few clothes, my passport and got all of my cash together.

Then came the moment I was dreading, I had to go into Devo's bedroom and get his money. As I walked in, I could smell him, the faint aroma of his aftershave. His room, as always, was very tidy, everything put away with care and respect, the very antithesis of mine, a stark representation of the divergence of our lives. I started looking around for the money; where was it? I was scraping around in the bottom of his wardrobe, and that's when I found his gun. I picked it up and looked at it; me against the Russians? I put it back before I got any more idiotic thoughts.

I eventually found the money wrapped in his old West Ham scarf, a scarf I hadn't seen for years. I took the money out and put it in my bag before I took a closer look at the scarf. I held it to my face, and I could remember when I last saw him wearing it. He would have been no more than twelve. A young boy excited to be going to watch his team play. I'm sorry, bro. Sorry for everything. I should have left you in bed that morning and done the fucking robbery on my own.

I took the scarf, hopefully, while I had it with me, I could feel that he was close to me.

I returned to my bedroom and decided to split half the cash into my bag and keep the other half on my person. I had about nine grand. At least this was one less thing to worry about.

Okay, time to leave. As I left my bedroom, I could see Mum watching the television. Should I tell her what was going on? Should I sit down and explain that she had lost her eldest son, a boy that if the truth be known, she couldn't give a toss about? I watched as she took a large swig of her beer can. I then took my phone out and sent Murray a text:

Cud you tell mum wat happened to us both pls?

I walked into the kitchen, peeled off a thousand pounds and left it on the table. If nothing else, Mum could have a good drink on me and be absolutely sure that's what she would do. I looked around the flat one last time. It had been my home since I was born. It hadn't always been a happy place, but I mainly had good memories and nearly all of them with Devo somewhere in the picture.

Sadness and despair suddenly washed over me. I knew it was time to leave. I decided that once the front door closed behind me, I would not look back. I dare not. If I was going to have a chance, I had to be resilient and brave; I had to look forward and be decisive.

As I stepped outside, I grabbed the door knocker, and without casting my eyes on the door, I slammed it shut.

Part Two

'The good Lord gave you a body that can stand most anything. It's your mind you have to convince.'
Vincent Lombardi

Chapter 37
Same Day

I arrived at the airport and booked myself onto the flight. Despite it being the middle of winter the plane was nearly full. I was the youngest passenger on-board by about fifty years and seemingly the only person who didn't need a piss every ten minutes. What was it about the elderly and their fascination with Benidorm?

I sat quietly looking out of the window. The old dear next to me had attempted to engage in some small-talk, but a few short answers had given her the message.

As the plane came down to land, I could see the lights of Spain. Fucking hell, what was I going to do with myself? I felt a million miles away from home and all alone, a lost soul in a foreign land.

I collected my luggage from the carousel and puffed my cheeks out as I walked through passport control and into the arrivals lounge. If my pick-up wasn't here, I was fucked. I glanced around, and sure enough, some dodgy looking geezer in his sixties stood there with 'West Ham' scribbled on the back of a piece of ripped card. As I approached him, the depth of his tan became more apparent. He was covered in fucking gold, and his skin looked like a lizard's, all thick and wrinkly. He looked at me suspiciously.

"Alright, mate," I said.

"Who are you?" he growled.

"Boleyn Bates."

"Show me your passport," he demanded.

I got it out and handed it to him. He looked at me and then looked at the passport.

"Follow me," he ordered.

And I did for about ten minutes. He was slightly nervy; kept looking around and walking several paces in front of me. Eventually, we arrived at his car; a smart looking Mercedes. He stopped as we approached.

"Pass me your mobile phone," he barked.

I reached into my pocket and handed it to him. He threw it on the floor and stamped on it.

"What the fuck are you doing?" I screamed.

"It's your very own tracking device. It would have led them straight to you. Now listen to me carefully, if you want to get through this then for the next four hours you ask me no questions and do exactly what I tell you. Have you got it?"

"Yes," I said realising I didn't have an option.

"Now Murray tells me you've got some cash on you?"

"Yes, I've got a bit," I said, trying to be coy.

"Good. Now pass me a grand."

"What?"

"I need a grand. I'm taking you to a place where you can hide which is going to cost a grand, so give it to me."

I was taking an instant dislike to this geezer. I peeled off another grand and handed it to him.

"Okay, get in the car and let's go."

I got in, and he sped away. He was driving like a fucking maniac down the motorway; he kept checking his mirrors and didn't speak to me for at least half an hour. Then he broke the silence.

"We're not being followed; I know that much. So, Murray tells me you're in trouble with the Russian mob, is that correct?"

"Yes."

"Fucking hell, I won't even ask what possessed you to mess around with them."

"It wasn't by design, I can assure you."

"The good news is I've got the perfect hiding place for you, it's in the middle of nowhere and the chance of them finding you, even assuming that they even know you are in Spain, is practically nil."

"Where are we going?"

"A long way from here my friend. Who are you now?"

"Sorry?"

"Have you decided on your new name? You can't use your old one."

"I hadn't thought about it."

"Well, fucking think about it then! This is the sort of shit you need to get your head around. Your new name, your new birthday, your fucking backstory, everything has to change. You left your old life back in London."

"I'll think of something."

"We will arrive at your new gaff in about three hours' time, so that's how long you've got to think about it."

"Joey, call me Joey. Joey Devonshire."

I had assumed the first name of my favourite West Ham player, Joe Cole, and the second name from my brother's unusual forename.

"Good, now you kick back and construct the rest of your story. Don't make it too exotic, just boring enough to be believable, oh and drop the cockney boy thing as well. You're a south Londoner now."

"Okay."

"And remember, never, ever trust anyone. Assume everyone you ever talk to is connected to that bunch of horrible cunts that will kill you in a heartbeat. Have you got it?"

"Yeah, I've got it."

'Never trust anyone' - with Devo dead and Murray hundreds of miles away, one blunt fact was staring me right in the eye; I currently didn't have anyone left that I could trust.

Chapter 38
Same Day

We drove for hours in total silence then eventually pulled off the motorway. Within ten minutes there were no street lamps; it was deathly quiet and scarily dark. As a Londoner, I had never appreciated that I was used to seeing night time awash with lights, the lights from lamp posts, houses, cars, bus stops, signs, they were everywhere. Here it was so dark and still, it felt like an altogether different planet.

We continued to drive for another half an hour, and it was clear that we were in the heart of the Spanish countryside. Occasionally, I would see the entrance to a driveway, but the houses would be half a mile away in the distance, the faint twinkle of lights from miniature windows like stars in the sky. Fuck me, where was I going?

He flicked the car's indicator, and we turned into a driveway. There was a sign up above a poorly constructed wall that I was just able to read:

Casa de las Almas Perdidas

Was this place going to be my home for the immediate future? He slowed down as he drove up the gravel, tree-lined driveway. As the drive curved to the right, I could start to see the lights from the building. As it became clearer, I could see that the building appeared as a large farmhouse. There was a grand, but old wooden front door. The farmhouse was two storeys high and had at least ten windows on each floor.

The car stopped, and I was instructed to get out and to take my bag. I retrieved it from the boot and followed him to the door. He knocked loudly, and it was answered quickly by a lady in her fifties. She acted like she was expecting him.

He stood talking to her in Spanish, and then he handed her the money. He then turned to me.

"I'll let Murray know you're alright. Remember what I said."

"I will and thanks."

"Good luck, son," he said with a serious, stern look.

And that was it. He got back into his car and drove away. I didn't know his name, and I had discovered nothing about him. It was a clinical meeting, and I was pretty sure I wouldn't see him again.

The Spanish woman greeted me in excellent English.

"Would you like to come in?" she asked.

I sensed she was a little wary of me. I suspected that given the story she had heard she would believe me to be dangerous. I don't know why, I mean, I had only been accessory to the manslaughter of a shopkeeper and was wanted by the Russian mob!

"Yes, please," I replied.

We walked into the sizeable, old-fashioned hallway. It had an unusual smell, maybe the lingering aroma of the food that had been cooked earlier. It was wood panelled and cluttered. The woman walked to a makeshift hotel reception desk. It was a free-standing table and on it were lots of leaflets, newspapers and a couple of magazines, those educational ones about big fucking rocks in South America. Behind the desk was a rack with some keys on it. Each hook had a room number above it.

"Where am I?" I asked.

"Did the man not tell you?"

"No."

"You are in Almedinilla in Andalucia. This is a commune. "

"A commune?"

 Do you know what a commune is?"

"No."

"We have a farm here, we grow all sorts of fruit and vegetables like oranges and olives, and we also keep cattle. People come here to stay with us for no charge. In return we feed them, and they help out on the farm. Your friend has given us some money so that you can stay here without having to work if you don't want to?"

"To be honest, I'm not sure farm work is my thing."

"That's no problem. Your friend said that some men are looking for you?"

"Yes, they are."

"They won't find you here, I'm sure. But, just in case, I would suggest you stay here in the compound. It will be safer, for the time being. We are busy here with the olive harvest, but luckily we have one twin room left. You can have this to yourself for the next ten days, but then you will have to share."

"Yes, no problem," I replied.

Fuck me, share - with whom?

"We eat breakfast between six and seven in the morning then we eat dinner between six and seven at night."

"What about lunch?"

"There is no lunch, as everyone is out working in the fields. There are shared bathrooms and toilets, one for each floor. There are plenty of books in each room, and you are welcome to read any of the books that you see around the place."

I looked around, and there were loads of shelves with books in, old looking books, thick ones as well which looked like they would take a fucking lifetime to read.

"Do you put on English television programmes?" I asked, tentatively establishing any levels of home comforts.

"Sir, this is a commune. People come here to escape. We have no television, no radio, no internet, no mobile phone reception, nothing. Sometimes even the electricity goes down for a few hours. We provide you with only the most basic of life's essentials, but we like to think that we make people feel comfortable."

"Okay." I replied.

I reminded myself of the need to be grateful; I could be sharing a bag with some breeze blocks at the bottom of the Thames.

"In your room, there will be a jug of drinking water, if it runs out just re-fill it from the vat outside. Please don't drink the tap water. There is a public phone in the lobby if you need to call home."

"Thanks."

Given what had happened today it was difficult to take this all in.

"The man told me that you had some money that you needed to keep safe?"

"Yes."

"We have a few security boxes, although generally, we don't get much call for them."

She reached under the counter and pulled out a small key on a fob.

"If you would like to put your money in box number six, it will be perfectly safe."

She invited me into a little back office where they were twelve small security boxes against the wall. I opened up the box with the key and then took the wad of cash out my bag, put it in the box, closed then locked it.

"I think it's best if you keep the key," she said.

She continued to act suspiciously.

"What is your name, sir?" The lady asked.

I paused. "It's Joe," I replied. "Joe Devonshire."

"Are you going to be alright?" she asked, with a concerned look

I considered the questions for a moment. "I'm not sure," I replied.

Chapter 39
Wednesday January 7th 2015

I woke up startled. As I had no mobile phone, watch or clock, I had no idea of the time. The light was pouring in through the thinly veiled curtains. While not hot, it was much milder than London, and my three blankets were sufficient to keep me warm.

This nightmare hadn't even begun to sink in. Life had drastically changed in just twenty-four hours. Yesterday I was in my bed in London, and now I was a fugitive on the run in a foreign country, hiding and trying to evade men that demanded me dead.

I looked around the stark, soulless room. I was lying on the bottom bunk of an old wooden bed. The room was decorated with unsightly dark green wallpaper. There was a sink in one corner, a desk in the other and in between a small wardrobe, a chest of drawers and a few odd ornaments scattered about. There was a fucking horrible painting on the wall which reminded me of our local doctor's waiting room.

I was busting for a piss but lay in bed feeling nervous. I knew roughly where the toilet was but felt awkward about getting up and using it. I was apprehensive about who I might bump into along the way. Knowing me, I was bound to open the wrong door and end up in some broom cupboard, which would then lock behind me leaving me to bang on the door before the lady downstairs let me out.

I tentatively ventured out of my room and poked around for a while before finding it. The clue turned out to be the picture of a toilet on the door. There was a clock on the landing which told me it was just before 8.30am. I'd missed breakfast, and I didn't even have the luxury of stale Coco Pops with water.

The toilet and the bathroom were separate, and both reminded me of home as they were grubby and old. The only thing missing was an ashtray full of Mum's dockers. As I walked along the landing, the house felt empty and silent. It felt like I was living in a place from a horror film. I suspected that anytime soon some mad bastard with nails hanging out of his face would start to chase me with a chainsaw.

There was no point denying it; I was as anxious as hell. I returned to my new, safe refuge and got back under the covers. I had to find a way of coping with this, but I was empty and lost. I drifted back off to sleep again and then woke up suddenly, having seen Devo's body lying in a casket.

I decided that this fucking nightmarish sleep was not doing me any good so I got dressed. I opened the curtains, which revealed a view out onto the farm. I could see a handful of people working. I pulled the chair from the desk up and just stared out of the window for the next couple of hours. It was a strange, calming feeling and I couldn't put my finger on what it was or why I got it. Maybe it was because, for the first time in about five years, I wasn't continuously playing with my mobile phone.

What was I going to do without it?

It must have been lunchtime, and I was getting ravenous. I went out onto the landing. It was just after midday. Fuck me; I'd have to wait for another six hours before I had dinner.

I had seen the dining room yesterday when I was making my way to my room. It was large with one big table and a load of chairs around it. I was going to have to sit and eat with a group of strangers. I wasn't good with strangers. I was a Cockney; I preferred my own people. Then there was the issue of food – fuck; they would be serving foreign muck. I was bound to hate it. I sat there doing that shaking your head thing. This wasn't going to work out. I needed another plan.

Perhaps I could return to London and see what enterprising death the seriously pissed off Russian mob have in store? Maybe they will disembowel me with a serving spoon before cutting off my limbs?

I then spent the rest of my day either sitting in the chair or lying on my bed. At least this situation was giving me time to think.

I wondered if Mum was okay. She'd have a grand in her pocket, so I expect she'd be fine. Murray would have been around and told her about Devo and me by now. Would she give a toss about Devo? Probably not given she didn't give two fucks when he was in prison. Would she miss me? I doubt it; she would be too pissed by now to remember.

Mum, for fuck sake, what a fucking waste of space and a pathetic excuse for a parent. Devo and I were a burden to her, a burden since day one. She was always far more interested in getting drunk or high than looking after us. I used to play truant from school, and she couldn't have cared less. 'I'll let you stay at home if you nip out to get some milk,' she'd say. Now for a lad who hated school that was the deal of the fucking century.

She never once badgered me to get a job; neither did she ever have a go at Devo for getting in trouble with the police. I doubted she gave a shit. Then there were the skanky fucking blokes she would bring back to the flat for sex. I could hear them at it as I lay in my bed. Fucking horrible it was. I used to have to put my headphones on to cancel out the noise. One morning, one of them sat at the kitchen table having a fag and a cup of tea. When Mum walked in it was clear she didn't even know his fucking name.

I wonder if I had offered Mum a deal of me staying or me leaving but giving her a grand, which one she would have taken? The money! She would have taken the money, every day of the week.

By this afternoon she would be pissed up on strong beer. She might have even headed out to a pub and flashed her cash around. If she were lucky, there would be one of her old flames knocking around and drunk enough to fuck her around the back of the pub. Mum – what a fucking joke.

I shivered slightly. I could feel my body aching. Was I coming down with something?

I could hear the voices of people coming back from the fields; there were all different languages being spoken. It was like being back in our local community centre.

Within a few minutes, a gong sounded, now that either meant the feature film was starting or that it was dinner time. I wasn't sure if I could face a room full of strangers.

Yeah, I could stay in my room and start a hunger strike against being harassed by Russian gangsters, maybe not.

Decision made and I tentatively walked down the stairs into the dining room. I could feel a cold shiver come over me. There were probably fifteen people sat around the table. I sat on a chair with no one sitting either side. I didn't look at anyone, and as I quickly gazed around, I realised that no one was bothering to look at me either. As I glanced passively around the room, I saw that everyone had that sort of hippy look about them. Bright, hand knitted jumpers, blokes with ponytails and nose rings and all that sort of shit; they certainly weren't like the locals from the Three Bells.

Why do they all dress like that? I could never understand it. Just because you eat fucking lentils and meditate, why do you need to adopt some fucking uniform? I was struggling to see how I was going to fit in here.

Somebody then sat next to me. I turned to see who it was.

"Hello," she said.

"Hi," I replied in a hushed voice.

She sat down, "I'm looking forward to this."

"To what?" I asked

"Dinner!"

"Oh yeah, same here," I replied, lying. I would, undoubtedly, fucking hate it.

"Picking those olives is hard work isn't it?" she asked.

"Oh, I don't know. I've only just arrived here."

"You'll ache after a day of doing it; it's backbreaking. Even though I can only do it for a couple of hours at a time, it still gets me. Good fun though, the smell of the fields are amazing."

A field that smells amazing! The only fields I've ever been in have stunk of fucking cow shit.

"Do they?" I said trying to be friendly.

"I think it's soup tonight," she said.

I plucked up a bit of courage and manoeuvred myself so that I could see her. She had dark Asian skin and this dazzling bright red, dyed hair. She was striking looking, and I noticed her tattoos. They were covering her neck, hands and arms.

"I'm Joe," I said.

Just then the door opened, and three people walked in with bowls of soup and started putting them on the centre table mats. I looked down at it with suspicion; it was this weird red concoction, which reminded me of Aldi chicken tikka masala sauce

"It'll be homemade tomato and paprika soup," she said. "Could you go and grab me a roll please?"

She pointed to a basket of bread rolls, where other hungry people were grabbing handfuls. One fella was suspiciously sticking a couple inside his hoodie pockets. A fucking roll thief, maybe I was going to fit in here after all!

"Yes, no problem." I went and got us both a roll and handed it to her.

We sat together eating our starter, which I have to admit tasted funny. I dunked my bread in the bowl once I had spotted someone else doing it. Not surprisingly it was the roll thief. If it wasn't for the fact that he had an earring the size of a Ford Mondeo hub cap, I might have believed we could become pals.

"My name is Elesha, by the way."

"I'm Joe."

"I know, you told me."

"Yes, sorry."

"It's no problem. How's your soup?"

"It's okay. I prefer Heinz, to be honest."

"What, rather than having it freshly made?"

"I've never really eaten freshly made food."

"What do you normally eat?"

"Stuff from takeaway places."

"Where are you from?"

"London. What about you?"

"Northampton."

"How long have you been here?" I asked.

"About two months. I have been here before though and thought it would be a great place to come back to."

"Are you on your own?"

"Yes. Are you?" She asked.

"Yes."

"I can tell. You look a little out of place, to be honest."

"I am out of place. I don't belong here."

"So, why did you come?"

"I had to." I was mindful that I was giving her too much information.

"Had to? What do you mean?"

"Just shit going on at home. I had to move out, you know."

"I get it. It's a good place to come and sort your head out. You'll be able to put things into perspective."

"I hope so."

We finished the soup and then we had some weird casserole, which Elesha enjoyed, but I struggled with. I had lost my appetite and was continuing to feel rough. I knew I was coming down with something; I could feel a thin layer of sweat on my brow. We talked a little more but without ever really getting to know each other. I got the feeling that she had a story that she was hiding as well. It was nice to be able to have at least one person here that I knew.

I wanted to stay and talk to her. She was pretty, and I realised I needed company, but after the casserole, she got up to leave.

"I need to go and lie down," she said.

"Will I see you here tomorrow?" I asked, desperate to cement our friendship.

"There aren't too many other places to eat around here, so I guess so. Maybe I shall see you out on the farm?"

"Maybe."

"You are going out tomorrow, aren't you?"

"Yeah, yeah. of course." I said, lying.

"Okay, goodnight then."

She then left. I slowly walked back to my room. What was I going to do all night? I looked at the clock. It was just after 7pm. Usually, I would be watching Youtube videos of cage fighting until about 3am.

I lay on my bed; whatever I was coming down with was getting worse. I was aching a little and felt cold. I got into bed and soon fell asleep.

When I woke up in the night, I was covered in sweat and shivering. I had a proper fever. I grabbed a towel and dried myself off. I then took the blankets from the spare bed and changed them with mine. As I did, the shivering became uncontrollable, and my teeth started chattering. I grabbed a sweatshirt from out of the wardrobe and put this on then I tightly wrapped the blankets around me.

I was sat on the edge of the bed. The door opened, and I could see a silhouette walk in.

"Dev, is that you?"

He walked in with a big grin on his face.

"You didn't think I'd leave my little brother all on his own did you?"

"Fucking hell, bro, I thought they had killed you!"

I got up and hugged him.

"I saw them coming from a fucking mile away mate, they were never going to catch me," he said,

"I thought I'd lost you."

"It's all going to be okay now."

"You're all I've got Dev. I hate it here. Can we go home now?"

"Of course we can. Grab your things and let's get out of here. It's time to go back to London."

"To London - but what about the Russians?"

"Oh yeah, the Russians. To be honest mate, it's not good news on that front."

"What are you talking about?"

"They're downstairs."

"What?"

"You see, they want to kill us both in the same room, only they want you to see me die first."

"What are you on about?"

He then suddenly became aggressive. "Running off to fucking Spain you clown, did you think they wouldn't find you?"

"Devo-"

"You never learnt a thing from me, did you?"

"What do you mean?"

"Murray sorted out a pickup from the airport; the pickup from the airport dropped you here. There were no breaks in the chain. You were so easy for them to find."

"Shit!"

"If you'd binned the fella off at the airport and gone solo you might have been alright; you might have stood a chance; we might have stood a chance, but not anymore."

"Bollocks!"

"Just how long did you think it would take them to catch up with you?"

"Fucking hell! I didn't think."

"You never fucking do, do you? You're a useless little cunt! Now we're both going to die."

"I'm sorry, Dev."

"Why did you come into my room that morning? You knew I wouldn't be able to leave you in the lurch. You fucking killed me that day, do you know that?"

"Please, Devo, don't." I went to hug him again and as I did I saw the blood seeping through his t-shirt.

"Fuck off and leave me alone! You're nothing to me now, nothing. I don't even recognise you as my brother anymore."

I woke up suddenly with sweat dripping off me. I had seen Devo as clear as day, the mole on his face, the detail of his teeth, everything. I wiped myself down again and then went back to sleep. I had a long series of feverish dreams; Devo was in all of them, the last of which involved us running down the street together, the big Russian was chasing us with a baseball bat. As we turned the corner, we realised we had run into a dead end. We watched terrified as he sauntered towards us and as he did he banged the end of a baseball bat on the road, a repetitive knocking sound, boom, boom, boom!

I woke suddenly. The knocking was coming from the door.

"Come in," I said in a total daze.

It was the lady from the reception.

"Hello, I just passed the door, and I heard you shouting out to yourself."

"I'm sorry. I'm not very well."

"You poor thing," she walked in and felt my brow. "You're burning up, and your blankets are all wet as well. Wait here."

When she returned, she had brought me fresh blankets, a pillow and a jug of water.

"Here. Let me change your bed for you."

"Thank you," I said

I sat on the chair while she stripped my bed and took the used blankets replacing them with fresh ones.

"This will make you feel comfortable."

I got back into bed. I was aching badly. I knew the nightmares would return. I fell asleep again and saw Devo in a coffin, worms wriggling around his skull. The coffin door slammed shut and then I saw the big Russian again; he grabbed my head and yanked it into a sink full of water. I couldn't breathe; he pulled my head up just as I thought I was going to drown. As I opened my eyes, I saw Murray. He was stood with the Russians watching as I was being tortured.

"Sorry, Bo it looks like I changed sides!" he said before he laughed at me.

My head was then thrust back under water. This time when it was pulled up, I could see my ex-girlfriend, Ashlee. She was standing with a child.

"Ashlee, I'm sorry," I said before my head was again dunked back under the water.

I woke as the light was on in my room. The woman had returned with a bowl of meat soup.

"This will make you feel better," she said.

"What's your name?" I asked.

"Tira," she replied.

I nodded then drank some soup.

"I can't drink anymore," I said after a few spoonfuls.

"You must. It'll help you. It's got chicken in it."

"Do you think my brother is dead?"

"Sorry?"

"My brother, do you think he is dead?"

"You have a fever, don't worry."

"Murray has gone to the Russians. He's going to tell them where I am."

"I will hide you from them."

"Can my Mum come here as well? I'll tell her to stop drinking."

"No more talking. Come on, get back into bed."

When I woke up, I felt like a sledgehammer had hit me, but thankfully the aches had subsided. I felt clammy with the sweat. Through blurred memories, I recalled Tira had visited me several times and looked after me. She had provided me with more care than I ever remembered getting from my Mum.

On the desk was a bowl of fruit, which she very kindly left for me. I was starving, and I looked at what was on offer. I'd never really eaten fruit. I decided to take a bite of an apple. The sweet freshness of it felt good. I sat on the bed, feeling relieved that the fever was subsiding.

I grabbed a couple of towels and went for a shower. I sighed with relief as the warm water cleansed my body. I felt like I had been in a car crash.

I returned to my room and slowly got dressed. There was a knock on the door.

"Come in."

It was Tira, "Ah, good you are up. Are you feeling better?"

"Yes. Thank you for looking after me."

"You've been out cold for pretty much three days."

"Three days? Fucking hell!"

"Dinner will be served in a few hours. I think you should try to come down and eat; it'll build up your strength."

"Yes, I will do."

I ran my hand over my stomach; it felt like I had lost weight. I hadn't eaten any takeaway food for nearly a week now. My body was probably going to start convulsing as I withdrew from fried chicken and kebabs.

I was looking out of the window and appreciating the beautiful sun when I caught sight of Elesha sitting on one of the benches. She was wearing shorts that exposed the tattoos that covered her legs. I wanted to speak to her; I needed some company, a warm, friendly face.

I left my room and headed out to see her. I walked through the double patio doors to where she was sitting.

"Alright? I asked.

"Hey, stranger! Where have you been?" she replied, with a warm smile.

"I've had a horrible fever. I've been laid up in bed for the past few days."

"Are you feeling better?"

"A little."

"Do you want to sit down?"

"Okay."

We then sat together and talked. She asked about my life, and I gave her a load of bullshit. It was for the best. I mean, who was this girl?

A couple of hours had passed, and as the other people came in from the farm, the gong sounded for dinner.

"Can I sit with you at the table?" I asked.

I knew I sounded like some pathetic, third-year kid at school but I was desperate not to be alone at the dinner table.

She smiled, "Of course you can, come on."

She then put her arm in mine, and we walked to the dining room together.

Chapter 40
Monday 12th January 2015

I had slept well and woke up feeling much better. I still had a faint layer of sweat over me and decided to head off for a shower. As I felt the tepid water cleansing my body, I remembered that through this whole ordeal an innocent man had lost his life.

The shopkeeper was going about his business that day. He was a hard-working man, making his living, paying his taxes, providing for his family and going to work, for what should have been a typical day at his shop. Only we rocked up and caused him such trauma that he died. That made me a murderer, simple as that. My actions had directly led to the death of my brother and the shopkeeper.

The shopkeeper – that was what I constantly referred to him as. I did not even know his name. It would have been in the newspaper article that Devo showed me; only I was more concerned with my own predicament rather than humanising my crime by giving this man the dignity of knowing who he was.

I returned to my room, lay back on my bed and closed my eyes. I needed to reflect. I had to sort this mental car crash out.

I asked myself a fundamental question: At what point did my life go so badly wrong? Was it when I started selling drugs? No, it was before that. Was it when I suggested the robbery to Devo, me as a young man desperate for a life of notoriety and crime? Or was it a long time before then, way back when I left school, when I left with no plans, no ambition and was just looking forward to a life of doing fuck all, scrounging off the state, taking money from the honest, hardworking taxpayer, then to steal off him and sell on what I had stolen to other scumbags like me?

Was this outcome an inevitability - should it be that a person, like me, who has never once in his life taken any responsibility be punished?

And now here I was; effectively a prisoner in some far away land, a man with the blood of two people, one of them my brother, on my hands.

I was a disgrace and an embarrassment, and I was ashamed of myself.

I knew that I had to somehow find redemption and escape this grief and torment. If I committed to change, then maybe someone would grant me a second chance? Maybe a higher power would provide me with an opportunity to do it all differently? I could be someone; I could work hard, give something back and maybe even assist someone that needed the help of another.

God, if I only had another chance. I would do anything for one more opportunity to put it all right.

But there would be no more chances. Life had been an opportunity, and I had failed to realise it. Now it was too late.

The damage had been done. I was standing in front of the judge and jury, and I was guilty of all charges. Should my sentence be to return to London to find Devo's body and then let the Russians have their time with me?

That was it. That was to be my punishment. It was clear. I deserved nothing better. A piece of shit kid from a piece of shit estate, the ending should fit the rest of the story.

I had made my decision, and it involved me signing my own death warrant. I was going to return to London. I just needed to figure out how I was going to get to the airport and then return home. I decided to go and have a walk around the farm to get some fresh air and to finalise my plan.

Knowing that I would shortly be leaving gave me a little more confidence. I walked out of the back of the house where there was an expanse of outbuildings with various old tractors and farm equipment. I strolled around and stuck my head into the different barns and sheds, there was hay in some, machinery in others; a few of them were empty, but it all meant nothing to me. I walked down the side of one of the buildings, and there was an odd looking wooden entrance where the door was slightly ajar. I opened it further and walked in. It was dark inside, and it took a few seconds for my eyes to adjust. As they did, I could see there were racks of wine bottles lining the walls. I started looking at them before I heard someone approaching.

"What the fuck do you want?" The voice said, in an aggressive cockney accent.

From out of the shadows emerged a small, scrawny teenage boy. He had horrible squinty eyes and a vile scowl. He couldn't have been more than five feet five, skinny and topless. His skin had this strange crinkled look to it. His head was close-shaven, and his torso was covered in small scars.

"Well, come on, what the fuck do you want?" he repeated.

"Nothing, I was looking around," I replied.

"That's a London accent, where you from?"

"South London," I said.

"Which part?"

"Lewisham. What about you?"

"Whitechapel," he said, abruptly.

Bollocks, he lived near me. Suddenly I found myself feeling uncomfortable. He might recognise me, or he might know Devo. I was quickly on my guard.

"Why are you nosing around here? This place is out of bounds." He continued.

"I was seeing what was in here."

"All this fucking wine, that's what."

He grabbed a bottle that was open and started drinking it.

"You can't get any other booze in this fucking place – here go on have a swig," he said.

"No thanks, I don't like wine."

"Neither do I, but booze is fucking booze. Go on have a taste; it looks like you need it."

I took the bottle and drank. I had tried wine before but wasn't keen; I still wasn't. I passed it back to him.

"They'd go fucking mad here if they found out we'd nicked any of their wine," he said.

"I had better get going," I said, feeling uncomfortable.

"Ah, stay here and help me finish this bottle."

"I need to get back," I replied.

"Why are you so twitchy - have you been up to something?" he probed.

"No, nothing," I said, nervously.

"Don't give me that. You've got a guilty fucking face. Have you been a naughty little boy?"

"I don't know what you are talking about," I said, anxiously.

He approached me, and as he did, I could see he had a false eye with no colouring on the pupil and a scar running down it.

"Cute aren't I?" he whispered and grinned showing his broken teeth. He then grabbed my sweatshirt, "I was at school, and some cunt slashed me across the face with a machete, he took my fucking eye out."

"Jesus!"

"You're not going to tell anyone I was in here, will you?" he asked.

"No, of course not."

"Good, because if you do, I'll take your eye out, you fucking south London cunt. Now get the fuck out of here."

He let go of my sweatshirt, and I slowly backed out of the store. As I did, his image disappeared into the darkness. I then turned and hastily returned to my room.

Chapter 41
Same Day

As I walked back to my room, I realised that the door was open. I approached tentatively, unsure of whom I would find there. It was a big, black geezer who was taking his clothes out of a large holdall. I slowly and slightly apprehensively walked in.

"Alright, bro?" I said.

He looked around and smiled. He was about forty years old, heavily muscled, and with a shaven head. The wear on his face and the look he had suggested that he had seen a bit of action.

"Good day," he responded with a smile.

"Can I help you?" I asked.

"Is this your room?" he replied.

"Yes."

"Nice to meet you, I'm your new roommate." He put out his hand, which I shook.

"I wasn't expecting you until next week."

"Yes, I was told I was required to come earlier."

"What, because of the olives that need picking?"

"Something like that."

He continued to unpack his clothes. They were all immaculately folded and crisp. He methodically hung them up in the wardrobe, making sure they were hanging perfectly straight.

"Feel free to move my stuff out of the way if you need more room," I said.

"I'm sure I won't."

I realised that all of my stuff was strewn over the table and the floor, as usual. I quickly grabbed it and moved it out of his way.

"Sorry about this," I said.

"No problem," he replied.

He carried a calmness about him, an assurance, which I seldom detected in a person.

"Where have you come from?" I asked.

"Originally?"

"Yes."

"Ghana. You?"

"London. Have you come from Ghana today?"

"No."

Silence after that.

"Top or bottom bunk?" I asked.

"Which one have you been using?"

"Bottom."

"I'll take the top one then."

"Sounds good. Do you snore?" I asked.

"Only when I'm sad. You?"

"Only when I'm drunk," I said with a cheeky smile.

"Given there is no alcohol here and that this is a place designed to make you feel happy, I think we can assume that we can both sleep peacefully then."

He looked at me and smiled. I smiled back.

"Hopefully," I said. "Have you stayed here before?"

"Not at this place, but I have stayed at similar establishments."

"Do you like them?"

"Kind of."

He was pleasant, but also cagey. My money was on him a having some colourful backstory, a little like myself.

"I'm Joe, by the way."

"Good to meet you, Joe."

I was waiting for him to tell me his name, but he didn't.

"Sorry, what's your name?"

He paused and then slowly turned around before looking me straight in the eye. "Kumasi. My name is Kumasi."

Chapter 42
Same Day

I was lying on my bed while Kumasi was sitting at the desk reading. Despite my initial reservations I was enjoying having some company. It was clear that Kumasi was a quiet, thoughtful character and this interested me, intrigued me even. I felt compelled to get to know him.

"What are you reading?" I asked.

Kumasi stopped and peered over the book, "It's called the Critique of Pure Reason."

"What's it about?"

"It's asking questions about the foundations of human knowledge."

"Sounds like heavy shit to me. Do you like stuff like that?"

"Another man's hypothesis on the meaning of life intrigues me."

"I don't read," I said.

"Neither did I until recently, but now I have realised it's one of life's wonders."

"What made you think differently?"

"The moment that I realised that it allows you to be transported to a different world."

"Oh right," I said, not having a fucking clue what he was talking about.

"Do you use social media, like Facebook and Twitter?" he asked.

"When I was at home, I was on them all the while."

"Doesn't that involve reading?"

"A bit, but I mainly prefer looking at film videos."

"That can still be enlightening."

"Not the ones I watch, bro!"

I looked across at him to see whether this had prompted a smile, but it hadn't, he just carried on reading.

"I reckon I'm only going to be staying for a couple more days then I'm heading back to London."

"Why's that?" he asked, continuing to read his book.

"Erm, my Mum's ill. I think I need to get back to check to see if she's alright."

"What's the matter with her?"

"Erm, she's got to go into hospital. Something's up with her breathing."

"How long have you been here?"

"Five days."

"And you've got to go back already. What a pity."

"Well, I think it's for the best, you know what I mean?"

He looked up from his book. "No."

"With her being ill and all that, I think I need to go home."

"You've got to do what you think is right."

He then moved slightly forward in his chair and presented me with a deep stare.
"You are doing what you think is right, aren't you?"
"Yes, I think so."
"Why did you come here?"
"Why? Oh, I thought I would have some time for myself."
"Why did you need to have time to yourself?" His tone had become a little interrogatory.
"You know."
"Who do you live with?"
"My Mum."
"Had you fallen out with her?"
"God no! That would involve actually having a conversation with her! No, Mum's a drinker, but she's not the reason I'm here."
"What about your Dad?"
"I've never seen the useless cunt."
"Why?"
"He moved on when I was a toddler."
"Did you miss him?"
"I never knew him."
"Do you think your life would have been different if you'd had a father around?"
"Maybe, I'm not sure."
"A boy without a father, it's like a boat without a rudder. He's the most important person a young man needs when he's growing up. He's his guide, his mentor and his conscience. What's worse is fatherless parenting seems to get passed down to the next generation, and so it continues. The cycle needs to stop. I wish, on just one occasion, I could do that.'
"A bit of support would certainly have been nice," I said with a smile.
"You never properly explained why you left home?"
"There was shit going down and all that."
"All what?"
"Shit things happening."
"'Shit things happening' – what does that mean?"
"Stuff going down."
"So, why here - why not clear off to the English countryside?"
"I wanted to get away from England."
"Wanted to or had to?"
"What do you mean?"
The atmosphere suddenly changed. Kumasi then moved a little further forward in his chair and looked at me. He spoke slowly.
"Did you decide to come here of your own volition, or did you have to leave London through necessity?"
Something was wrong. The question was too intrusive. "Are you with them?" I whispered.

"With who?"

"Are you here to kill me?"

"What? No! Why, is somebody seeking to kill you?"

"I'm in trouble, big fucking trouble."

"Do you want to tell me about it?"

"I'm scared, bro, really fucking scared."

"What are you scared of?"

"I've got men after me. Men who want to kill me and the real reason I'm here is that I'm hiding."

"Hiding. Do you want something?"

"What?"

"So am I."

Chapter 43

Same day

The gong went for dinner and Kumasi and I walked downstairs. I saw him grab a couple of pieces of fruit and a bread roll then strangely he left the dining room.

Elesha walked in, and I gave her a wave. She waved back and then came over to join me.

"Hey, how are you?" I said.

I couldn't disguise my pleasure in seeing her beautiful smile. I knew I was falling for her; I was getting that glow every time we met. She approached me smiling, but slightly out of breath.

"Hey, Joe!"

She kissed my cheek. A little ripple passed through me. I had to avert my gaze and regain my composure.

We sat down and immediately started chatting away. Elesha told me about her day and how she had picked olives for a couple of hours then had to stop because she was tired. She explained how she suffered from asthma and this made her wheezy and lethargic.

The starter arrived, cold meats and cuts of cheese. The main course was some fucking horrible casserole again with vegetables. In the interests of appearing to be appreciative I made periodic humming noises to falsely suggest that I was enjoying it.

"Have you seen that scrawny cockney lad knocking around?" I asked her.

"No, what lad?"

"I was having a nose around today and ended up in one of the side buildings where they store the wine they make. I stuck my head in, and this fucking horrible fucking geezer threatened me."

"What!"

"He said he was going to take my eye out if I told the owners that he was helping himself to the wine."

"I haven't seen him. You would have thought he would be here now having something to eat."

"I bet he's pissed out of his head and fast asleep next to one of those big fucking cows."

"They're bulls, Joe."

"It's the same thing," I said with a wink.

After dinner we went outside, as it was a lovely mild evening, we sat on a bench under the tree and stared up at the stars. Ah right, so this is romance, I had previously believed it to be sharing a doner kebab and having a cheeky grope around the back of the boozer.

"I'm thinking of heading off in a few days," I said.

"Are you?"

I was pleased to detect an element of disappointment in her voice.

"I might stay though. It all depends on whether my Mum needs me to go home or not, you see she's very ill."

I was telling more fucking lies. I felt like a fraud.

"Who will I have dinner with?" she asked with distinctly puppy dog eyes.

"I'm sure you'll find someone else," I said, fishing for a compliment.

"You're probably right." she responded.

"Hey!"

I pretended to give her a friendly punch. We both paused and looked at each other. I was dying to kiss her, but I didn't know how she would react. I didn't want to spoil it as she might knock me back leaving me feeling like an idiot.

"I've got a new cellmate, babe."

"Cellmate!" she laughed. "Who is it?"

"That big fella who walked into the dining room with me, Kumasi's his name. Seems like a decent enough bloke."

"I didn't see him."

We sat for a few seconds in silence. I looked down at her tattoos; there were hundreds of little mini designs, a patchwork of ideas all cobbled together on her very own organic canvas.

"You've got a lot of ink on you. When did you start getting them done?"

"As soon as I realised I no longer liked the person I saw in the mirror."

"What was up with that person?"

"I had badly let someone down. I had allowed someone to take a terrible path in their life and I should have stopped them, only I didn't. I've lost them now. I doubt I'll ever see them again and I suspect something bad will happen to them if it hasn't already."

"Who was it?" I asked.

"Somebody that was very close to me."

"So, why the tattoos?"

"To change the reflection, to see someone looking back at me who doesn't remind me of the person that came up short, when it mattered most."

I started to look at the detail of her tattoos. It was a collage of art, quotes and symbols.

"What does the Arabic writing mean?" I asked, pointing at her arm.

She looked at me and paused for a few seconds.

"Lost my Will to live."

"Have you?"

"I lost it some time ago."

"Why?"

"I've just told you."

We sat in silence for a few moments.

"Have you got tattoos?" she asked.

I didn't have any tattoos; in fact, I had nothing of any interest to say about me at all. My life back in London was woefully shallow; a void of nothingness; of fucking around all day and rarely leaving a two-mile East End radius.

"No." I eventually replied. "There is nothing to see."

"Maybe someday, then," she said politely.

"Maybe," I replied.

I continued to look at her tattoos; they were beginning to fascinate me, I subtly turned her arm to read the writing on the underside.

"That one hurt like hell," she said. "But it was worth it."

"Can I take a look?"

"Sure."

As I she rolled her arm back I saw the writing, which had tears dripping from the letters. 'Will I let you down', it read.

It was clear that whoever she had walked away from the pain that she felt was torturing her.

"This is my favourite one," she said.

She then pulled her top down just below her collarbone, exposing more writing, this time intertwined with barbed wire. It read; 'Will I always Love you'.

Hurt, pain and weird questions inked all over her petite body. This thing was eating away at her. I was intrigued as to precisely what and who it was but dare not ask.

"So, how come a good looking girl like you, hasn't found a fella then?"

"I've found loads of fellas, just not the one I have been looking for."

"Who are you looking for?"

"Based on my experience of life, so far, someone that is loyal would be a good start."

We then continued to look at the stars. I thought that if she were interested in me, then she would return the question, but the moment passed.

"What star sign are you?" she asked.

I secretly fucking hated this question, but in the interests of charming an attractive lady, I played along.

"Aquarius and you?"

"Cancer."

"I always thought that was a scary star sign."

"That's a different meaning. It apparently originates back to a crab which was supposed to attack Hercules."

"Is that the geezer whose strength was in his hair?"

"No, that geezer is Samson."

At that point I decided to move the conversation away from Bible studies, otherwise, I could be rapidly exposed as the thick fucker that I am. A trait, I suggest she probably won't find attractive.

"What's your tipple?" I asked her.

"What?"

"If we were back at home and were to meet up in a flash bar, what would be your drink?"

"Champagne."

"Champagne, shit girl, you aren't messing around, are you?"

"Could you afford me?"

"Fucking right, I could. Could you handle me?"

She replied in a Cockney accent, "Fucking right I could."

We laughed and then we hugged. I held her in my arms, this gorgeous, petite, tattooed princess. Wow, she smelt good. I hadn't embraced a woman since the night I finished with Ashlee.

"Come on," she said, "I'm getting tired, take my arm and escort me to my room."

Was this going to be my lucky night? I could feel those erotic butterflies fluttering in my stomach. It had been a while since I had felt them, and boy, I'd missed them. I held my arm out, and she took it.

Alas, it was a false alarm. My belle, Elesha, was out of breath and by the time we arrived at her room I had to settle for a kiss on the cheek and that look. That look – I know the one, the look that says I am interested.

As I returned to my room, I realised that maybe I did have an option. Perhaps Elesha was a reason to stay here. My prospects of trying to become her next boyfriend were after all better than my chances of returning to London and evading the Russians.

Perhaps, she could give me a reason to make this work.

Chapter 44
Tuesday 13th January

I was awoken by the bleep of Kumasi's alarm clock. Within seconds he kneeled on the floor. He had his eyes closed and was silently mouthing words. I stared at him, fascinated. He appeared to be praying which is something, outside of a church, I hadn't seen anyone do.

After about ten minutes he stood up and drank some water then stripped off his loose shirt and stood just in his pants. As the light shone through the gaps in the curtains, I could see bullet wounds over his body, four, five, six of them. Fucking hell, this fella must have seen some serious action. He then got down on his knees and started to perform press-ups, but not the jerking ones we used to do at football practice; he was doing these in almost slow motion. Each up and down movement was taking about ten seconds. After about three minutes I could see the strain in his face, but he kept going, eventually collapsing on the floor.

He then performed the same routine with stomach crunches and then some weird dips that he did from his bed onto the floor. This peculiar, meticulously executed routine continued with more slow exercises. I could see his ripped muscles straining, as was his expression, but throughout his workout, he never made a sound.

Eventually, he gathered his towel and headed off to the bathroom.

I rolled over and went back to sleep.

When I woke up, he had gone. It was mid-morning, and I was facing a full day of total, mind-numbing boredom, yet again.

By noon I decided to go out to get some fresh air. I walked out into the yard and went to sit on the bench where Elesha and I were last night. I was hoping that she would finish in the fields early and come and find me.

I sat looking at the sky. It was cloudy today. I waited for her, but she didn't come.

As I gazed out to the farmland, I could see the muscular figure of Kumasi approaching. I waved to him, and he gestured back and walked towards me. I was pleased to see him, and I gave him my customary greeting:

"Alright, bro?"

"Good afternoon."

"What are you up to?"

"I'm heading in. It's going to start raining in a minute."

I looked up at the sky. "Who are you, a fucking weatherman?" I joked.

"I can see the cloud formation overhead. Trust me; it'll rain and heavily as well. A good time for me to do some reading, I think."

"I'll come back in with you."

I followed him to the room. Even within the short time I had known him, I was gaining a warm sense of comfort being in his company. He was intelligent and compassionate, but I guess I also respected where he was now in his life, given his past. I wanted to know his secrets, and those bullet wounds only served to intrigue me further.

We arrived back at the room, and I looked out of the window to see that the rain had started and that people were running in.

"You were right," I said.

I doubted that he was like Mum and would give me the old, 'told you' line.

"What's it like working out in the fields, then bro?"

"It beats walking the streets of Ghana with a machine gun thinking I am some big-time gangster."

"Is that what you were?" I asked with a noticeable level of excitement and intrigue.

"I'm afraid so."

"What was it like?" I asked.

"How old are you, Joe?"

"Twenty-two."

"I'm guessing that the thought of being a feared gangster appeals to you?"

"No -"

He interrupted, "Don't worry I would have thought the same at your age. But then one day you wake up, and you think to yourself, is this all I am? My life was just about reputation, fear, and violence. And those people who didn't fear me, well, they wanted to kill me. I realised that it was a pathetic existence."

"I wanted to be someone, back in London," I admitted.

"Did you?"

"My brother was a bad boy; he used to pull jobs, get up to no good, he did time in prison and all that. I wanted to be like him."

"Why?" he asked.

I shook my head, "I don't know."

"I bet you do," he replied.

"No, seriously, I don't know."

"The reason is pretty much always the same," he said.

I turned and looked at him. "Go on then," I invited him to tell me.

"It's because you had nothing else in your life, so it might have been the one thing you could have done that you might have got some credit for."

I shrugged my shoulders, "I don't know about that."

"Well, think about it, if you were good at something, say playing the piano, then you would have focused your efforts on developing this as a skill, eventually maybe making something of yourself as a pianist; earning a reputation; making some money and everything that goes with it. But most of us aren't born with great skills, which is why some of us choose to become well known, not through the good things we do, but the bad. Making ourselves infamous is a way to do that."

Fuck me, he was right. In retrospect, I initially didn't want to pull the robbery at the European Store for the money. I wanted to do it for the street cred. Afterwards, I would have wanted everyone at the Three Bells to have known it was me that had done it. It would have been Devo and me; two brothers in an area where siblings had a reputation of being feared. I wanted to have geezers point at me from across the bar and whisper my name because then I knew they were taking me seriously. I wanted a reputation. Of course, I did, I wanted to be somebody and took the only route I thought possible. He had nailed it, and I had suddenly realised the futility of it all.

He continued, "Anyway, I digress, you were about to give me a platinum-tipped reason why you can't go out and work in the fields."

"It's not really for me," I replied, lamely.

"Why?"

"I'm a city boy; we aren't used to working out in the fields."

"But you are used to working?"

"Yeah, oh yeah, I was working when I was back in England."

"Doing what?"

"In a garage. I'm a mechanic."

"A mechanic?"

"Yeah, yeah, I've been doing it since I left school."

"Well done. What type of vehicles do you mend?"

"Cars, obviously!"

"What's obvious about that?"

"Well, what else do you mend in a garage?"

"Heavy goods vehicles, motorbikes, motorhomes, but of course, working in a garage you would know that."

"Yeah, yeah. I specialise in sports cars," I said, brazenly lying through my teeth and digging myself a bigger fucking hole.

With that Kumasi held a stare towards me, "That sounds good," he said slowly.

"It is." Who was I kidding? "So I'm guessing you didn't have a proper job back in Ghana?"

"I was the leader of a gang."

"Fucking hell! What type of gang?"

"The worst type of gang."

"What, like you were involved in drugs and guns and all that?"

"And worse."

"Shit. Like what?"

"You don't want to know."

"So, did you leave Ghana by choice?"

"It's complicated, but let's just say I departed very quickly."

"Or what would have happened?"

"A lot of pain, I expect."

"What had you done?"

"Things that meant people wanted me dead. "

"I know what you mean."

"Why would anyone be hunting down a sports car mechanic?" he asked.

"I got involved in drugs."

"Was this before or after you started to mend cars?"

He asked me with a slightly sarcastic tone. He had sussed me. I lowered my voice, ashamed that I had lied, again.

"There were no cars, bro. I've never been a mechanic. I've never been anyone. I'm a loser, a waste of space. The only person I had that meant anything to me is dead and it's my fault."

"What are you going to do about it?"

"What do you mean?"

"Twenty-two years old and you've given up just because you've made a few mistakes, is that what you are telling me?"

"I've got no one Kumasi; you don't understand. My brother was the only person that meant anything to be, and now he isn't here, and it's all because of me."

"So, that's it then. Game over, lights out, draw the curtains and all this despite you being healthy and having the rest of your life in front of you."

"I've got nothing. Now all I do is sit in this fucking shit hole all day, waiting for dinner time."

"And what did you do back at home all day?"

"What?"

"When your brother was alive, and you were back at home, what did you do then?"

"You know, stuff."

"'Stuff?'"

"Yeah, you know."

"No."

"I'd hang around the estate and that."

"At twenty-two?!" he probed sarcastically.

"It was better than being in here," I said, defensively.

"Hang on; you've painted this picture that life was good back then, that it was somehow richly fulfilling. I'm interested to learn what made it so?"

"Well, I used to hang out."

"You've already said this, but what exactly does 'hang out' mean?"

"You know?"

"No."

"It wasn't like this."

"What was it like? Convince me."

"Convince you of what?"

"That it was ever good. That you haven't, in some small way, created this smoke screen that life, before whatever went down, and you had to leave London, was this bed of roses, because I'm not sure I am buying the story, my friend."

"At least I had my brother though, at least he was around."

"And now he isn't, so it's time to put the 'closed' sign up and cease all further trading?"

"No," I said defensively.

"Or was it up anyway?" he asked.

"'Closed' sign, what are you on about?"

"I'm talking to an under-achiever, that's clear. You're someone who hasn't done anything meaningful with your life, and it's simply easier to clutch onto a terrible thing that's recently happened and use that as an excuse for the past and what's even worse, the future."

"Okay, you tell me what I can do then?"

"And you think that will work?"

"You seem to have the answer for everything else," I said, now visibly getting irritated.

"We can stop this conversation right now if you want. It doesn't mean anything to me."

I sighed, "No, sorry, go on, please, I want to hear what you've got to say."

"I'm telling you what I am seeing. I do not intend to give you the answer for anything."

"Then can you please give me the fucking answer, because right now I am walking around with this fucking guilt on my mind and I can't see any light at the end of the tunnel."

"I don't have the answer. You do."

"I don't though! That's just it. Will you help me? Will you tell me what I need to do?"

"Listen, how many people do you think go into a doctor's surgery every day to be told that whatever is wrong with them is down to their lifestyle. They overeat, they smoke, or they drink too much. The poor doctor sits there and does his best to get them to change and, maybe for a few days afterwards, with his advice resonating in their head they do. Only they don't sustain it. They simply revert to doing what has become their habit."

"You're losing me, bro."

"You want to change, is that correct?"

"Yes."

"And you want me to tell you how?"

"Yes."

"Then that makes me the doctor in this equation, and as I have already told you, it doesn't work, it would be a waste of my time, and I'm not a person that likes to waste time. I might not have very much left."

"At least help me?"

Kumasi sighed. "Tell me, what do you want your life to be?"

"To do something, to stop feeling fucking useless, to prove to my dead brother than I can make something of myself."

"Then you need to be clear exactly what that means. Where is your destination? How will you know when you have arrived there? And then you need to sort out what steps you need to take to get there."

"That's what I need your help with."

"I'm not the doctor, remember?"

"So, I need to work out what I should be doing with my life?"

"That would be a good start."

"Okay, okay. I get it."

"But you have to mean it; you have to want to achieve those things. Otherwise, it won't happen."

"I understand."

"Remember my friend; the vast majority of human beings are weak and pathetic. They spend their entire lives seeking change and it simply never materialises."

"I'll try my best."

"And while you are at it, think about your values as a human being. I found this very useful when I realised I wanted to change."

"Values, what do you mean?"

"If you were a tree and I was to cut you in half, what values would I see? I would like to think that if you cut me in half nowadays you might see traces of kindness, discipline, a desire for education and respect for my body. These are values that I now live my life by. I don't always succeed, but I always try."

"Who told you to do that? Is that the religious stuff you do?"

"It's got nothing to do with religion. My values were created and developed by me, and I am the only person who stands in judgement of them."

"What's that praying you do in the morning then?"

"It's not praying."

"No?"

"I am reflecting on my life. I say sorry to everyone I have ever hurt; I am saying sorry for the years I wasted in my life doing bad things, taking drugs, drinking, taking people for granted. And most of all, I am saying sorry to my mother, who passed away, believing her only son to be a bad man. I reflect on the challenges that lie ahead that day and make sure that my inner demons don't destroy my plans."

I could see that Kumasi had a tear in his eye.

"I hope my mother she sees me now and I pray that I have finally made her proud. Why don't you do that, Joe, make someone proud of you?"

"I will do, Kumasi. I will do," I said.

Kumasi then walked over to me and stood close.

"What would you do if someone gave you an opportunity to peer into your future, would you take it?" he whispered

"Yes, of course, I would."

"Take a careful look at what is around you, my friend. Learn from your experiences and act upon them."

"Okay," I said.

"People like us are volatile and erratic, and the road that lies ahead can be fraught with danger because of our inclination to veer off-track at any time. We can soon become lost amongst our worst inner demons, and when this happens, they can pull us down to depths that you never imagined and a safe return from this point can be almost impossible."

I was hanging on his every word. "Okay," I said, again.

"Remember, the greatest test that any of us will ever face will be to conquer ourselves. If you are prepared to accept this as one of life's truths, then maybe you are prepared to face this challenge and to not hide from it any longer. But it'll be, without question, the longest and hardest fight you'll ever have."

Chapter 45
Same Day

I had spent the rest of the day on my bed doing something I had never before done; I was contemplating the rest of my life. What should my values be? Could I alter the trajectory of my life and be heading for a more positive direction? Was I prepared to accept the challenge that Kumasi talked about and face up to who I was, and then seek to become a better person?

I had spruced myself up with a shower and treated myself to a splash of duty-free aftershave. It said 'eau du toilette' on the bottle, which confused the fuck out of me, given it didn't smell like any toilet I had been in. I was listening out for the gong, which would be my cue to meet up with Elesha. I was looking forward to it. As it had stopped raining, I had planned for us to sit outside again on our bench. I loved our conversations and the passive flirting that we engaged in. I wasn't sure whether she was attracted to me, but one thing was for sure, I was in with a chance, a chance which may very well have doubled now I was wearing my eau du toilette.

The gong sounded, and I rushed down for dinner. I got us a pair of seats away from where everyone else seemed to congregate. I sat patiently for ten minutes, but there was no sign of her. The starter appeared, but still no show. By the time the main course of road kill stew appeared, I had given up and left the dining room feeling deflated.

I went outside and sat on our bench on the off chance that she decided to skip dinner but would come down and look for me.

"Are you waiting for that tattooed bird?"

Out of the darkness the horrible Cockney kid appeared.

"No, I was just chilling out."

"Are you sure? I've seen you two together. You're drooling all over her like a pathetic puppy. You think you're in with a chance don't you?"

"No, we're just friends."

"Fuck off are you. But, you've got no chance, pal. She's well out of your league."

Despite him being no more than seventeen, he strangely intimidated me. He had a very threatening presence, a lot like a Troy or Cazley.

"Well anyway, I'm off to bed," I said.

"What, and miss out on this fucker?"

He pulled a huge spliff out of his pocket.

"Where did you get that from?"

"I know a fella in the next village who can get it for me."

He lit up. I could smell the sweetness of the cannabis. I had missed it. He took a big drag then passed it to me; I couldn't resist. We then smoked the lot leaving me feeling wasted.

"It's fucking world class gear, that is," he said.

"What's your name?" I asked.

"Billy. Yours?"

"Joe. What's your story then?"

"The Old Bill back in London wanted to speak to me about something a bit naughty. I wasn't too keen on a spell in a detention centre, so I split."

"What did you do?" I asked.

He pulled his finger across his neck, smiling while he did so. Was he joking? Probably not, this geezer looked capable of anything.

"What about your family, do they know where you are?" I asked.

"I've only got my Mum. I'll suppose I'll drop her a message at some point and let her know that I'm alright."

"Do you ever see your Dad?"

"Never set eyes on the cunt. I don't fucking want to either. What about you?"

"Nah, he left when I was two. I'm like you; I've just got my Mum." I said.

"What's she like?" he asked.

"She's an alcoholic waste of space to be honest."

I felt a bit bad saying that, but it was the truth.

"What about your Mum?" I asked.

"She's a good woman, but I lived in a rough area, so I suppose that's why I turned out like I am. She didn't seem to resist too much when she knew I was leaving though. I suspect she was glad to see the back of me."

"When do you think you'll see her again?" I asked.

"I'm not sure I ever will."

"Do you reckon it would have been different if your dad had been around?"

"Maybe, I don't know," he said, shrugging his shoulders.

"It's weird to think our dads are out there somewhere, going about their business, doing their thing and not giving a toss about us," I said.

"They never wanted anything to do with us, so fuck them both, I say."

I had a feeling that I had exhausted the civilised conversation that I was going to have with Billy and made it clear that I was off to bed.

He then grabbed my arm, "You owe me twenty quid for that."

"For what?"

"That spliff."

"Twenty quid, are you having a laugh?"

"It's twenty quid, you cunt. Make sure you have it with you the next time I see you, otherwise there'll be trouble."

He stared at me in a menacing way; it was clear that he wasn't joking.

"Twenty quid, or else we're going to fall out, have you got it?"

He then walked away, his scrawny figure disappearing into the darkness.

Chapter 46
Same Day

I returned to our room distinctly stoned. I walked in, and Kumasi was sat in the chair reading.

"Alright, bro?"

"Good evening." he turned to me and pulled half a smile, "from the look of your eyes it appears you've had a good night."

"I bumped into someone I knew, and we shared a smoke, you know what I mean?"

He went back to his book. "Fair enough," he replied decidedly disinterested.

"I bet you don't approve, do you?"

"Of what?" he asked, continuing to read his book

"Of me getting high."

Kumasi chuckled, "You do exactly what you like, my friend. I only judge myself, not others. I thought I had made that clear to you."

"Perhaps I should make that one of my values, 'likes to get high.'"

"Maybe you should," he replied, his gaze still firmly on his book.

"That and being a lazy little cunt, that'll work, won't it?"

He didn't answer me; instead, he continued to read. I was childishly trying to get a rise out of him. I immediately stopped, feeling like the idiot that I was.

I decided to take a fresh approach, "I was thinking about what we were talking about earlier, you know, about my values and all that, I decided that I would like to be known as a hard worker."

"Do you?" he said, still disinterested.

"Well, it's a good thing isn't it?"

"Is it?"

"You said as much earlier."

He then slowly put his book down. "So, you're going to try to copy me, are you?"

"No!"

"Because it's easier than having to think for yourself, isn't it?"

"I'm trying to get into this, bro."

"I think you've got me confused with someone who gives a damn about you and your little self-help enterprises."

"What?"

I could feel his mood changing from the laid back Kumasi, to something very different.

"I don't want to get dragged into your world, or anything that involves you. You're a loser. I can spot that from a mile away. So how about you clear off and play in your own sandpit." he said.

"Alright, bro, take a fucking chill pill will you!" I said.

"And stop calling me 'bro' as well. I'm not you're 'bro'. To be my 'bro' you've at least got to have some balls. You've got none."

I lay on the bed, feeling raw, he had hit a nerve but what was worse was that he was right. I recalled Devo's reaction when he had told me about his first day working in the warehouse and I asked him if he could try and get me a job there. There were similarities in how they had both responded. They cited that I was a weak, pathetic character. Having admitted to myself that something had to change I was taking the soft option of trying to hang on to someone else's shirt tails and hope they could pull me out of the shit-pit that I was slowly sinking in. But why should they? I was somehow delegating my responsibilities to someone else because it was easier than having to assume full accountability myself.

Unfortunately, with Kumasi, I had tried to cock my leg up the wrong lamp post, and he had sniffed me coming from a mile off.

It's a horrible feeling the moment you have it confirmed that you are a loser. I'd had it a few times, but coming from a man I had met just two days ago, it stung in a very different way.

I decided in the morning that I would speak to Tira and see whether I could have a different room. Things had turned toxic so it might be for the best.

But that's what I always do. Rather than face my problems and have the courage to resolve them, I push them to one side and forget that they matter and most importantly, assume absolutely no responsibility.

Maybe it was time to do the opposite of what I would usually do. Did I have this in me? Did I have the commitment and dedication to change?

Perhaps it was time to find out.

Chapter 47
Wednesday 14th January 2015

I woke up to Kumasi's bleeping alarm clock, and within minutes, he was performing his morning routine; knocking out torturous sets of press-ups. Once he had finished I decided to break the ice.

"Sorry about last night, Kumasi. You were right, by the way."

"Right about what?"

"Right about me, and right about everything."

"I'm sorry for my part in the discussion, as well."

"Can we move on?"

"Today is a new day. If you have had as many arguments as I have had, you would know why I never bear a grudge."

He offered me his hand to shake, which I gratefully accepted.

"I want to change you know; I want to be a better person. It's just that I feel gutted about my brother."

"Don't use that as an excuse, use it as a reason."

"You're right. Could I come out to the fields with you today?"

"To work?"

"Yes, I want to work. I want to stop being lazy. I'm ready to face the challenge."

"Of course you can. Look I'm going for a shower, you get yourself ready then we shall have breakfast and head out together."

"Okay, great!"

After he had left the room, I lay on my bed and anticipated how the rest of the day would play out. I hadn't done a day's work in my life, so how the fuck would I be able to do eight hours of graft?

Worst still, I was convinced that whatever task I would be asked to do I would somehow fuck it up. I would pick the olives in an incorrect way or put them in the wrong place; I'd even damage them somehow. I just had a track record of getting things wrong, and when it happened, it knocked me backwards. I would withdraw into myself; say that I wasn't bothered when I was. It would hurt like hell; then whatever I was doing, I would just quit.

I painfully remembered being at school in year 9 and Mister Warner, our science teacher, giving us practical demonstrations. He thought it was great fun to invite me to show the class how the experiments needed to be performed. He knew that I would get it wrong and so did everyone else. It was hilarious for everyone in the room, except me. I used to dread the lessons, wondering whether I was going to get humiliated. Eventually, I just stopped going and with that any academic interest I may have had in the subject vanished.

Mister Warner, you fucking wanker! I would pay good money to bump into you again, let's see if you'd be laughing after that.

It was situations like this that had deflated me and rinsed my confidence. But as Kumasi said, I was showing no balls and now was the time to step up.

I got ready, and we went down for breakfast. The dining room was busy with people helping themselves to food. There was fruit, bread, cheese, ham – this wasn't exactly a bacon and eggs affair. I had a glass of orange juice, ham and cheese. I was feeling nervous, and I picked at my food while Kumasi sat quietly, eating melon, grapes a banana and a small piece of cheese. Not a word passed between us. I wondered what he was thinking. Did he think I would quit? Was he laughing at me inside? No, that wasn't his style. Kumasi wanted me to succeed; that's who he was.

Once we had finished, I noticed that he took his plate back to a side table and wiped his place with a cloth. It was immaculate and ready for the next person to use. I did likewise. Someone came and waited to sit down as I was cleaning away the crumbs that had strayed off my plate onto the tablecloth. They thanked me for doing this. I nodded and followed Kumasi out of the room into the backyard of the farm.

We walked towards the fields where I could see endless lines of trees. There were a couple of people getting tools ready for the day's work. I slowly approached them, starting to feel awkward.

An older man walked up to me.

"Hello, do you speak English?" he asked with a Spanish twang.

"Yes."

"Is it your first day in the fields?"

"Yes, it is."

"Have you picked olives before?"

"No, you'll have to show me, I'm sorry."

"There's nothing to be sorry about. Come with me."

I followed him to where there was a man, and a woman stood at an olive tree. There was tarpaulin on the floor, and they held these weird sticks in their hands.

"This is Peter and Antonia. This is-"

"I'm Joe."

They were both friendly and greeted me warmly. They then showed me how to use these weird sticks to shake the branches from where the olives would fall onto the tarpaulin. You would then collect the olives and place them in trays.

Peter handed me a stick. I turned to look for Kumasi, but he had disappeared. I then started work. After a few minutes, Peter offered me some encouragement about how many olives I was shaking off. They were both very kind and friendly.

By mid-morning, a man approached us with a tray of drinks. I was encouraged to drink water, which I did. I also had a cup of coffee that was darker than Kumasi and nearly as strong.

"It's how the Spaniards like to drink it," Antonia said.

At lunchtime, the man came back with some bread rolls, some with ham in, some with cheese. I had one of each. I sat on my own under a tree. I felt knackered, absolutely fucking drained. I had been shaking trees and picking olives up from the floor for four hours, maybe more.

Peter and Antonia then carried on for the afternoon session. I sat, feeling flat and de-motivated. Fuck this, for a game of soldiers, I thought. I'd paid these cunts a grand to stay here, not like these fucking freeloading hippy twats. I'm not standing here all day doing this shit. I slowly walked back to the farmhouse.

What a load of fucking shit - fucking olive picking! I sat on the bench.

"Oi, have you got my twenty quid?" It was Billy.

As it happened, I had. I knew I would bump into him sooner or later so took it out with me.

"Here you go," I said,

"Nice one." he took it from me and pulled out another huge spliff. "Have a look at this fucker!"

"If you think I'm paying you twenty quid to go two's up on that you can get fucked," I said, still narked.

He lit it up, took a couple of drags then offered it to me.

"Here, you go, have this one on me."

I accepted it and took a couple of heavy drags. I could immediately feel the welcome lightness in my head.

"You've got sweat on you. Hang on a minute; you haven't been out working in the fields have you?"

"Yeah."

He laughed, "You fucking mug!"

"Tell me about it."

"You won't catch me getting involved in any of that shit, I can tell you."

"I thought you needed to help out in the fields so you can stay here for free. How do you get around that then?" I asked.

"Want to know a secret? They don't fucking know I'm here."

"What?"

"I sleep in one of the barns. There are so many people mingling around here no one ever questions me."

"You cheeky fucker!" I looked at him, and he smiled. "So how can you afford to buy this gear?" I asked.

"I nick stuff off the farm then sell it to some geezer in the village. Wine, fruit, olive oil, shit like that."

He steals stuff from a place that opens its door to the public; that is built on goodwill and trust. He was a horrible little cunt, but a horrible little cunt with a quality dealer. His gear was fucking spot on. We sat and smoked another spliff until I could barely walk, then I trudged back to my room where I crashed out on my bed.

When I woke, it was dark and silent. I lay still, the drugs still providing me with a calm peacefulness.

Then I sensed someone, someone looking at me, someone close. I quickly turned my head round; in the dark, I felt his presence within arm's reach of my bed.

"Is that you Kumasi?"

I heard him take a deep breath; I was sure it was him. I asked him again, "What are you doing, why are you sitting there?"

"You're like a paper airplane trying to fly in a tornado." he said.

"What?"

He then made the strange and realistic sound of wind with his mouth, "Poor Joe, trying to fly but getting nowhere, just going round and round in circles."

"I'm sorry."

"It's so funny, I mean, you couldn't even do a full day's work."

"I was knackered, I had to stop."

You didn't stop, you quit. You gave in to him, didn't you? But, let's be frank with one another, spending the afternoon getting high on drugs is about all you're good for."

"It won't happen again; I just got tired. I need to get used to it. I'm going to do a full day tomorrow. I give you my word."

"Your word!" he laughed, "That's the funniest funny thing I have ever heard. You're not worth jack, so what value does that make your word?"

"I don't know."

"And how do you think the girl felt?"

"What girl?"

"She just sat there all alone tonight. Every time the door opened, she turned to see if it was you. I was inclined to tell her not to waste her time with you any longer."

"I'm sorry."

"Let me ask you, Joe, have you ever let someone down before? Have you not been somewhere important when you said you would be? Is this scenario familiar to you, or are you going to tell me that this is the first time it has happened?"

"Leave it will you. I'll see her tomorrow."

"Do you see how quickly you can brush your fuck-ups under the carpet. 'I'll see her tomorrow,' you just move on and never worry about the repercussions."

"What do you want from me, Kumasi?"

"Nothing, I'm just going to pull up a ringside seat and watch you."

"Watch me do what?"

"Like a sad, unwanted dog in a weighted bag, tossed over the bridge into the river. That's what you are, and I'm afraid I'm not going to watch you sink to the very bottom, because, after all, that's where you belong."

Chapter 48

Thursday 15th January 2015

I woke up to Kumasi performing his routine, which was unrelenting in its intensity. I lay watching him as he was pushing himself to his very inner limits. When he finished and went off to the shower, I got up. Maybe it was time to turn the corner, to replicate the life changes that Kumasi had made, and perhaps the right place to start was to copy his exercise regime.

I assumed the press-up position and started to do them slowly as Kumasi did. After eight repetitions my arms started shaking, and my whole body appeared to be convulsing. I managed nine and a half reps.

I turned over and did the same with sit-ups, again getting to ten before feeling knackered. I quickly concluded that I wasn't cut out for this shit. Years of filling my body with rubbish food, booze and soft drugs had taken its toll.

I decided to assemble a list of the areas where I needed to improve. While contemplating this, I sat with my hands down my pants fiddling with my bollocks. It was then that I realised that fiddling with my bollocks while thinking, was one area that needed to be eradicated.

The first barrier to tackle was the issue of my laziness. My first goal was to complete a full day out in the fields, picking olives. I needed to prove to myself, and Kumasi, that I could do it. But, I knew it was going to be hard. After I had done half a day yesterday, I felt like a sucked orange, washed up; spent. Kumasi was right; I had become a habitual quitter. Whether it was going to school; playing football for the local team; or even fucking olive picking, whatever it was, I would start it, then begin to lose interest, and then quit. This was why I had subconsciously decided that it was easier not to start anything new rather than to risk starting it and inevitably jack it in.

Quitting is something you might readily invite into your life; you'd sit it down, give it a drink and then make the mistake of offering it a room for the night. You'd then spend the rest of your life trying to get rid of it, like a drunken squatter.

I was desperate for someone to push me; someone to motivate and offer inspiration. Maybe Kumasi would be that person? I needed someone to make me do things, to give me no option and to force my hand. I mulled over asking him to be that person. I think he would accept; he would embrace the opportunity to watch me grow, to know that it was through his coaching that the improvement had been achieved. That's what I would do; I'd ask Kumasi.

I felt euphoric as I had found a solution. This would work. Kumasi would become my mentor. My mind drifted to the American films I had watched where coaches would be demanding more from boxers and American football players. Shouting and screaming at them; getting them to train harder. Sweat would be dripping off them, and it was a sign of their improvement, their achievement, their ability to win the battle with the mind. This is what Kumasi and I could be like. He could whip me into shape; scream at me to push myself harder and further, eventually hugging me once my goal had been achieved. We'd run up the steps of the building together, and as we turned around we'd embrace the crowd!

Within minutes Kumasi returned, his towel around his waist, his toned muscles rippling against his scarred flesh.

"Hey Kumasi, I've got a favour to ask you?"

I was struggling to hide my optimistic grin. He stood there, with his back turned, methodically applying skin lotion.

"What's that?" he said, with a distinct lack of enthusiasm.

"I reckon I need a coach, someone to kick my ass when I'm acting lazy."

"You reckon?"

"That's what I need, bro, someone to get in my face and to make me get shit done."

"And you think that will help?"

"It's got to be worth a try isn't it?"

"Why not?"

"So, I was thinking -"

He interrupted, "Whether I would be your coach?"

"That's it! I'll listen to you, Kumasi. You've been there and done it and all that. I can learn off you."

He turned around and looked at me, "Are you confident that this will work?"

"Yeah definitely, I think this could be my turning point."

"You won't let me down though will you, Joe? I mean I'll be counting on you."

"No way, bro! I won't let you down."

Kumasi then just looked at me and shook his head. "You've been awake for about ten minutes, and this is the best you can come up with?"

"Yeah, and?"

"You just don't get it, do you?"

"What do you mean?"

"Stand up will you please?"

"What?"

"It's not difficult, stand up."

I stood up and as I did Kumasi yanked me by my t-shirt and thrust me against the wall. He lodged his massive forearm under my chin, crushing my windpipe; he then used his strength to lift my entire body off the floor. I couldn't breathe.

"Look me in the eye." he said.

I was gasping for air.

"Look me in the eye, you mother fucker!"

I looked at him fearing he was about to take my life.

"I'm looking at a fucking weak, pitiful loser, who comes up with bullshit plans and ideas all the fucking time. Now listen to me, and listen to me good. If you want to change, you fucking make it happen. Don't pass the burden to me or anyone else.

You get it straight in your head, and you either do it, or you don't fucking do it. But don't involve me or anyone else in the fucking process. You hear me?"

I was gasping for air.

"I said do you hear me?"

I did my best to give him an affirmation.

He then just let me drop to the floor where I lay sprawled out taking shallow breaths.

Kumasi then just continued to very slowly and methodically get dressed. I grabbed the side of the bed and hauled myself on to it. The fucking mad bastard had nearly killed me!

I lay checking my windpipe hadn't been crushed as Kumasi left the room.

I was going to show this cunt, and it was time for me to stop rolling over whenever the going gets tough.

I got myself ready and went down for breakfast. Kumasi was sitting alone. As I walked in, he glanced at me and then looked away. I grabbed some food and made a point of sitting next to him.

After ten minutes I leant into him and whispered, "I'm going to fucking do this, you know."

He leant back to me and in a hushed voice replied, "I don't care."

Chapter 49
Same Day

It was a clear day out in the fields, the sun was starting to break through, and the atmosphere amongst the other workers was, as usual, convivial. I was determined to maintain a positive mindset; setting myself mini goals to complete during the morning. This kept me on-task and motivated. I had been working flat out until the lunch break, and I had taken a couple of ham and cheese rolls from the ham and cheese rolls guy and was sitting under a tree, quietly reflecting that at this point yesterday I bailed out; quit and turned my attention to the less rigorous pursuit of smoking drugs. But my 'lazy bastard' light was flashing, and the thought of doing it again appealed to me.

"Guess who?" from behind, I was approached by Billy, "I thought you'd thrown the towel in on this fucking game?"

He stood over me, so I found myself staring up at him.

"I thought I'd give it another go."

"Who the fuck in their right mind does this sort of shit all day? Come on; follow me I've got a stash of top-notch, rock 'n' roll gear back at my den. Let's go and get fucked out of our heads."

"I'm alright, bro," I said shaking my head.

I didn't need this temptation thrust at me while I was flagging.

"You what!"

"Seriously, I need to do this. I can't just sit around for the rest of my life smoking fucking dope."

"What's the alternative? Working your bollocks off for fuck all – are you a fucking mug or what?"

"I'm staying here, bro."

"You won't though, will you? You are what you are, don't bother to fight it. People like us need to stick together."

"I need to fight it. I don't want to be that person anymore."

"Fine, fuck you then. I'll have an afternoon kicking back smoking gear, feeling fucking great, while you stay out here breaking your back picking fucking olives."

He then started laughing, "See you later, olive picker."

He walked off, thank God. I puffed my cheeks out. 'Olive picker,' fucking hell, was this it for me? I mean, he was right; I wasn't even going to be getting paid.

I contemplated the whole issue of not getting paid for this work, was this the issue or just something that I was somehow using as an excuse for why I should quit, because work represented effort and commitment, whereas I just preferred being a lazy cunt?

Would it be any different if I was getting paid? Perhaps I would then question the rate of pay and would deem it insufficient and then still quit? And what is the correct rate of pay for an olive picker? Whatever it was after a few weeks I would think I was worth more. I would manufacture some gripe that would allow me to exonerate myself when I did predictably quit. I would then slightly exaggerate the story when telling others to make them think I was hard done by and quitting was the right and only thing to do.

I considered this further; maybe quitters claw for excuses, any excuse because it entitles them to convince themselves that there was nothing wrong with ceasing to do something that is fundamentally positive. In life, you can pretty much find a reason to quit anything if you think about it for long enough.

And yet how many people openly admit that they quit a job because they are fucking lazy and weak and prefer to bum around all day? No one, because there is always another reason and that reason is generally someone else's fault.

I stood up and found myself doing that thing where I shake my head. I looked across the field to see people working away. Then I saw Kumasi. He was going for it, all on his own, demonstrating a strong work ethic and rock-solid discipline.

But he wasn't showboating; he wasn't doing it to impress anyone else. This fella did it because he had made a conscious decision that this activity, along with other activities that he chose to do, would result in him being the person that he wanted to be. They contributed to his values; defined him as a person and, as a consequence, he lived a life of far more significant fulfilment than I.

He was an inspiration to me. He was a little like Devo, only different and better as his edges had been knocked off. He had searched hard for the shining beacons in his life and had found the road map to happiness, while the rest of us had to settle for a lifetime in the shade. He had not looked for fame or fortune, but instead just wanted to be at peace with himself and he had created his private universe where those conditions prevailed.

I had leant on him for advice, without ever seeking his permission and I had felt rejected and hurt when rebuffed by him.

But he was my beacon, he provided some dim light at the end of my dark tunnel, and I knew I must follow him because the alternative did not bear contemplation.

I recognised the consequences of misreading my map of life and ending up heading into a dark cul-de-sac. More than ever, I could see the stark differences between the life choices I had been presented with.

I walked back to one of the olive trees from where three people were picking away, and without any acknowledgement, I joined them.

Chapter 50
Same day

The day was coming to an end, and I had completed my first ever full day at work. I wearily trudged back to the house. I hadn't noticed his approach but walking at the side of me was Kumasi. He didn't acknowledge me, but I was determined to let him know of my achievement.

"I did it!" I exclaimed.

He turned to look at me, "So you did."

"I bet that surprised you?"

"Forgive me if I don't start polishing your gold medal just yet."

He was becoming a far cry from the genial man that I had been introduced to. This guy had the potential to get right under your skin if you irritated him.

"You don't think I can do this, do you?" I asked him.

"It's your path, why don't you walk it alone, unless you're one of these people who constantly need an audience applauding them every time they don't fuck-up."

"Give me a break will you!" I snapped.

"Oh, so you *are* one of those people."

"A bit of support would be nice."

"A bit of support, leading to what? You will eventually fuck-up, you always do."

"I won't this time. I'm going to turn this around, Kumasi. I'll show you."

"I'll be so proud of you," he said sarcastically.

"Go fuck yourself!"

I made my way to my room where I lay on my bed feeling shattered. My eyes were starting to close, but I didn't dare not nod off and risk missing Elesha. I decided to get up and have a shower, clean myself up and get ready.

As I stood in the shower the water felt soothing on my aching body. I wished I had my mobile phone; I wished I could lie on my bed and fuck around, playing a game, flicking through Facebook, watching Youtube videos and wasting hours just chilling out. Still, at least I had my meeting with Elesha to look forward to.

I returned to my room and got ready. Kumasi was sitting quietly reading. I ignored him; I couldn't believe he'd been so negative towards me.

The gong sounded, and I headed straight off, keen to arrive first in the dining room so I could secure a couple of places away from the fucking hippy, free-love gang. As I entered the dining room, Elesha was already there, alone. I noticed a strange pallid look on her pretty face.

"Hey," I said, as I approached.

"Hey Joe," she said, in a strained manner.

She managed only half a smile.

"Are you okay?" I asked.

"Yeah, why?" she replied.

"I don't know; you look a bit pale."

"Sometimes I feel like the life is being sucked out of me," she said.

"What do you mean?"

"Do you ever feel like you're running out of time?"

"I don't know," I replied.

I was confused, what was she going on about? She placed her hand on mine and smiled. I smiled back.

"Tell me; it's going to be okay, Joe?"

"What is?"

"Just tell me it's all going to work out."

"I don't know what you're talking about though."

The starter then turned up; it was slices of ham and melon. Fucking melon; who eats this shit? I watched as Elesha picked up her slice of melon. She looked at it, lovingly, before biting into it then she closed her eyes to relish what she was eating.

"Is that good?" I asked.

"It's so fresh. Why don't you try it?"

"I'm not keen, do you want mine?"

"Shall we swap, my ham for your melon?"

"That sounds like a good deal to me."

"I agree, your fresh, juicy, nutritious melon, for my slice of processed pork from an animal that has probably never seen the light of day."

"I don't eat fruit."

"You were never given fruit to eat when you were a kid, were you?"

"No."

"I didn't think so."

"My Mum didn't like it."

"And therefore, nor do you. Still, it's not your fault; taste is genetically handed down you know?"

"Is it?"

"Of course, it isn't! You've got it in your brain that you don't like fruit and now you accept that as being the case."

"Have I?"

"I was the same; my Mum told me never to try olives; she said I wouldn't like them. When I finally did try them, guess what? I fell in love."

"So the moral of the story is, don't listen to a fucking word that your mum says?"

"I wouldn't say that, but I think you have to treat everything you've been told with a little care."

We finished dinner then walked out into the fields and found our way to our favourite bench. We sat and stared at the stars, talking.

"This is officially our bench now," she said.

"Is it?"

"Look," she then turned her back and revealed a small, but clear etching she had made in the wood.

Joe + Elesha x

"Thank you," I said, struggling to contain my gushing smile.

It was cold this evening, the coldest I had known in the time that I'd been here. I could see that the sharp air had chilled Elesha. I took my sweatshirt off and gave it to her.

"Thank you." she said softly.

As she put it on, I gazed at her, her beauty, the mystery of her tattoos, her long flowing hair. I became transfixed by her and realised I had missed the intimacy of another.

"Are you okay?" she asked.

I kicked my head back; I was aching to tell her how I felt.

"I'm fine," I replied.

I saw her shiver a little; I lifted my arm up.

"Do you want me to keep you warm?" I asked.

She slowly and hesitantly moved her tiny body towards mine. I put my arm around her and squeezed her petite frame, just a little, just enough to make her feel safe. Her fragrance wafted over to me. I took a long slow smell. She then put her hand on my chest.

"I can feel your heart beating." she whispered. She then squeezed me, "Is it beating faster now?" she asked.

I waited for a while before answering, "Maybe just a little." I leant towards her forehead and softly placed a kiss on it.

"I did a full day out in the field today," I said proudly.

"Well done," she replied, insincerely.

"I'm feeling pretty pleased with myself."

"You are speaking as someone who hasn't done many full days of work."

That comment knocked me a little off balance. I had moved the conversation down an unfortunate track.

"Well, maybe not as many as I should have done."

There was a pause. I sensed she was waiting to say something.

"I know something, Joe."

"What's that?"

"I know how this story ends."

"How does it end?"

"You'll let me down."

"What?"

"You'll let me down when I need you."

"I'd never do that."

"I'll cry out for you, and you won't be there."

"I will be, I promise."

"You've never kept a promise though, have you?"

"Of course I have."

"It's just a word you use. You might even believe it at the time, but then it's meaning to you disappears."

"What has made you say that?"

"I've seen your weaknesses."

"What weakness?"

"We all have weaknesses, but in some people, these are more pronounced. I met someone once like this. I overlooked what was right in front of my face, and what followed was a horrible mistake."

"I'm not like that anymore."

"Sure you are, and deep down you know it."

She then turned and looked me in the eye, "You know what you are, and you know what you are about, and to say anything to the contrary is a lie. This is a charade, all of it. You're a charlatan. You're playing at this," she said

"What?"

"And you've had the chance to sparkle, the chance to do the right thing, but you have always chosen not to take it."

"What chance?"

"It's time for me to go now," she said, disentangling herself from my warmth.

"Why are you saying these things?"

"Look up at the sky. Tell me what you see?"

I looked up, "Lots of shining stars," I replied.

"Look closer, then."

"What am I looking at?"

"I need you to look at the mass between the stars. It's the blackness; the emptiness, the bit that connects up all the sparkles, but somehow never gets to shine. That's the bit that I see when I gaze up." She then stared at me intensely, "and that's what I see when I look at you."

Chapter 51
Friday 16th January 2015

As I woke, I could immediately feel the soreness in my muscles. I felt shattered. The previous day's work had taken its toll on me, good God, one day of work and look at the state of me.

Kumasi arrived back from his shower, he was like a fucking robot, always the same, ready and prepared to face what was before him without ever questioning whether he could, or he would. He never appeared to consider the weak option; he had conditioned himself to eliminate any possibility of talking himself out of doing what he knew to be right.

I had to get up; I had to get myself out into the fields. But the fatigue was engulfing me. I briefly closed my eyes….

I woke up suddenly. Kumasi had departed, and I panicked. I knew I couldn't afford a slip. Failure was waiting for me, yet again. I had to prove to myself that I was capable of embracing the challenge; I simply had to get up.

I quickly got ready and ran out of the room; it was just after nine thirty and I had a chance that I could get out into the fields and salvage this situation. I ran past Kumasi, who didn't appear to notice me. I arrived with the usual group and just started work. No one commented or seemed to mind that I was a little late.

Within half an hour the adrenalin had worn off, and the fatigue kicked back in. There was just one more day, one more day then it was the weekend, where I could come up for air and relax. Come on; I can do this; I needed prove it to myself.

The fella I was working alongside was wearing a watch. Every ten minutes I would glance at his wrist; checking the time, fuck me, the day was dragging. I just couldn't summon any energy. I desperately needed to stop, to rest, to be back in the room, to have another afternoon being lazy, just laying on my bed, drifting in and out of sleep.

It was finally lunchtime, and I sought solitude under a tree with my daily ration of ham and cheese rolls. I had to be on my own because I knew he would come, and despite pretending to the contrary, I wanted him to.

"Look at the state of you." he said, again stood over me, wielding the power he had nurtured.

"Please leave me alone," I said, recognising my futility.

"You've not got an afternoon of this shit left in you."

"I need to do it," I said pathetically.

"I'll tell you what you need, a toke on the gear I've got back at the den. It's fucking mint! You can have a nice afternoon, kicking back, floating away on this stuff. It'll make you feel like the king of the world."

I held my head in my hands. I knew he had got me and I was about to surrender.

He knew it as well. He offered me his scrawny hand, and as I took it, he pulled me to my feet.

I followed him, in silence. He took me to the back of the outbuildings, away from those people working in the fields. Here the air changed from the fresh smell of pine groves to the thick odour of manure and livestock. Disused farm machinery was strewn across the ground, the rough concrete yard itself a mesh of animal shit, mud and hay.

I followed him to a derelict wooden shed, an appendage to the side of an even bigger outbuilding. As he opened the rickety, ill-fitting door, it scraped across the concrete ground, a dilapidated entrance to a murky world.

We walked into the darkness, where the air was filled with the sweet smell of cannabis. Billy flicked a light switch on a lamp, which provided me with the first glimpse of his filthy empire; a drugs den the size of a garage. There were two mattresses on the floor, a smoking bong, ashtrays and roll-ups everywhere. Everything about the place was wrong. Even the flickering lamp was gaining its power not from a plug but bare wires, flimsily hanging out of a socket.

"Sit down there," he growled, pointing at one of the mattresses.

He was seemingly unable to speak with anything other than an aggressive, hateful tone. He pulled out a burner and some foil, he then rummaged around a chest of drawers he had between the two mattresses and pulled out a little bag of brown powder.

"I don't do that shit, bro," I told him.

"You mean you didn't do that shit."

"Weed only. I'm not touching that."

"Relax, we're not injecting it, let's just smoke a bit."

"No, no way, bro."

"Have a fucking dabble you pussy. If you don't like it, then don't have anymore."

He then went about his business, placing the foil over the flame before sucking the smoke up through a thin plastic tube. He took a heavy intake of the smoke before passing it to me.

"And trust me, you will fucking like it," he said with an abhorrent grin, exposing his broken teeth.

I took the plastic utensil from him and in doing so, acknowledged that it was time.

This was just about to stop being a cheeky spliff while stood on the balcony back at home.

Playtime was about to end.

This was the real deal, and I knew the stakes had suddenly become high. I was en-route to an altogether different place, where self-control was at a premium. A place you only visit when you need to escape whatever torment was eating away at you. It was time to escape my torment, to finally suppress any sense of what might be right and to let go.

It was time to cross over.

We all cross over at different points in our lives; we just don't know it. For me, it certainly would not be the first time I had moved from one place that I knew to be right to another, that I knew wasn't.

The first day I had skived off school.

Stealing that packet of sweets from the newsagent.

The drag I'd taken on the cigarette at the school disco.

The spliff I had smoked while joy riding a stolen car.

Denying the existence of him.

The first time I had sold weed.

The robbery I had done with Devo.

The man we had killed.

It was all crossing over.

And so it came to pass. I took a sharp intake, and I had added another string to my bow of amoral acts.

Within seconds the feeling hit me; I had been lifted onto a magic cloud.

I passed him back the pipe.

He looked up at me with his vile visage and smiled. "It's fucking fantastic isn't it?"

He repeated his action and handed it back to me; I took another sharp intake before I lay back on the mattress.

"I've got to admit, this beats picking fucking olives," I said.

I lay in a stupor of unbelievable calm and euphoria. I finally felt at ease. I had turned my back on my torment and had surrendered to this macabre haven. I closed my eyes and savoured the tranquillity.

This must be how a rehabilitated alcoholic must feel when he buckles and has his first drink, the same sensation a struggling dieter experiences when they sit and scoff a plate of cakes, the reformed gambler, putting his whole week's salary on a horse race, to get that feeling back, the instant gratification and to finally escape the false hope.

Life had beaten me, and I had sought solace in an ocean of artificial serenity. I smiled, as I knew I had quit the challenge. I had not the courage, nor commitment to fight it. While most had faced the same trial they had offered resistance and clambered for dry land, while I had allowed myself to get sucked to the bottom of this ocean where, with a little luck, I need not come back up for air.

I was in a minority of people that spend their lives plagued by their pathetic weaknesses.

As I woke, he was doing more of the same; again he passed me the pipe which I took, gleefully. Then the magic returned. I was on a rocket rushing out of orbit. I lay open-mouthed on the mattress. I felt like this small piece of the universe had stopped spinning. It was calm and soothing, and I felt free. Free of any burden, free of any expectations that life places on you. Free to detach myself from my fading moral compass.

I opened my eyes again; the sunlight that had been piercing through the missing splinters of the shed had been replaced with darkness. I tried to get up, but my legs buckled. I stumbled and fell back onto my mattress.

"You're not fit to go anywhere, stay here," he said.

"I need to see Elesha."

"What, looking like that? Don't make me fucking laugh. Anyway, we've got some more of this shit to smoke."

He began to cook up the next batch.

I'd let myself enjoy this incredible freedom for the rest of this evening, but that would be it. I had to return; I had to believe that I could swim to the shore and beat this. I would file this away as a 'one-off', nothing more than a blip. I would learn from it. I would grow stronger and try again. I would pull myself together. I would do it for Elesha. I needed her, I pleaded for her soothing soul. With her around me, my tormented life made sense. Being with her allowed me to conceal my weaknesses and her beauty would be a distraction from the horror of the one thing that I knew I faced, but had always denied: my future.

We smoked some more, then some more and so it continued. We never spoke; instead, we just lay on our decaying mattresses locked in the confines of our drug fantasies.

I saw the face of the shopkeeper, his last breaths before his passing. I wondered whether in that final moment he knew his fate. I wondered whether he blamed us.

Then I saw the big Russian; I stood close to him. I could feel his power, his majesty, his aggression and hatred. A man whose sole purpose was to inflict pain on other men. And of course, I saw the face of my brother. He was looking at me shaking his head, appalled at what I had become. He was mouthing words to me, but I couldn't tell what he was saying, so I approached him slowly.

"It should have been you," he said.

"I know," I replied.

I received another rush of euphoria, then Elesha. I could see the back of her head, her gorgeous red hair flowing down her back. I reached out and stroked it, and as she turned around, it was Ashlee. She was crying, sad tears rolling down her pretty face. I was trying to say sorry to her, but the words wouldn't come out. I felt the floor tremble, and as I looked down, I saw the earth that I was stood on had become detached. I was moving away from her, our two worlds becoming disconnected and me, without the strength of mind to do anything. I screamed out to her, like a baby, reaching out my hand for her to take and for her to save me, but she just stared passively and did nothing, like I had done, all my life.

I woke suddenly. The morning sunlight was coming through the wood panels. Billy was flat out. I got up and left the den. I still felt fucked as I walked into the house. I could see Elesha walking into the dining room for breakfast. I wanted to call out her name, to have her look round, to walk up to me with her big smile. I wanted her to give me that special glow, just one more time. But instead, I let her walk off, and I was like a ghost watching the world going on but incapable of affecting it.

I slowly and awkwardly climbed the stairs to my room. I needed to see Kumasi; I would plead for his help, ask him to help prevent my seemingly inevitable descent down this dark spiral. I arrived at our door and tried to turn the handle, but it was locked. I tried it several times before knocking.

I had a sense of urgency as I could feel his faint presence. I knew that he risen and was on his way to get me.

"Kumasi! Kumasi!"

I implored him to open the door. I tried it again, starting to panic now, as I knew I was running out of time.

"Kumasi, please let me in, I'm begging you."

I could feel him, getting closer. The game was nearly up. I started to shout, feverishly wrenching at the door handle.

"Kumasi, it's me, let me in for fuck sake!"

I then felt a hand on my shoulder; it was Tira, "Joe, are you okay?"

"I can't get into my room."

"You don't look well. What's the matter?"

"Just let me in, will you. I need to get in." I said, in a state of extreme panic.

"Have you been drinking?"

"I need to get in; please help me for fuck sake! This is my only chance. Get a fucking spare key and let me in."

"No, I can't. I'm sorry."

"You have to."

"I don't have to," she said calmly.

I then grabbed her, "You have to you fucking witch, open the fucking door and let me in!"

She pushed me away from her. "I'm not letting you in."

I was resigned to my fate. "Then, it's over."

"I know. I'm sorry," she said calmly.

"You've killed me, Tira."

"It will have been your choice."

"He's coming for me, and this was the only place left where I could hide."

"You don't want to hide though, do you?"

"Please open the door for me, so that I can have one last chance."

"You've had that. Now go back to him. It's where you belong. It was always your destiny."

I was desperate to regain control, but the narcotics had overcome me, strangling my mind, suffocating my logic, drowning the last drop of spirit left in my beleaguered body. I stood staring at the door, unable to rationalise the situation.

I gave out a pathetic whisper, "Please let me in, Kumasi."

Dejected, I turned and walked away, all hope had vanished. I approached the stairs; their descent would represent the fading grip I had on my life. I had to check one more time; maybe he would empathise with my anguish and prevent me doing what he told me he had done himself. I turned around to look at the door one last time, and I realised that it was now fractionally ajar.

A soft ray of light shone through the tiny gap.

I sensed there was someone stood behind it looking at me.

"Kumasi, Is that you?"

I walked slowly towards the light, not wishing to frighten whoever was behind it; I wanted them to see my desperation, to take pity on my plight. But as I got within a few feet, it closed, and I heard the key from the inside locking it.

I walked downstairs and stopped at the glass window of the dining room and peered in. Elesha sat on her own, quietly eating her breakfast. I stood and watched her for a while before I gently tapped on the glass. She looked up but did not notice me. I went to knock again but hesitated. There was no point. I had lost. It was time to leave. After a brief period of worthless resistance, he had finally won.

It was no longer a predicament, for it had been decided.

The uncertainty had disappeared. My future, against the spectre of the darkness that I knew would lie ahead, now yielded a strange clarity and the torment of expectation at that moment finally ceased.

I turned and walked out of the house.

He was waiting for me, as I knew he would. As I approached him, we didn't acknowledge one another. We didn't need to. I despised him and knew him to be flawed but had come to surrender to his offerings.

We made our way back to what was to become my netherworld.

We returned to the den.

Chapter 52

Saturday 17th January 2015

I woke up on the lumpy mattress, feeling chilled. I had no bed covers, and my clothes were scarcely protecting me from the sharp morning air. I looked across at Billy who was already skinning up. I watched as he carefully completed his routine and lit the spliff. He took two deep drags before passing it to me. I took it and did the same. The gear was intense, and it soon made me high.

"We're running out," he said.

"Can you get some more?" I replied.

"I'm out of cash; you'll have to get some from your safe."

"How do you know about that?"

"Get a grand. The fella down the village has taken in a new shipment. He's got all sorts of goodies in; let's fill our fucking boots."

"I'm not getting a grand out!" I tersely replied.

"It's a grand or nothing. You either get it out, or you can fuck off back to your African pimp."

I felt for the safe key in my trouser pocket. Fuck it, what else was I going to spend the money on?

I took the last few drags of the spliff then uneasily got to my feet. I ambled back to the house where thankfully no one was around. I walked in quietly and went to my safe. I took the money out and counted a thousand pounds. As I turned around Kumasi stood there in front of me.

"What are you doing?" he enquired.

"What does it look like?!" I snapped.

"Is this what you want?"

"I don't know what I fucking want anymore, Kumasi, that's the problem."

"Then it's only right that you should fly near to the sun because you need to feel it burning your wings."

"What?"

"Just don't get too close. Otherwise, you may never return."

"I don't know what the fuck you are on about, and by the way thanks for not letting me in yesterday, that was nice of you."

He smiled, "I always enjoy it when the weak find a reason to blame someone else."

"Fuck you!" I said.

"Remember, Bo, not too close."

I walked away, turning around to catch another glimpse of him. 'Is that what you want?' he had asked. What did I want? I wanted my brother back; I wanted the shopkeeper to be alive; I wanted to talk to Mum about antiques, I wanted my Pot Noodle ashtray. I wanted it to be all back to normal again, but instead, this mess and I was stuck right in the middle of it, unable to reach to the sides to climb out.

I headed back to the den and handed Billy the money. There were no demands; no threats should he never return and no acknowledgement of what I would expect him to buy. I just gave it to him, because I had capitulated.

He passed me a spliff and then left. I took off my sweatshirt and t-shirt and lay on the mattress and smoked it. I allowed the hot ash to fall on my chest. I needed to experience the pain as it touched my skin. I needed to hurt myself. My self-loathing had finally risen to the surface.

Later Billy returned sporting a toothy smile and a bag of drugs. He ripped it open, so the contents spilt out onto the floor. Pills, powder, weed, syringes the fucking lot.

"We don't need to leave this place for fucking ages now," he said.

I picked up a blue pill, which had a tiny white dove on it.

"Take your time with them because it'll kick you like a mule."

I grabbed the water and knocked the pill back. What did I have to lose?

As the spliff wore off the pill kicked it.

I looked out from a broken panel of wood. I could see Elesha trying to work. She was picking up olives and stopping every half a minute or so and standing up straight. She was in pain. I could see the anguish on her face. I wanted to go to her aid, but I knew I couldn't. My body tingled, and I had lost control.

I just lay back on the mattress and went back off into an induced state of unconsciousness.

I woke, hours later. I couldn't face reality and instead had opted to escape it. I found a different coloured pill. This one was red with a white cross on it. I swallowed it and then kicked back on my revolting mattress and waited for it to perform its magic.

I looked at Billy, "Food?" I asked him.

He shook his head, "Not in here."

I smiled, and my head rolled back. I looked up at the ceiling and the broken wooden roof. It was a different pill and a different sensation, but equally as otherworldly.

Later I woke up to the intense churning of my stomach. I jumped to my feet.

"What's the matter?" he said, startled.

"I need the toilet."

"Don't go outside, for fuck sake. They'll see you. Go over there."

He pointed to the corner of the shed, near the door. I ran over and dropped my trousers and pants. Hot, fizzy fluid left my body and splattered the floor and wooden side panels. Billy just looked at me with a smile on his face.

"Have we got any bog roll?"

He smiled and threw me my sweatshirt.

"I can't use that."

He walked over and ripped it, ripped it again and then gave me a section of it. I took it and wiped. I then wiped my hands on my trousers.

The smell was putrid.

I lay back on the mattress and curled up to the foetal position. The air was turning cold, and I was shivering, shirtless and distressed.

'We don't need to leave this place,' he said. And I didn't intend to. It was our shelter from what lay outside, but a place that we both desperately needed to be rescued from.

Chapter 53
Thursday 22nd January 2015

I knew he would initiate their use, it was just a matter of time, and now that time had come. I had inwardly declared that I would decline at all costs, but any point of sensible reason had long since passed. I could now see my destiny and needed to accelerate the process.

He knew when to do it; he had perfected his timing. I knew that he could anticipate my every thought now, what I was capable of and what I was prepared to do. He would be aware of how much I now despised myself.

The world to us was now a place outside, to which we had become alien. Our world was here, in these claustrophobic confines.

He knew everything, and like a parasite, he was sucking out of me the last fading elements of life. He was slowly torturing me into a state of mental paralysis.

I sat on the bed and watched him take the syringe out of the plastic wrapper. He threw me a piece of thin rope. I needed no instruction. I felt like I knew only too well the routine. I wrapped it around my arm suffocating it of its supply, teasing the veins to the surface like worms reacting to birds pecking at the soil.

It was the bottom rung of the ladder, a place for the tormented. I had often wondered how anyone could end up like this, but then I realised that each had their own story, their own pathway, which somehow conjoined to the same place, a dark place where a person goes to escape.

After it was liquefied, it entered the syringe. He then passed it to me. As I took it, I briefly gazed at him.

He pulled a disgusting smile, the expression of a person watching cruelty. Should I pass it back to him, did I have the conviction to get up and leave? I was standing on the steepest cliff face I could imagine, seemingly destined to jump, but right at the last minute; I had aroused an element of doubt that may save me. There was something left deep inside, some level of hope. If I could raise this courage to the surface, then I had some foundation that I could re-build myself on. I could return to my room and plead with Kumasi to help me.

Fucking Kumasi.

I detested any admiration I had for him. I was desperate to know him when he was lost, when he hated himself, when he was ready to experience pain just to escape. The disciplined, moralistic, hardworking man I had met was not someone I could or wanted to connect with. I couldn't any longer; it was too far away from where I was now.

He passed me the syringe.

I then pricked the needle deep into my throbbing vein and watched as my blood infiltrated the drug forming a potent mixture.

I plunged the toxic heroin deep into my defenceless body.

I smiled as I mouthed silently. "I hate you."

He silently mouthed back, "I know."

Chapter 54
Sunday 8th February 2015

I was woken by a strange fizzing sound coming from the plug socket. I looked down at the bare loose wires that were making the noise. I pulled them out, and the room went dark. I foraged on the floor for water, but instead, I felt a hard round tablet. I grinned to myself as I popped it into my mouth and swallowed.

My hands felt the soft texture of the mattress. I stroked it imagining it to be some intimate contact. I remembered the feeling when I was in bed with Ashlee, and she would get up and go to the toilet. The warm glow I had knowing that she would shortly return and we could again be together.

When she would walk into the room, I would smile as I saw her beautiful naked breasts approaching the bed. We were two young people, two young bodies, intertwined in infatuation and lust.

Within a month we started to share the word 'love.' We would use it seriously at times and insincerely at others. I remember the first time I told her that I loved her. I believed it was true, but how did I know? When is the word 'love' really a substitution for the infatuation you might feel in a new relationship or when does the longevity of a toxic association mean that the word 'love' equates to your coexistence becoming nothing more than a habit that needs to cease?

How can you say something that important to someone unless you knew it was true? That it had a definition and you could judge your relationship against this. And yet we casually commit to another human being and tell them they have entered the ultimate sanctuary without any level of certainty.

Did I love Ashlee? Do I love Elesha? Does a handful of beautiful encounters with her warrant me starting to think of our relationship in terms of love?

Why do we even have to use the word 'love'? Is it a pseudo-adult progression from the school playground, when you would announce to someone that they were your best friend? Do we say it to make the people that we feel close believe that they exist in your intimate social hierarchy? Why do we crave for the need for verbal confirmation of somebody being in love with us, when surely actions and intimacy would suffice?

But I had a marker; I had something that I could judge it against because I loved Devo. I pined for him when he was in prison like I pined for him now. That was love, in its purest form, unconditional and unrelenting. Every other relationship in my life was going to be second to this, I was sure of it.

He walked back into the den and fiddled with the wires; the light came back on. I watched him pick up a bottle of water and drink it with such ferocity that half of it ran down his chest. He swilled the last mouthful around his gums before spitting it out on the floor.

"Spit some on me," I demanded.

He took another swig, washed it around his gums again before pissing it out of his mouth all over me. The bacteria riddled fluid washing all over my withering, pitiful body.

Chapter 55
Friday 27th February 2015

I hadn't left the den for approaching six weeks. He had been to replenish water, but I had always remained guarding our dwindling supply of drugs, evermore paranoid of what was outside.

Having not eaten since I had entered the den, I had become very weak. After the first couple of days I hadn't missed food, I hadn't missed anything in truth. I just lay on this soiled, disgusting mattress all day, dipping in and out of consciousness. I had not spoken to him for weeks. I acknowledged his sparse conversation by either nodding or taking what he offered to me.

I could feel the bed sores on my back and the scabs that had appeared on my face. I now vomited regularly; a greenish decaying substance that was desperate to leave my body. The last remnants of anything that could sustain me had long since been flushed out.

I ran my finger over my gums; they were bleeding profusely. I looked at my arms and studied the scabs and track marks from the intravenous injections. I lightly touched them and noted that at least a couple of them were turning septic. He had told me that they would eventually become gangrenous.

The rain started to come in through the roof. I quickly moved our stash to the cupboards before manipulating the mattress into a 'V' shape enabling me to shelter under it. The cold rainfall on my chest instigated a cough and I knew that phlegm would follow. This had been the pattern for several weeks.

I was in a tragic state. I guessed that within a week, maybe two I would be dead, and I could escape the punishment that I was inflicting on myself.

I wished I could see Devo again; I missed him so much. I sat on the cold floor and called out his name.

"Devo, I need your help, bro, I need you to come for me."

Maybe we could spend one last day together at home; we could have bacon sandwiches and a mug of tea before we went to the match. We'd have one final drink in the Three Bells. I could buy Murray a present, something special to make up for the Christmases that I missed. I'd get him a signed shirt. I'd hang around the training ground for weeks before and get the players to sign it, one by one. I smiled as I thought of it, of us all in the pub together, laughing and joking.

I spoke out loud, again, "Look what I've got you, Murray!"

He'd smile back, take the present and open it in front of the pub.

The Brigadier would come up and inspect it. He'd nod at me, an acknowledgement that I had done well. Devo would look on with pride. His little brother had got something right for a change.

"It's from both of us Murray, me and Dev."

Devo would then wink at me, put his arm around my shoulder and kiss my cheek.

"Good boy, Bo, good boy."

I'd smile back at him.

Then we'd call around to see our Mum. We would check she was okay and make sure she had some cans of beer in the fridge. I'd put my arms around her and forgive her for all the things that she did that I ever resented. I would tell her that I understood and appreciated that life for her had been a struggle. I would reassure her that she was loved. I'd explain to her that I was sorry for leaving without explaining. We'd watch one last antique programme together.

I'd call out, "You were right Mum, forty quid, that's all he got for it." I'd make her say, 'told you,' one more time. I longed now to hear her say it. I'd then grab a can of beer from the fridge, a nice cold one, just how she liked them. I would stand in the doorway of the lounge and watch as she opened it and took a huge swig. Then I would open the front door and leave.

Suddenly I got this strange urge. I needed to go outside, needed daylight, needed to watch people, needed to see healthy people enjoying their lives. I knew my time was up. I had to reach out and touch something real, something that was alive and flourishing.

I got to my feet for the first time in days and tried to walk. My legs hurt like hell, the muscles had shrunk to nothing. I limped to the door of the den, and with a substantial physical effort, I scraped it open. The daylight hit me. I hadn't seen or felt it for weeks. I slowly walked out into the yard where the rays of the sun were piercing my eyes. The pain in my feet and legs was excruciating as I tried to walk. I dragged myself to a low wooden fence, which I leaned on for support. I watched as people worked in the field, happy people, enjoying life.

I should have stayed in London. It was going to end anyway. At least I would have been with people I knew.

My eyes scanned the fields. Maybe I would see Elesha one last time? I'd see her beauty as she toiled with the labours of the day. I yearned to see her. I needed to watch life before death, to glimpse at someone who shows resilience despite physical challenges. If I could see her one last time, then that would be enough. I would then return to the den, and that would be it. I would peacefully let the end happen.

My miserable fucking end.

I again looked across the fields, but there was no sign of her. I panicked, and I started to become anxious. I called out her name, as I had Devo. I could at least say sorry to her. But she wasn't there. And it was for the best. I'd had my opportunities, and every one that came along had something in common with the last one - I had let them all pass me by.

I felt lightheaded and nauseous. Sweat started to gather on my brow, and I began to tremble. I wiped my nose, and there was blood. I felt a wrenching from deep within my stomach, and I threw up while draped over the fence. My vomit was a deep red colour. There was nothing left of me; my body was now rejecting its own fluids.

I looked around one last time then glanced to the heavens. I suddenly felt my legs buckle, I gripped the fence, but I had no strength, and almost in slow motion, I could feel myself falling backwards and as I did I closed my eyes in resignation.

That was when I was scooped up, like a child in the arms of his father. From within the deep annals of my memory, I had finally remembered something about my dad. I remember him gathering me up as an infant. I remember his warmth, his strength and his security. For just one occasion and on just one day, I now recalled the moment vividly. I smiled as I looked up at his face. He looked back at me and winked. He winked like Devo used to wink at me.

I could feel myself being transported. I felt a warm glow cascade over my dilapidated body. Someone had come to help; someone knew I was in trouble and needed to be saved. My head rolled back, and as it did, I stared into his eyes, his big brown eyes and I smiled as I whispered his name.

"Kumasi."

Chapter 56
Friday 4th May 2012

I was lying in my single bed with Ashlee in my arms. I had met her from work and taken her back to our flat. Mum was down the pub, as was Devo, and we did what we always did when we had the flat to ourselves.

I had initially been a little embarrassed about bringing Ashlee back to my home. She lived in a smart terraced house and her dad, a builder, had done a great job doing it up. Our dad wasn't a builder, and our flat was a shithole. She didn't seem to mind though, and it became our regular shag pad for the three months that we had seen each other.

Ashlee was beautiful. She was curvy; gorgeous, brown curly hair and with a big smile – I adored her. She had cut my hair a few times before I plucked up the courage to ask her out. She wore a little name badge on her top, 'Ashlee Brookes', I think that she liked that I remembered her name when I went in to see her.

The significance of this evening was that it was the first occasion that a crack appeared in our hitherto, perfect relationship. I should have guessed that it was going to come along, but as always, I was too slow and too fucking stupid.

"I need to go home," she said.

"Why? Stay here; it's Friday night."

"I've got bookings all day tomorrow, flat out from nine o'clock."

"Don't go in babe, you can call in sick, and we can spend the day together."

"You know I can't do that."

"You can, do you want me to call in for you? I can pretend to be your dad."

"What are you doing tomorrow?" she asked slightly confrontationally.

"Fuck all; probably just wait around for you."

"Like you did today?"

"I suppose."

"And like you did yesterday, as well."

"Where's this going?" I asked.

"I'm just wondering whether you're intending to spend the rest of your life doing nothing, that's all."

I tried to brush it off with my usual cockiness, "Don't worry about me babe, I'll get a job when I'm ready."

"And when will that be?"

"I don't know, come on Ashlee, don't break my balls about this, you know I'm a lazy fucker."

"And that was fine back then when this was just a bit of fun, but now it worries me."

"What do you mean?"

"We've been seeing each other for three months now, and I love you to bits, and it's only natural that my eyes drift into the future."

"And what do you see?" I asked, setting myself up for a fall.

"You and I in our own place together, but I see myself working my butt off all day and you sitting at home smoking dope."

"If we got a place together I'd be working and paying for stuff, I promise."

"And that sounds convincing, but I don't see it happening. You never look for a job, the Jobcentre keeps sanctioning you, and then you get no money for a couple of weeks, then you sign on again. It seems like a hopeless circle."

She had evidently given this much more thought then I realised. Once again, my naivety shone through.

"Okay, I'll get myself a fucking job, stop going on about it."

"What job?"

"I don't know, any fucking job, will you get off my case, like I don't get enough stick already from Devo."

"It's a Friday night, Bo; we should be out having a drink somewhere, then a bite to eat, doing something nice with our time, instead, we're around here, like we are every week."

"It's because I haven't got any money."

"I know; that's my point! Have you not been listening to anything I have been saying?"

"Alright babe, now let it go for fuck sake."

She then got out of bed and started to put on her underwear.

"What are you doing?" I asked.

"Going home."

"Why? Come on babes, don't be like that."

"Can I tell you something, Bo, my Mum and Dad keep asking me when they are going to meet you."

"I'll meet them whenever you want."

"I don't want you to."

"What?"

"My dad will ask you what you do for a job, and you'll have to tell him that you're on the dole."

"I can make something up."

She turned and looked at me, shaking her head "You just don't get it, do you?"

"I'll walk you back to your house," I said, desperate now to paper over the cracks of what had become a damaging exchange.

"Don't bother. You stay here. You must be knackered given how busy you've been today."

"Shall I meet you after work tomorrow?"

"If you want," she answered, insincerely.

"Look, you're right. I'll make this up to you, I promise."

I got up and put my arms around her.

"No more being lazy. I don't want to lose you, babe, you mean everything to me."

"Don't do it for me, Bo, do it for yourself."

"I will do babe. I'll show you. I'm going to sort my shit out from now on." I turned her around and looked her in the eye, "I promise."

Chapter 57
Friday 27th February 2015

As Kumasi carried me up the stairs I could feel myself dipping in and out of consciousness. Every jolt was crushing through my fragile body. I heard the door to our room being opened. The familiarity of the setting and the scent was reassuring. I was softy lowered onto my bunk like a child who had been carried from a car back to their cradle.

As I opened my eyes, I saw Kumasi talking to Tira.

"We need to call a doctor," she said.

"No doctors," Kumasi replied.

"If we don't get him seen soon, he's going to die."

"Leave him with me," Kumasi calmly replied.

"You're not medically trained. He needs urgent attention; I'm going to call for someone."

I could sense the urgency in Tira's voice.

"If you do that, he will be killed. Dangerous men are hunting him down, and hospitals keep records."

"He needs medicine," she said.

"I have medicine. I know what he needs. He needs an antibiotic for the infection, and we need to hydrate him with saline solution. I will take care of that."

"You have that with you?"

"Yes," he replied.

"If he dies it will be your fault."

"If he dies, it will have been his fault," Kumasi replied.

"I still think he needs to see a doctor."

"There will be no doctors, and this will be the last conversation we have on the matter. Now can you go, please? I will let you know in the morning if I need anything."

I managed a half-smile. Kumasi was going to look after me, and this provided me with a sense of safety. I could see him going through his bags and getting out tablets, drips, all sorts. Who was this fucking guy?!

I just let him do his stuff as the drip pierced my skin. I managed to swallow the tablets. It all felt extraordinary, like a bizarre dream. I knew the withdrawal was going to be lousy. I had spoken to friends who had done it, and I realised it would soon be upon me, but right now I felt very calm.

Kumasi pulled a chair up next to me. He placed his big palm on my forehead. He looked me in the eye.

"If you pull through then always remember this moment, my friend. It will serve you well," he said.

"I flew very, very close to the sun, I think it's burnt my wings," I replied in a fragile voice.

I felt tired now. I looked at Kumasi, and our eyes met. I wanted to say sorry to him. I knew I was drifting away, unsure whether my ruined body would give up during my sleep and never let me return. And as we continued to stare at one another, I did the only thing that I had the strength left to do; I gave him a wink.

Chapter 58

Saturday 5th May 2012.

I woke up and predictably it was the afternoon. I checked my phone, but there were no messages from Ashlee. This was unlike her, and I knew that the tide was turning against me.

I decided to drop her a text:

> **Hey babez, I'll meet u after work and take u 4 a drink.**
> **CU @6. Love you xxx**

I got out of bed and walked into the kitchen where Devo was frying up bacon.

"Alright, bro," I said.

"Alright, mate. I saw your new bird last night; she's a bit tasty, isn't she? You'll need to keep an eye on that one."

"Tell me about; she's started breaking my balls about getting a job."

"I bet she has, you lazy little cunt. At least this time you might listen."

"Whatever."

"Guess, what you're doing this afternoon?"

"What?"

"I've got you a ticket for the West Ham game."

"It's Millwall, isn't it?"

"It's going to get proper naughty. Now let's have our lucky bacon sandwiches, and then we'll get down to the Three Bells. Today's going to be a fucking good drink."

"I've got to meet Ashlee at six, bro. I'll have to clear straight off after the game."

"No problem."

As usual, we met Murray and the other lads down the pub. I felt like there was a dark cloud hanging over me. I had found the argument with Ashlee strangely upsetting. That was the day that I realised that I had deep feelings for her. I desperately didn't want to lose my girl, but she was looking for something in me that I didn't know that I was able to provide.

When you sign on the dole for a sustained period, you lose any sense of aspiration. You get used to cutting your very limited cloth on the fifty odd pounds you get every week. You get into a routine as to what that money can and cannot buy you. You get used to saying 'no' to invitations that you cannot afford, and after a while, it doesn't bother you. You look at people with nice cars, expensive clothes and see them heading off on fancy fucking holidays and you stop feeling jealous. You just cannot relate to it anymore. It's out of reach, something that only happens to other people and something that will be impossible to achieve.

Then there is the lethargy, the constant tiredness, the lack of any routine, the hours of lying in bed doing fuck all. You hate it, and you hate yourself for it, but the thought of doing anything else scares the shit out of you.

I was scared. The promise I had made to Ashlee about getting a job terrified me. I didn't have a clue what the next step to achieving this was. No one had ever told me. I had just been left for years to fend for myself and as someone with no confidence and no self-belief, I did what people with no confidence and no self-belief always did in that situation - fuck all. Absolutely fuck all. I was rotting away in a solitary world, hoping that no one would notice.

After the game, we headed back to the Three Bells. The atmosphere, as ever, for the Millwall games was very tense. There was the smell of beer and trouble in the air. I decided to have a quick pint to allow the crowds to disperse before I headed off to meet Ashlee.

West Ham had won, and the pub was jumping. Devo was standing on a table singing, and the whole pub was joining in. The Brigadier was there and in great form. Every time I looked at him, he was knocking back another chaser.

I got a tap on the shoulder, "Alright stranger?" It was Murray.

"Alright, bro?"

"We've not seen you here for a while. Where have you been?"

"No money, bro," I said. There, I was at it again.

"Devo tells me you've got a new bird."

"She's a fucking diamond, Murray."

"Bring her down, Bo. It'll be good to meet her."

"You keep your dirty mitts off her, you randy little cunt!" I replied.

Murray looked at me and winked.

I tentatively approached Devo, "Dev, sorry, bro, I've got a favour to ask you?"

"What's that mate?"

"I wanted to take Ashlee for a drink after she finishes work, but I'm skint."

Devo did nothing more than stick his hand in his pocket, pull out a twenty-pound note and hand it to me. He never made any eye contact though. I could sense his irritation. He was getting tired of giving me hand-outs.

"Thanks, bro, I'll give it back to you when I get my dole money through."

He didn't respond.

Suddenly there was a bottle thrown through the window. Millwall had arrived. The door of the pub opened and there was a flurry of punches exchanged, and bottles then started flying everywhere, it was proper scary stuff. The Millwall mob had been followed by the police as there were flashing lights everywhere. The police had their batons out and were wading through the group. Predictably, my brother was in the thick of it.

After about a minute or so, order was restored. Millwall were outside behind a police cordon, and The Three Bells pub was throbbing with West Ham songs as we were goading the Millwall fans. Bottles continued to be periodically thrown. There was glass and beer all over the floor. It was total chaos.

The pub was barricaded; no one was getting in, and no one was getting out. Murray activated his battle plan A and out came the plastic pint glasses and ban on bottles. He operated a well-oiled East End machine.

I looked at the time, 6.30pm. Ashlee would have left work and gone home. I had no credit on my phone, so I couldn't text her. Bollocks! I couldn't leave the pub to go to her house, and even if the Old Bill let me out, I wouldn't make it one hundred yards down the road before the Millwall mob attacked me.

I stayed and drank and then drank some more. Devo's twenty quid had gone, and I was pissed.

I left the pub around ten o'clock staggering. Perhaps I should go round to her house and say sorry and explain what had happened? Not a good idea.

It was home time. I had fucked-up, again, and I was only too aware that the sand was slipping between my fingers.

Chapter 59
Thursday 10th May 2012

I hadn't heard from Ashlee since Friday night. I knew she would be mad at me for not coming to meet her on Saturday. I was still skint which meant I was still out of phone credit. Things were cooling off rapidly, and I couldn't let that happen. I decided to take the bull by the horns and went to her place of work.

As I walked in I looked over to see her snipping away at some old dears pink hair. I explained to the camp looking fella on the front desk that I needed a word with her. When she walked over to me, it has to be said she looked none too pleased.

"What are you doing here?" she asked, decidedly irritated.

"I need to see you. Look, I can explain what happened on Saturday, it wasn't my fault."

"It never is, Bo."

"Please, Ashlee, can I meet you after work so we can talk?"

She paused. "Okay, meet me in Manhattans bar at six."

I left knowing she was mad at me but as she was prepared to meet up then I was still in the game. I had a slight issue in that I had no money so I wouldn't be able to buy her a drink. Fucking hell, I don't half make things difficult for myself.

I killed a bit of time by just dossing around the local shops. As I didn't have any dosh, I decided that rather than embarrass myself and sit in the bar with no drink, I would wait outside.

She arrived just after six and saw me waiting for her.

"Don't tell me; you haven't got any money?" she asked.

"Sorry," I replied feeling awkward and embarrassed.

"I'll buy you a drink," she said plainly irritated, again.

We sat down, and I decided to play the apologetic hand.

"Ashlee, I'm so sorry about Saturday, Devo treated me to a ticket to the West Ham game and I -"

"I'm pregnant."

"What?!"

"I found out on Sunday."

"How far gone?"

"A couple of months or so."

I was gobsmacked. "Fucking hell!" I said.

"Quite."

"How do you feel?" I asked.

"I've always wanted kids, but I'm not sure this is what I had in mind."

I put my hand on hers. "Look, babe, I know you've been pissed at me for the last few days, but you know I love the bones of you."

"You and me, parents – how does that make you feel?"

I knew a trick question when I heard one and now was the time to be positive, to show I was committed because I knew this was what she wanted to hear.

"Good. It makes me feel good. We can make this work, babes. Come on; you know we can."

"But look at you, Bo. You've turned twenty, and you haven't got two ha'pennies to rub together. What are we going to do, apply for a council flat in a high-rise and bring our kid up on an estate? That's not going to happen."

"I told you, I'm going to pull my shit together. Now I'm more determined than ever."

"I want to believe you, Bo. So, why don't I?"

"You need to trust me on this, babes; I'll be there for you. Fucking hell, I'm going to be a dad!"

I detected a faint smile from her.

"I know, and I'm going to be a mum," and with that followed the tears. I hugged her and stroked her hair.

"It's going to be alright babes; everything is going to work out."

We got up to leave, "Bo, you can't tell anyone."

"Can't I?" I asked, a little miffed.

"No, not until I've had the 12-week scan. Then we can let everyone know. You have to promise me that you'll keep it a secret."

"I promise."

"I mean it, Bo, no one. If you start spouting off about this, I'll never forgive you."

"Fucking hell, alright, message received loud and clear. Mum's the word, literally."

When we were out on the street, I grabbed her.

"Come here, will you."

I pulled her towards me and kissed her. There was warmth between us. We shared something special. She was my girl, and I was determined to look after her. As I walked towards our housing block, I looked up at it. Was this where we were destined to live, the three of us, which would probably become four, five, even six? Was Ashlee right? Would my kid just become a younger version of me like I was becoming a younger version of my dad?

I needed to believe in myself; it was time to stop acting like a boy and to become a man. My time had now come.

Has it though, has it really? Me a Dad! I can barely look after myself. I couldn't iron a shirt, cook a meal, drive, I knew fuck all about fuck all, and now I was going to be a dad. I had to admit it, I wasn't ready, and yet again, I was scared.

Chapter 60
Monday 5th July 2012

Eight weeks had passed and I'd like to say that I had changed; I would like to say that I had got a job and I was saving hard for our family; that I was starting to act like a man, rather than a boy, but this would be a lie. I was, as ever, jobless, skint and going nowhere. I talked a good game, but I had no intention of putting any of my lame ideas into action.

Our relationship had turned fractious. I knew I would lose her; she was slipping away from me, and I felt powerless to do anything. She had already told me that unless I had found a job before the birth, then she would bring the child up at her parents' home. I was a boy waiting for a miracle to happen. I was stuck in the middle of a maze, and I hadn't got a fucking clue how to get out of it. Looking back I needed a guide; I needed someone to help me.

I was ill-prepared for all this adult shit. I liked playing Xbox games and watching Youtube videos. What did I know about getting a job, changing nappies and paying fucking bills?

Today was the day of the scan. I had arranged to walk around to her house then we were going to head off to the hospital for the 9am appointment. I had set my alarm for 7am, which was unheard of. I had to show Ashlee that I was committed to this.

I had been true to my word and had told no-one about the pregnancy, not even Devo. In truth, I was too scared anyway. It was a problem that I couldn't get my head around, and in reality, I was probably in denial about.

I had been awake at 3am playing Xbox and was worried about sleeping through my alarm.

I need not have been.

I was awoken by the noise of the front door crashing in; then there were the screaming sounds from the SWAT team rampaging into our flat. The door of my bedroom was then flung open, and three of them charged in instructing me to put my hands on my head. They were armed and very excited. I knew straight away who they were after, and he was asleep in the next bedroom.

Devo was placed in handcuffs, and the three of us were asked to wait in the lounge while they searched the flat. He looked worried; I knew they would find something. I looked at him, and he shook his head and mouthed the words, 'That fucking slag.' Someone had grassed him up.

Within ten minutes a very satisfied looking detective walked into the lounge with a bag of gold watches in his hands.

"Well, well, well, what have we got here then? Were you thinking of opening your own jewellers, Devonshire?"

"Go fuck yourself," Devo said. He wasn't going to take it lightly. "And tell that fucking grass that he's got it coming to him."

"Please don't talk like that about him. Since we found a load of stolen gear in the back of his van, he's proving to be a most useful police asset. Now take these two down the nick."

"It's got nothing to do with Boleyn; you don't need to get him involved," said Devo.

"Then he's got nothing to worry about."

Oh bollocks, I was heading off to the police station where I would spend hours trying to clear my name. I turned to the detective and knew that I was going to need to beg.

"Look, bro, you heard him, whatever he was involved in had nothing to do with me. Is there any chance we can do this another time, I urgently need to be somewhere?"

"I can't help you, mate," he replied.

"I'll come straight down to the station afterwards, please? I'm begging you."

"Take him away."

Chapter 61
Same Day

I was waiting for her in the bar when she walked in looking pale. There was something the matter; maybe something was up with the baby?

"You alright, babes, you don't look very well," I said.

"I'm okay," she replied, unconvincingly.

"Listen, you won't believe what happened this morning; we got raided by the Old Bill -"

"I'm getting rid of it, Bo."

"What are you on about?"

"The baby, I have decided to get rid of it."

"But, you can't."

"I can, and I am. I've booked myself in for a termination."

"Look, Ashlee, it was out of my hands today, the Old Bill came around and nicked Dev, they took me to the station as well."

"I can't even bear to look at you anymore."

"I haven't done anything though, babe, they let me go."

"You haven't done anything. You're right about that."

"This is our baby; you can't just do this without us talking about it."

"It's my baby, not yours. You were just the donor. I've made my mind up."

"Can't we at least talk about it?"

"There's nothing to talk about. Look at yourself; you're a waste of space. I don't know what I ever saw in you!"

"Why are you being so horrible to me?"

"The thought that you might always be in my life and be the father of my child. No, no way. It's just not going to happen."

"You can't do this."

"It's over, Bo, you, me, whatever is inside me, everything. It finishes now. There's no reason for us to see one another again."

"Fuck you then, Ashlee - fuck you! You go and kill our fucking baby then. Good for you. Go on, murder it."

"Listen to you. You've had two things to do while I was pregnant; one was to get a job the other was to come with me to the scan. And guess what? You've failed on both."

"I told you why."

"It's just bullshit excuses. Aren't you embarrassed? Don't you look at yourself in the mirror and see that you are a schoolboy failing to grow into a man?"

"No, I look in the mirror and wonder whether I could do better than you," I said vindictively, but not meaning a word of it.

"I don't have the energy for this, or for you. Look, I'm sorry it's turned out like this. Please don't contact me again. I've been out at lunchtime and bought a new mobile phone with a new number. You won't be able to text me."

"For fuck sake, why don't you move to another country while you're at it?"

"Goodbye, Bo."

She got up and left. I sat there in total shock, but as the dust quickly settled I had to admit that I was feeling relieved, I had swerved a bullet. I would have been a terrible parent. I would have been no better than that poor excuse of a human being who left me when I was an infant.

I was irresponsible. It would have been a child raising a child. From a paternal point of view, it would have been a disaster. No, it was for the best. It was a sad admission, but a truthful one.

I was becoming fabulously honest at admitting my old failings. It somehow gave me a 'Get out of Jail free' card for assuming no responsibility, and once you got used to flashing the card a few times, you didn't seem to mind anymore. There was no more loss of pride; it was a passport to continue being pathetic.

And that, make no mistake about it, was what I was.

Chapter 62
Sunday 1st March 2015

I opened my eyes and saw Kumasi seated a few feet away from my bed. He noticed that I was awake and brought to my mouth a beaker with a straw in it.

"Drink a little." he said.

It was sweet and cold and tasted good. He took it from me. I tried to talk although initially, no words would come out. My throat was dry, and I was very weak.

Eventually, I managed, "Thank you." My voice was very faint.

"Try not to talk."

"Am I going to make it?"

"Just."

I put my hand out. I needed to feel human contact. He waited a short time before taking my hand in his large grip.

"What's your name, Kumasi - I mean your full name?"

Kumasi smiled, "There are people who would pay good money for that information."

"It can be our secret," I whispered.

"You've already told me your secret, so I guess I owe one in return."

"Have I?"

"You were talking in your sleep. I'm sorry about what happened between you and Ashlee."

I smiled. "Where did I get to?"

"She had finished with you and had told you that she wasn't going to keep the baby."

"Yes, the baby," I said, drowsily.

"It must have been difficult for you."

"That's not the end of the story."

"No?"

"Give me your full name, and I'll give you the ending."

Kumasi squeezed my hand and then stared at me for several seconds. His eyes were piercing mine with an intensity I had never before seen. It felt like his soul was somehow entering mine. He was almost struggling to get his next word out.

"Isaiah."

He let go of my hand and breathed heavily like he had been on some strange journey.

"My name is Isaiah. Kumasi is just where I come from."

"Isaiah, that's an unusual name. Give me some more of that juice, and I'll tell you the rest of the story. I will warn you, as with everything in my life; it doesn't have a happy ending."

Kumasi moved the beaker to my mouth, and I drank some more. It was an unusual concoction; this time I tasted a little bitterness.

"What is it?"

"A nectar, something I made myself from several ingredients. Something that will help you regain your strength."

"I think it might be working." I smiled at him. "I'm sorry, bro."

"For what?"

"For putting you through this. You shouldn't have to be here looking after me."

"I was where you are once, you know?"

"Yeah?"

"Yes, I came close to dying twice. The first time was when I had been peppered by six bullets, the other time when I decided to start smoking crack."

"And you pulled through; look at you."

"I stopped being a dick and realised that life was worth something."

"I wish I was you, Kumasi."

"Trust me; you have my spirit in you, you've just got to find it."

"Jermain," I said.

"Who?"

"Jermain."

"Who is Jermain."

"She kept a big secret from me."

Chapter 63

Friday 6th December 2013

I was on a bus heading down to the Jobcentre for my weekly signing on trip. I had been to visit Devo in prison the day before, and our meetings were starting to affect me. I was getting home and feeling more and more detached. Any support network I may have enjoyed had all but disintegrated. Mum was now living in her own world, showing zero interest about us, and I was feeling more and more depressed with all aspects of my life.

No money, no prospects, a brother in prison, an alcoholic mum and now here I was on my way to the Jobcentre to get a load of hassle about not doing a proper job search for the sake of just over fifty quid a week.

I was sitting on the bus contemplating how this fucking bullshit conversation at the Jobcentre would play out and then boom! I spotted Ashlee from the bus window. I hadn't seen her since she had dumped me and told me that she was going to have an abortion. Only here she was walking down the street pushing a pram.

Fucking hell, was that my baby?! The bus was travelling in heavy traffic, so she kept catching it up. I was getting strange looks from people on the bus as I was out of my seat and walking up and down the lower deck to get my best vantage point of the pram. I did the maths on when she told me she was pregnant, the approximate date of 12-week scan and yes it seemed to match with the baby being in a pram.

After she broke up with me in the bar that night I just assumed that she would make good on her word and have the abortion. I had never considered that she wouldn't. I mean, given how adamant she was, why would I?

But why did she change her mind? Maybe the baby wasn't hers? No, it had to be. She would have been at work otherwise. Maybe the baby wasn't mine? Maybe she was seeing someone else, and that was why she finished with me? That didn't make sense either. If she had been, she would have never told me about the pregnancy and dumped me. I needed to somehow get confirmation without having to confront her.

Her place of work! That's it. I would play dumb, go in and ask for an appointment with her and see if they would tell me anything. I got off at the next bus stop and ran around to the hairdressers. I was pretty sure they wouldn't recognise me as her ex.

I walked in all matter of fact and approached the front desk. Some young girl appeared from the back and gave me that familiar, slightly forced greeting; "You alright there?"

"Yes, sorry, I used to come in here and have my haircut by someone called Ashlee."

"She's on maternity leave at the moment I'm afraid. Can I book you in with another stylist?"

"I remember now, she was pregnant, wasn't she?"

"Yes, she won't be back for a couple of months I'm afraid."

"Okay. I might get her a card for when she comes back. Oh, by the way, do you know what she had?"

"Yes, she had a little boy."

Chapter 64
Sunday 1st March 2015

"She had given birth to a nine-pound baby boy, my boy, my son, Jermain."
I noticed that Kumasi looked perturbed.
"Jermain - did you go around and see him?"
"I would like to tell you I did. I would like to tell you that I held him in my arms, gave him a kiss for the first time, even bonded with him. But you know me better than that, don't you? That's why a fuck-up merchant like me ends up in a mess like this."
"Did you contact Ashlee?"
"She wanted me out of her life, bro. The abortion, fucking hell, it was just her way of ending it and making sure I never had cause to go back to her. That's what happens when someone has poison in their lives; they have to get rid of it."
"How did you feel about being a father?"
"I just went into denial, again. I never told Devo, never told Mum, never told anyone. In fact, you're the first person I have ever told. I just hid my head under the pillow and pretended that it had never happened. After a while, I stopped even thinking about him. I knew he was safe and despite what she did to me, I knew that Ashlee would be a great mum."
"Don't you think your son might need a father one day?"
"What, someone like me? Look at the state of me, bro? I'm a fucked-up smack addict. If I went outside right now, the slightest breeze would knock me off my feet. No, he doesn't need someone like me in his life."
"You've been to the edge of hell, you've stared down the abyss, and maybe you're underselling what you can do for that boy? Maybe all this means something - maybe it shouldn't be in vain? You can teach the boy a lesson, tell him what you've been through, help him, guide him, take an interest in the positive things he does."
"I can't, bro. I'm a fucking kid. I think as a kid; I act like a kid, I always have been. By the age of twelve, he'll be telling me what to do; he'll be embarrassed by me."
"Why, were you embarrassed by your dad?"
"I don't remember him?"
"What nothing at all?"
I then recalled my memory of him picking me up, cradling me in his arms as Kumasi had done.
"Well, maybe, one thing."
"Tell me about it?"
"He held me once, held me in his arms. "
Kumasi edged himself a little closer to me. "Tell me what it meant to you?"
"Everything, it meant everything."
"So he held you on just one occasion, and it meant everything?"
"Everything," I replied.

"And yet, you choose to turn your back on your son."
"It'll be for the best."
"Why?"
"It just will."
"Convince me."
"It just will be."
"Convince me."
"I'm better off out of his life."
"Convince me."
I shook my head. "I can't go there, bro."
"Go where?"
"I can't."
"Can't what?"
"You know."
"Tell me."
"Don't, Kumasi, please don't."
His big eyes were fixed on me. "I want you to tell me."
"I'm scared."
"I know you are, but it's okay."
"It's not okay," I said
"It is okay. It's time to let it go." he held my hand again.
I was beginning to cry, "It's so fucking difficult, you know?"
"But so easy to say it. It's time to face it." he squeezed my hand. "Now is the time."
"I was so scared of letting him down."
"Because you were let down?" he asked.
I looked at him with tears in my eyes and nodded. "I couldn't do it to the little lad."
"It's okay."
"Do you think he'll understand?"
"I don't know."
"When he grows up, what do you think he will think of me?"
"What do you think of your dad for not being there?"
"I needed him, Kumasi, I needed him to be there for me."
"Then you have your answer."
"I wish I could go back."
"To when?"
"To the first time, I met Ashlee. To know what I had, to appreciate the value of it and to understand what I needed to do to keep her. Then I would be at her side now, the three of us. Me working, providing for my family, giving Jermain what he needs; to be there when he cries."
"Then you're a wiser man now, and that cannot be a bad thing."
"If I pull through this I'm going to change; I'm going to get my shit together."

"Why?"

"Why? Because I need to!"

"For whom? Are you intending on going home and trying to make up with Ashlee?"

"That boat's sailed, bro. Anyway, if I step foot back in London, then I'm a dead man."

"For whom then?"

"Elesha. She's my beacon; she's my hope. I need to prove to her that I won't let her down. I've let one angel slip through my fingers; I won't let another one go." Kumasi edged even closer to the edge of the chair, "You already have," he whispered.

"What are you talking about?" I asked.

"Elesha died last night."

Chapter 65
Thursday 5th March 2015

I woke up with the withdrawal effects kicking in. I was shaking and sweating and feeling nauseous. I looked at Isaiah as his big hands reached out and pinned my shoulders to the bed.

"It'll be okay," he said comfortingly.

"Let me go."

"I can't."

"There's no point. You should have left me out in the field. Why didn't you?"

"Because there was still life and I'm a believer."

"She told me it would happen?"

"Who?"

"Elesha, she warned me, and I did nothing."

"I've been exactly where you've been my friend. You must search for the flickering of stars in the dark sky."

"How am I ever going to escape this?"

"Well, at least you are asking yourself the right questions."

"But what's the answer?"

"You honestly think there is one reference point for this, do you? One solution, one set of answers that can be applied to the whole population."

"Isn't there?"

I could feel the sweat now rolling down my brow. Isaiah wiped it with a cloth.

"You aren't suggesting that everyone is the same? Maybe if we were, then yes, but alas, the good Lord made seven billion very different and extremely complicated souls each with their own DNA on how to make a mess of this fabulous gift that we know to be life. It's just that some have learnt to control it, some have learnt not to be bothered by it, and some are ignorant of it. Then there are people like you and I. We are seekers. We know something is not right, and we seek to change it. But if we are not careful, we are blind as we approach this strange wilderness, and we don't see what actions we need to take. Sometimes we are lucky enough to have our eyes open, and we know what the actions are only we don't undertake them because we are weak. But this much I have learnt; everyone has their own peculiar wilderness, you will have yours, and it'll be unique to you, you have to understand it, and you have to identify it, and when you have, you then have to venture into it alone."

"Am I in my wilderness now?"

"No. You are at its entrance. It's now your decision as to whether you go in. I think your eyes are open, but I'm not sure whether you are strong enough."

"I know I'm not strong enough."

"Not now, but you can be. You need to get better. You need to believe that you can go in, you have to give yourself your best possible chance."

"Have you come out of your wilderness?"

"No, but a dim ray of light from a star shines a little more on me each day."

"I need help," I said.

"You need strength."

Isaiah then got up and walked over to his bag. He poured a little liquid into a small cup; precisely measuring it out. He returned to my bedside and gave it to me to drink.

"This will help you with the fever you'll get. It will allow you to think about your wilderness and whether you dare to face it."

I drank the liquid, and within a few minutes, I felt relaxed and calmer.

Chapter 66
Tuesday 17th March 2015

I had been convalescing for over a fortnight. Isaiah, to my knowledge, had never left my bedside. Every time I woke I saw his face, every moment that passed I felt a little better. Every day was punctuated with a cocktail of tablets, juices, a little food and just a drop of the magic liquid that would help to keep away the horror of withdrawal.

My conversations with Isaiah would last for hours a day. We would talk about anything and everything. I learnt about his life in Ghana, as he learnt about mine in London. We both opened up. We would laugh and joke, try to make sense of the past and what we have learned from it, I even told him my real name. And yet all the time we talked he never directly told me to do anything. He only ever offered gentle guidance, telling me how he resolved issues in his life. He would provide me options or a viewpoint, but without ever being overbearing. When our conversations ceased, I would reflect on them, trying to gain some order to them so that I would be able to apply what he had told me to my life. Those hours, those days we spent together would stay with me forever, indelibly etched into my memory.

I felt blessed for the time we spent together.

"How long will you stay here for?" I asked

"Until you get better."

"Then what?"

"Who knows?"

"It's your choice though isn't it; don't you plan where you go?"

"I will somehow find my way to a place. I no longer plan; I go with my instinct."

"What do you do for money?"

"That's not a problem; I used to be a gangster, remember!"

"I don't know how I can thank you for getting me through this."

"I do."

"What's that?"

"Don't put yourself through it again," he replied with a smile.

"Okay, I'll do that." I smiled back at him. "Will you ever return to Ghana?"

"No. The only people I know there are not nice."

"Family?"

"No."

"Are you lonely?"

"I'm too busy to be lonely."

"Too busy doing what?"

"Fighting my demons, they follow me around all day, as they will follow you. Just be ready for them when they call."

"Do you believe in all that spiritual shit?"

"What shit?"

"Fucking demons and angels?"

"Not like in the movies, but everyone has their own demons and angels. They are very real my friend. They circle us all day; they especially like to latch onto people where they can sense weakness. They will suck the blood out of you if you let them. Drugs, alcohol, obesity, gambling, laziness. Anyone with a weakness will get offered these things safe in the knowledge that they will take them and then spend the rest of their lives fighting to resist them. It is all the work of demons infiltrating weak people."

"What do you do when the demons come along?"

"You can only control them. And that is why every day is a challenge."

"To beat your demons?"

"Absolutely, and if I don't consciously fight them, then they will gravitate towards you like a pack of wolves hunting down the weakest deer."

"Isaiah, I think I might be ready for a walk around, I want to feel the daylight, to get some fresh air. Will you come with me?"

"I've been waiting for you to ask. I've been waiting for this day to come."

Chapter 67
Friday 20th March 2015

I was woken by Isaiah's bleeping alarm. I hadn't heard it for weeks. Had he switched it off during my recovery? It carried on bleeping, and for once he hadn't turned it off. I instinctively knew something was amiss. I jumped out of bed and checked the top bunk; it was empty

He had gone, departed, all of his things, every trace of him had disappeared, as if he had never been here. The sheets on his bed had been immaculately folded. All ready for the next guest. The only thing that remained was his alarm clock; one piece of solitary evidence of his stay with me.

I sat on the edge of my bed and an emptiness entered my stomach.

I knew that would be the end of our time together. I knew I would never see him again.

He had vanished - but why? No explanation, only the merest of hints and no goodbye. I hadn't even heard him packing up in the night.
Where had he gone?

I sat on the bed seeking answers to many mysterious questions. Had he left me? What lay ahead for me now and could I manage without him? Straight away my selfishness kicked in. I grinned, as I knew he would if he could read my thoughts. He knew me better than anyone; he could second guess my next thought, my next movement and my next emotion, just as Billy had done.

I pondered a little longer before I realised that I needed to get a grip on the situation and take control.

I got down on the floor and began to undertake slow press-ups, not many of them, but it was a start. The same with sit-ups and the other exercises I had seen him perform. I needed to feel his spirit, and I needed to feel a connection with him.
I then sat on the floor and closed my eyes. I said sorry to Devo for what I had dragged him into, I apologised to Ashlee for being a poor excuse of a man, and most importantly I asked forgiveness to my son for not being there for him; for letting him down.

I was about to stand up before I realised I had forgotten something. I closed my eyes again and said thanks to Isaiah. For what he had done, for what he had taught me, for looking after me and for mending my broken soul.
I then went for a shower and when I returned I organised my belongings in the room so that they were tidy, immaculate even, and as I performed each task I did so slowly, mindfully and methodically.

I picked up the trousers that I was wearing when Isaiah had brought me back here after I had collapsed in the yard, when he had carried me like a lost child. They were heavily soiled, ripped and ragged. I threw them in the bin pushing them down as far as I could, suffocating their relationship to this chapter of my existence, an existence that had brought out the very worst of my weaknesses.

Don't forget the key to the safe! Shit, the key was in these trousers. Panicking I retrieved them from the bin and feverishly went through each pocket, pulling out the lining which such force that I ripped the stitching.

It had gone; someone had stolen it from me. Billy, who else?

That vermin had nicked it and had no doubt cleared the money out of the safe. What was I going to do? I couldn't bear to face him or to have to talk to him, let alone confront him and even then he would deny any wrongdoing because he was a lying, stealing bastard.

I decided to let it go; I didn't need any money. I would stay here now and make a simple life for myself, working hard on the farm and resting in the evenings. No drugs, no booze, no temptations, no torment, no fear, just a clean and simple life.

I sat in the dining room eating breakfast alone. I ate only fruit and a piece of wholemeal bread. I drank water with a slice of lemon. I enjoyed the calm silence. I watched others but without attracting attention. In all, I must have sat for an hour, lost in my thoughts, contemplating my uncertain future.

I took a sharp intake of breath and exhaled very slowly. It was over now. I felt clean and energised. My mind felt cleansed. I would pour only positivity into it now. I had come so close to death, and I knew that the strain that I had put on my body would no doubt have taken years off my later life, but I could face the future now, not deny it.

Isaiah was right; I was a wiser man because of what had happened. In fact, for the first time, I felt like a man, not a child. I felt a certain maturity to how I observed the world, how I viewed the people who lived in it and most importantly how I saw my existence.

I knew I didn't have all the answers, but at least I was prepared, finally, to listen to the questions.

I ventured out into the warm fields and worked for as long as I could. After a couple of hours, I had to stop. It was no big drama, my weak body was predictably buckling under the physical pressure, but I would slowly strengthen it. I would become stronger than ever.

I slept in the afternoon under a tree, and as I woke I looked down at my arms, my scabs had all but gone. The traces of the darkness I had experienced were disappearing.

My body was miraculously healing itself. The ultimate paradoxical organism, capable of so much that was good but everything that was bad.

I walked back to the farmhouse, and as I walked through the lobby, I took an orange from the fruit bowl. I returned to my room where I slowly ate the segments while I looked out of the window.

Sometime later my door then opened and in walked a man. He would have been aged late forties, maybe fifty. He had greying hair and was a big, portly build. He sported a ruddy, friendly face.

"Hi, you must be Joe?"

"Yes," I said, a little surprised.

"Nice to meet you, I'm Warren."

"Oh, pleased to meet you." We shook hands. He had a firm grip with his well-developed, strong hands.

"Are you staying in this room?" I asked.

"Yes. Tira tells me your last room-mate has moved on and there's a bunk going spare."

"So it appears."

"Good to hear it." He put his suitcase down and sat on the chair, pouring himself a glass of water.

"Phew, it's getting hot out there."

"Where are you from?" I asked, as I couldn't place his accent.

"Sheffield, and you?"

"London."

"Have you been here long?" he asked.

"It feels like a lifetime," I said.

"Like that, is it?"

"Have you visited before?"

"I come over here every year. I'm a mechanic. I mend the farm machinery."

"Nice one."

"This is my twenty-first year, not that I'm counting or anything, but I had time to kill on the coach over here, so I worked it out."

"Happy twenty-first birthday," I said.

"Thank you."

"What's the story then?" I asked.

"The story? Well, I came over here one year, met some lovely people, learned to relax a bit, and I have returned ever since."

"What made you come over here in the first place?" I asked.

"Long story, it was a while ago now, but, let's just say it involved my best mate, a girl and a nasty argument."

"I'm on your wavelength there, bro."

"It wasn't nice. Still, I've never met anyone since and after a couple of years of coming here I decided to return every year. I love coming out, and I like the climate as well."

"Apparently, it gets hot in the summer, doesn't it?"

"Boiling, but it beats a Sheffield summer. Now, top bunk or bottom?"

"I'm on the bottom."

"Fair enough."

"Do you snore?" I asked.

"Only when I'm drunk? Do you?"

I deliberated the question, "Only when I'm unhappy," I replied.

Chapter 68

Tuesday 24th March 2015

I had explained to Warren that I had a quirky morning routine of exercise and stretching. He didn't appear to find this unusual. He was open-minded, and I quickly warmed to him. I got the feeling I could tell him anything, and he wouldn't be shocked.

So, every morning my alarm clock would go off at 5.05am, and I would carry out my routine while Warren slept. As I went through the prescribed session, I felt his spirit around me. It was like Isaiah was in the room not judging me, not even checking on my progress, but just observing.

After a few days, I realised that my morning routine was the only positive thing I had ever stuck to in my life. I had previously vowed to make significant life changes, but they had never transpired or simply never stuck. It's funny how we always seem to descend back to the place we came from. It's like we are pre-conditioned to always act in a certain way. But maybe, just maybe, I was proving that you can bring about positive change. It just needed a lot of effort. It felt like I was reversing the turn of a wheel, but it was resisting, and I had to keep pushing hard.

I had never previously contemplated my life in any detail. The deepest thought I ever had was working out who West Ham were going to play up front on a Saturday afternoon. I knew why I was re-programming my mind; it was because of Isaiah - I missed him. I longed for one of our conversations, to further explore his perspective, to listen to how he made sense of the world, to tap into how he had become almost bulletproof to life's annoyances, and how he had found light in his wilderness.

I wondered what he was doing. He had told me he was a nomad so he would be in some faraway land, a place I might have heard of, but had no idea where on the planet it was located. That's where I imagined he would be. He would arrive knowing not a soul and yet fit right in.

He would be helping someone, that much was almost a given. He will have found another lost soul; maybe they will have been forced upon him. I suspected he was a magnet for them. That's what he did, despite his apparent reluctance to want to do so. It was as if he was obligated, contracted even.

Warren was a good man. I recognised from day one his strong work ethic and his passion for mending things that were broken. I admired him for that. A piece of damaged farm machinery would be taken into Warren, and it would eventually come out working again and able to continue farming the land. From the passionate manner in which he talked about his work, this gave him an enormous sense of satisfaction. I had never mended anything before in my life. I had broken a lot of things, a hell of a lot of things, but after that, they had been discarded.

Warren was a perfect roommate in many ways although maybe a little untidy. I was starting to notice his disorder against my exacting habits. All my possessions were neatly put away, out of sight, whereas Warren would leave some of his clothes lying around. However, not for the first time, I remembered one of Isaiah's many lessons; only judge yourself, not others.

I had completed my first full day out in the fields and was feeling pretty pleased with myself. I knew that I had to take it easy in the afternoon, but I had made it through to the end. This was a real milestone on my journey to recovery.

I was getting there, getting back to where I was before the horror of what had happened in Billy's den, only this time I was in far better mental and physical shape.

When I returned to the room, Warren was there rigorously washing his hands in the sink, desperately trying to remove the deeply ingrained oil.

"Ah, just the man! Now then young, Joe, have you got any experience of mending machinery, bikes or cars or anything?"

"No. I used to like the idea of being a mechanic when I was a kid, but like everything else it never happened."

"Blimey, you've got a low opinion of yourself, haven't you?"

"With good reason, bro let me assure you."

"But at some point, you thought you wanted to be a mechanic?"

"Yes, but that was a long time ago."

"It couldn't have been that long; you're not that old!"

"You know what I mean."

"Why did you think you wanted to be a mechanic?"

"I can't remember."

"You can't remember?"

It felt like Warren was pressing me for an answer and as usual, this made me feel uncomfortable.

"I don't know; I think it was because I liked cars and wanted to do something that meant I was around them."

"You liked the idea of getting your hands dirty then?"

"Bloody hell, where's this going?" I said light-heartedly.

"We've got too much work on in the shed. The machinery is old, and it's breaking down all the time and we can't mend it quick enough before the next lot comes in."

"What and you think I could help you? Are you having a laugh!"

"I wouldn't expect you to be mending stuff on day one, but you could do a bit of fetching and carrying. That would be a start; then, after a while, I could show you some of the basics."

I then started to panic as my fear of failure was kicking in. I was groping for an excuse, something to tell him that would mean he'd leave me alone. Picking olives was boring, but I knew what I was doing. I had passed the point where I could fuck anything up. It was comfortable now, a nice straightforward, mundane job which suited me fine.

"I don't know mate; they need me out in the fields."

"They seemed to manage fine when you weren't there."

I looked at him sternly.

"Don't worry, Joe, I know all about it, Tira told me. It's okay."

"It was a bad time."

"I get it. Come on, roll me another excuse."

"I'm not sure Warren. You've been doing that shit for years. You'll pretend to be patient, but when I fuck things up, you'll want to get shot of me."

"Sorry, I didn't realise you had experience of working with machinery before?"

"I haven't."

"And yet you so graphically describe your failure, like it's happened before."

"I know it will."

"You know it will?"

"Can we drop it, please?"

"Of course we can. I know that look anyway."

"What look?"

"That look."

"What look are you talking about?"

"You've had the confidence beaten out of you, son."

"What do you mean?"

"You know what I mean. You are certain you'll fuck everything up and therefore, it's safer not to try. That'll have been the work of a parent, or was it a teacher at school? Perhaps I'm overlooking a close friend? Why don't you tell me which one?"

"I don't know what you're talking about."

"Sure you do."

"I don't."

"Someone beat the confidence out of you didn't they?"

"You're talking shit, bro."

"They made you feel small, and it got to you, got you to because you were only a kid."

"Seriously, bro, I don't know what you're talking about."

"And that feeling has never left you, has it? It follows you around every day, strangling the life out of you."

"Don't Warren, leave it."

"Who was it?"

"Don't go there, bro, I don't want to talk about it," I said sternly.

Warren moved closer to me, "Who was it?" he asked insistently.

"Why are you doing this?"

"Who was it?"

"A teacher."

"There you go."

"He fucking killed me."

"What was his name?"

"Mr Warner, the fucking wanker!"

"I know, I can see what he did to you."

I found myself getting emotional, "He thought it was funny as well."

"Of course he did. He had no idea of the impact it would have on you. That was his crime."

"I hated him for it."

"So you should. How old were you?"

"Young, just a young boy."

"And yet you carry the pain and damage around, even today."

"I want to let it go; I've always wanted to let it go."

"Then maybe it's time to."

"I'll try. I just need someone to help me."

"Then that's what I'll do. Come on, have a go, make a few mistakes and be safe in the knowledge that, provided you give me one hundred percent commitment, I will only ever support you."

I knew this was a great opportunity, but the usual demons were still holding me back.

"Can I think about it?" I asked.

"Take as long as you like."

As I turned away, I swear I saw the briefest flash of Isaiah's face. He was looking stern, like when I had annoyed him. It had startled me.

I acted without further hesitation.

"Warren, fuck it; let's give it a go!"

Chapter 69
Wednesday 25th March 2015

After breakfast, Warren and I headed off to the 'shed' as he referred to it. However, it was anything but. The 'shed' was a massive outbuilding packed full of tools and various pieces of farm machinery. There was also an old flatbed delivery lorry, which Warren reliably informed me stills runs. Warren introduced me to the other fella who worked there, Marcos, a Spaniard, aged in his thirties, who was employed full-time by the commune.

It was clear a warm friendship existed between Warren and Marcos, and I was surprised to hear Warren conversing with him fluently in Spanish, albeit with a strange south Yorkshire twang.

I felt like the new boy at school who was out of his depth, a little anxious and desperate to please. I suggested making them both a coffee to kick things off, and I was pleased when this was well received. Marcos then sorted me out with an ill-fitting, grubby set of overalls which I quite enjoyed wearing. It made me feel industrious and purposeful. For my first task, Warren had me sorting through some old parts. As I did, he would tell me what the part was and provide a short explanation of its function. He then gave me a demonstration of how to strip a tractor engine. It didn't make much sense, but I nodded along with him and appeared interested. After that, I was tidying up around the workshop.

But I couldn't hide the fact that I didn't feel that I fitted in and my quit light was flashing. I considered telling Warren that it wasn't for me and then heading back to the fields. Was this an alternative? I had to think of the long game. I had no money, and I couldn't return to London. Casa de las Almas Perdidas was my home now, and I had to make this work.

Didn't I?

It was lunchtime, and thankfully the fella with the baps called in, cheese and ham – obviously. I ate these and then went and had a walk around. The shed was close to Billy's den, and I felt myself getting dangerously drawn towards it.

I was a recovering drug addict, a tag that would now follow me around for the rest of my life. I craved the feeling of getting high, of escaping and having my mind wander to another, better place. I walked up to the back of the den then started to approach the last few yards slowly. Was he in there? The light was off, and it was pitch black. I walked up and looked through a thin gap in the wood panelling. I stared in trying to figure out through the darkness whether he was there. Suddenly his face appeared right next to mine on the other side of the panelling. I jumped back in surprise. I waited for him to say something, but nothing.

"Leave me alone," I said.

He said nothing back.

"I want my money back, can you hear me?"

Still, there was no response.

Should I go around to the entrance to see him? What would happen if I re-entered the den? This wasn't an option, and I had to forget about the money. I then heard a hissing noise like a snake coming from the den. Was this him?

I approached a little closer. It was him; I was sure of it. The sound continued, it was getting clearer, why was he making it? I knew that I had deserted him, used him even and then left, but I had to stand my ground and be strong.

"I'm not coming back to you," I said. The sound continued. "You won't break me, Billy."

I decided to leave him and knew that returning to the shed was the only thing to do. I walked away with the vile sound of his hissing reverberating in my ears.

Our meeting affected me. I had sensed my weakness edging back in. I was right in the middle of my wilderness, lonely and lost, I could feel him coming at me, but I didn't know from which direction. I knew I was weak. I knew that I would probably buckle and take the wrong turn. However, by acknowledging this, by staring at my demons straight in the eye, it had galvanised me. I had seen his face and remembered what he stood for. I sensed closure and knew the time had come to turn my back on him.

I finally connected with what discipline was about and now understood all of Isaiah's teachings.

I returned to the shed. As I walked in, I noticed that Warren turned and smiled.

Fuck me; he didn't think I was going to return.

Warren then beckoned me over.

"Come over here Joe; I'll show you how to change the brake shoes on a vehicle."

Chapter 70
Wednesday 8th April 2015

I had been working in the shed for two weeks, I wasn't exactly ready for the formula one pit stop just yet, but I was undertaking basic tractor maintenance.

The farm had three tractors, and every couple of days I would check the radiator levels, clear any shit out of the sediment bowl, and so on and so forth. I now had a routine, which meant I could be productive and every day I learnt a little more under the excellent supervision of Warren and Marcos.

I was continuing to eat well, doing my early morning exercise and spending a moment every morning closing my eyes and saying a few words to those close to me.

On Sundays, a rest day at the commune, I would kill time by coming to the shed and tidying up. I would then sit under the trees and enjoy the feeling of the sun beaming down on my face between the branches. I'd always position myself so that I could feel the heat. I'd often go and sit on the bench where Elesha and I would sit. I would run my hand over her carving of our names.

My life was simple now, but had more structure and purpose. As a consequence, I was far more content.

Occasionally, I'd see a cat that would walk around the farm. He would come and sit by me for a stroke. Some days I would look out for him, just for some company.

Some company, any company in fact, would be nice because I had become lonely. The only two people I talked to were Warren and Marcos, and this was always about work. They would mostly speak in Spanish, so more often than not I didn't know what they were talking about. Sometimes they would laugh together, and even though they didn't mean it, I would feel left out.

In the evenings, I would sit alone on our bench. I would keep looking out for her still disbelieving that such a beautiful young person could be taken so early. I spent far too much time contemplating loss. I would look up at the stars and remember what Elesha had said. I wondered whether she would still have the same opinion of me or whether she would now feel that I was shining, just a little.

Of course, the thought of surrendering to him again would enter my head. I then remembered lying in bed and Isaiah looking after me.

To return to the den would be a disgrace to him and what he did for me. It would disrespect the days he nursed me back to health and provided me with guidance.

I had finished work, eaten dinner and I was sitting on the bench looking out for the cat. I needed to see it, to give it a stroke, to have a living thing enjoy my affection. Then from out of the darkness, Billy appeared.

"This gig isn't working out for you, is it?" he said in a typically confrontational way.

"Leave me alone," I replied, defensively.

"You don't want me to though, do you? You've never wanted me to. You even told me to take your money so you could never escape."

"What?" I asked incredulously.

"That's what you said to me when you were fucked out of your head on smack."

"I didn't mean it; you should give it back to me."

"I'm using it to buy a fresh stash of gear, amigo, and you're welcome back at any point to get stuck into the fucker."

"Fuck off, will you."

"Then the money is mine, mine to do with as I wish with it." He then grabbed me by the throat, "And I'll warn you now friend, you set one foot in the den looking for it, and I'll gut you like a fucking fish. You hear me?"

"I hear you. Keep the money, but leave me the fuck alone!"

"Never! I'll always be following you around, you weak-willed fucking pussy. I spotted you on day one; I'd got you in my sights. I knew I'd have some fun with you and I have, only it won't stop here, you see. You'll be back."

"Don't be so sure about that."

"What because you've changed the oil on a fucking tractor, you think that means you've escaped me?"

"I'm not trying to escape you, you fucking leech, I'm trying to keep you under control."

"Control - now that's funny! When have you ever shown any control - when have you ever shown yourself to be anything other than a selfish little prick?"

"Let's see."

"Oh, by the way, while your African pimp was mopping your brow your bird was crying out for you as she died."

"What?"

"Didn't you hear?"

"Hear what?"

"She collapsed out in the field. Apparently, she was born with a fucked up heart. The word is she knew she was going to snuff it at some point, only when that point came you weren't around."

"I don't believe you."

"Believe what you want. It wasn't a nice death. Apparently, her heart suddenly stopped, and in the next sixty seconds, she knew that she was going to die. That's when she called out your name."

"No!"

He then laughed, "It's something else to add to your long line of fuck-ups, isn't it?"

"What have I gone and done this time?" I was distraught.

"The den door is open to you. You don't need this sort of shit on your conscience. Come and escape it. Let your uncle Billy take away all your pain."

It seemed the only option. I started to follow him as he walked back to the den.

Once again, I was unable to face my future, and I knew that by returning to the den I would be lost forever.

Chapter 71

Friday 9th October 2015

I resisted.

I knew it was the only way. I embraced the spirit of Isaiah and what he stood for. For the next six months, I worked hard and continued to learn my trade under the excellent tuition of Warren. I was eating well and regained some of the weight I had lost, but I kept off the layer of puppy fat I had when I arrived here. My body was strong now, strengthened by regular exercise, a healthy diet and the work I was doing. I felt mentally sharper as the learning I was undertaking was waking up parts of my brain that I can only assume were lying dormant.

It was all positive.

I still felt isolated and lonely, but I occupied my spare time in a variety of ways. I had even started to read; I was reading twenty pages per day as a strict target. It turned out the library here stocked some decent books. I tended to favour the ones that were made into films. I could somehow relate to them better.

Billy used to turn up now and then, but we never interacted. He would stand nearby and stare at me when I was feeling tired or getting anxious. He would ensure that he was in my eye line just in case I was prepared to show weakness.

I grew to feel sorry for him, and that made resisting him easier. I learnt to control my emotions and to ensure that no action was driven by spontaneity. I remained faithful to my values. They had become an essential part of whom I was and where I was going.

The mindfulness that I had practised when I was tidying up my room was also permeating into other areas of my life. I would methodically carry out tasks in the shed, noting every action, every touch, every sense. When I sat on our bench I would take in the scenery; the weather and the smells. When my friend, the cat, visited I would stroke it slowly, feeling its soft fur on my hands.

I had embraced a different life; I started to get an enormous sense of pride when I reflected on my journey. I knew Isaiah would have approved. He would not have been gushing, but he would have smiled. I suspected the big man would have seen something of his transition in what I had achieved.

My target was to be able to repair and service a tractor without the help of Warren and Marcos. To do the job independently, be left to get on with it, trusted to do it properly. To achieve this would mark a significant milestone in my life.

But as ever, just around the corner was a bombshell, a game changer, something that would disrupt the progress, something that would require a monumental decision from me; a decision that would decide my future.

Chapter 72
Monday 12th October 2015

I had just finished work for the day and was on my way back to my room to rest before dinner. As I walked through the lobby, Tira called me and beckoned me over to the desk.

"Something has been delivered for you," she announced.

What? I started to panic. Who knew I was here? This was sure to be bad news. She was rummaging around under the desk before producing a postcard.

"Here it is." She checked the name one more time, "It just says 'Joe', but it must be for you."

She handed me the postcard.

The design on it was a typical London tourist collage of Big Ben, the Tower of London and the rest of it. I flipped it over. It had the Queens head on the stamp.

Written on it was:

> **Joe,**
>
> **I have found your son.**
> **He needs you, urgently.**
>
> **I.K.**

Isaiah! He'd gone to London and found my son. How would he have done that? He would have had to have tracked down Ashlee, but how? Why did my son need to see me? He must be ill. 'Urgently,' he had written, fuck, something was very wrong.

I took the postcard and returned to my room. I needed time to think. I had to remain calm and work this through.

I lay on my bed trying to unravel this logically. Isaiah was evidently in London; he would then have to have actively found Ashlee. How would he do this? He didn't have a surname, and he didn't know where she lived. The East End of London is a very densely populated area; you simply couldn't go around looking for someone by the first name, not knowing what they looked like and expecting to find them.

But Isaiah was a streetwise, clever, cunning individual. An old gang leader, he had his wits about him. He was capable of anything. He had also referred to me talking and telling stories when I was scarcely conscious. I could have told him her surname, mentioned a street name, the name of the hairdressers she worked in, anything. With that sort of information, it would be easy for him.

Fucking hell, I didn't need this. I had no way of getting hold of Isaiah and finding out more. Maybe it was a joke? No, that just wasn't his style.

I had to believe this was the truth. 'Urgently' – whatever it was couldn't wait. But the fact remained that I was not in the child's life. Whatever had happened to him, I could not affect this. If the worst happened, I might never find out and what I don't know wouldn't harm me.

I also had three major problems, if I decided to act on this information, and return to London I was a wanted man, and I would be dead within days. Even if Jermain was ill, what good would a murdered father be? This would only compound an already bad situation, wouldn't it? The second problem was that the police, like the Russians, were also after me for the robbery. The final problem was that I had no money. Bar walking back to London, how the fuck was I going to get home?

Fucking hell Isaiah, why have you done this? My mind cast back to home, to Ashlee, to Mum, to Murray. They were all just a two-hour flight away, and that seemed pretty close right now. I could see them all again, one last time. I could make my peace with Ashlee and hold my boy before the Russians got me.

But that would be a suicide mission and why would I want to do that? I was making some progress here; I was getting some level of order into my life. I had come through a traumatic period of addiction that had nearly killed me. Why would I want to return to certain death?

I lay on my bed thinking this over all night. I needed the counsel of Isaiah, ironic given that it was his postcard that had instigated this predicament.

Then it dawned on me; suddenly it became apparent. I *had* received the counsel of Isaiah. He knew the danger that I would be in if I returned to London. As a former gang leader, he knew how this would play out. Having found Ashlee and Jermain, he was telling me what to do. It was important enough for me to take the risk.

I then knew that should I return to London, to see Ashlee, and that whatever the urgency was, the decision will have been vindicated. Isaiah would never have written to me otherwise.

I trusted him with my life and therefore the decision was made.

By hook or by crook, I was going to find a way to return to London.

Chapter 73
Tuesday 13th October 2015

I woke after only a few minutes of sleep. After a period of relative peacefulness, my turbulent world was again spinning at double speed. Would it ever stop?

I was still kicking the decision around my head, but whichever angle I looked at it I realised that I had to return to London. I had to see Ashlee, and I had to be united, at last, with my son where I would help him in any way I could.

Maybe I would not be welcome? Perhaps Ashlee would not let me near Jermain or even tell me about anything about any trouble he was facing. She most likely would have got wind of the robbery and perhaps the problem with the Russians. She could say everything was fine and ask me to be on my way. If this were the case, then the door would still be open to return here, and again escape the ruthless Russians before they could capture their prey.

The Russians will have known for some time now that I had escaped London, so if I returned I might have a brief window before the penny dropped and the lynch mob came after me. By then, I might be on the plane evading them, again.

But I had two big problems; firstly I hadn't got a fucking clue where I was in relation to the airport. It was miles away given the drive took between three and four hours. Secondly, I didn't have any money for the flight, the train back to the East End or anything I would need when I was there. I had the few quid that was knocking around at the bottom of my bag but the real dosh had been stolen by him.

I needed to find a solution.

Murray! That was the only way out of here. I'll have to ask Murray for the money. I'll ring the Three Bells, tell him I've got to come home, and ask him to weigh me in for the plane ticket. He can book it for me, ring the geezer in Spain and get him to pick me up and drop me off at the airport, where I can collect the ticket. It was a bit cheeky, but this was Murray, and he would understand.

If I managed to sort things out in London, I would have to rob the money to pay him off and then get back out here. Not a particularly pleasant thought given my track record of crime, but I would have to somehow get hold of some dosh.

I might even go and see if Mum had any change left out of that grand that I gave her. The thought of it made me smile. She would have spent that fucker within two weeks of me leaving. No, unfortunately, not for the first time in my life, Mum was going to be of very little help.

Okay, it was time to initiate the plan. I went downstairs and got Tira's attention. I gave her the details of the Three Bells pub and asked if she could get the telephone number, stating it was urgent. She disappeared into the back office where I heard her make a call before she returned with the number scribbled on a piece of paper.

I then gave her a couple of quid in exchange for a few euro coins and headed off to the public telephone that was in the lobby. As I did, I became nervous. Ringing

Murray was re-connecting with the East End and moreover the Russians. If word got back that I was coming home, then I would be a dead man.

The very fact that I was still alive now, with no sign of the Russians, was because Murray was the one person I could trust. This stage of the plan was plain sailing. The heat will only get ramped up when I set foot in London. I gulped at the thought of it. It would be like walking a tightrope in a hurricane. Once back in London I could get captured and killed at the drop of a hat.

I picked up the receiver and dialled the number. The call was connected, and the phone was ringing. This time of the day it would only be Murray, or maybe the cleaner who would answer.

The phone rang and rang, but there was no answer. Shit!

I sat down and waited for no more than five minutes before I called again - nothing. I repeated this six or seven more times. Where was he? It would be nine o'clock London time. He could be anywhere; down the cellar, in the shower, getting his shopping, having a shit. I needed to chill out!

I then decided to go to the shed and start work, but I was preoccupied, and within ten minutes I was back at the phone, calling again and again - still no answer.

I then decided to give it a couple of hours. It would be opening time soon. A couple of the old lads would be tapping at the door with their copies of the Racing Post in their hands, all ready for a couple of pints of bitter before betting twenty or thirty pence on a crooked greyhound race.

Just after noon London time and I returned to the phone and made the call. Again it rang.

"Hello, the Three Bells, can I help you?"

It was a ladies voice, which wasn't familiar to me.

"Oh hello, can I speak to Murray please?"

"He doesn't work here anymore, I'm afraid, can I help?"

"What?" I was hit for six.

"Did you want to speak to him or was it business relating to the pub?" she asked.

"Do you know where he is?"

"I don't, I'm sorry. Are you a friend of his?"

"It's Bo; he might have mentioned me."

"I never met him, I'm afraid, I'm sorry. Maybe if you call into the pub some of the locals here can tell you more."

I slowly put the handset down.

Chapter 74
Same Day

I returned to the shed. That was the end of that then. I was going nowhere. Warren approached me, "Alright?"

"Yeah, bro, sorry, I needed to call home. Something's kicked off."

"Is everything okay?"

"Not exactly."

"Anything you want to talk about?"

"I'd better not. Thanks anyway. Right, let me crack on, Marco, are you getting the kettle on then?"

There was no point mulling it over anymore. It had been decided; I was staying here. However, this didn't answer the question of where Murray had gone? He'd had the pub since I was born. Had he had enough and quit? He wasn't involved in the aggro with the Russians, so there was no way that he would have become involved was there? I then started to think the worst - what if the Russians had found out that he had helped me leave the country? Fuck me; he could be dead. The woman on the phone had said that he didn't work there anymore, as to what had happened to him, the answer was anything. It was more than a little odd.

As I started work one stark reality dawned on me, I would probably never see my son. I would be here forever. A fugitive stuck on a fucking olive farm. If I stayed here, I'd never earn any money, and I'd never return to London.

This was hopeless. What the fuck was I doing? I was a man without any plan. At lunchtime I sat out in the fields, the gorgeous sun beaming down on me. Warren came over and sat with me, something he'd never done before.

"What's this problem then?" he asked.

"You don't want to know."

"Try me."

I puffed my cheeks out, "Where do I start?"

"How about starting with how you arrived here - there's some trauma behind that, isn't there?"

"I did something bad. I did something very silly, and an innocent man lost his life. After then, it turned sour, and some bad people came after us. My brother got killed, and I had to escape before they killed me as well."

"Now what's happened? - Do they know you are here?"

"I fucking hope not! No, it's nothing like that. I got a bird pregnant some time ago. We fell out, and I never got to see my kid. Now I get a message that suggests he's in some sort of trouble."

"What sort of trouble?"

"That's it; I don't know."

"How old is he?"

"Nearly two."

"A two-year-old in trouble, that sounds like he could be ill or something."

"That's what I'm thinking."

"Only you can't go home to see him because you're scared those fellas will come after you."

"Believe it or not no. I can't go home because I haven't got any fucking money to get home and not only that, and you'll laugh at this, but I don't know where the fuck I am, Warren. Some geezer picked me up from the airport and dropped me here."

"What, so you've been here all this time, but you don't know where you are?" he started to laugh.

"I know, it's fucking stupid isn't it?"

"Did you not arrive with any money?"

"I had several grand, all locked away in the safe behind reception, but some fucker stole it."

"And then cleared off, I assume?"

"No, he's still here."

"What? He nicked your money, and he's still here? Then go and get it back from him."

"I can't; he reckons I let him have it when I was fucked up on smack."

"It's your money sunshine, why don't you go and get it back?"

"Because this kid's a fucking psycho, Warren. He's already told me what he's going to do to me if I try to take it."

"I know what I would do if I were you, I would find out where he's hidden the money, take it back then get on my way before he notices."

"Get on my way, where? I've told you, I don't know where I am. I'd leave through the front gate and end up wandering around the outback of fucking Spain for the rest of my life until I starved to death."

"Okay, how does this sound, I'll take you to the airport."

"What?"

"If you're serious about this, I'll take you."

"What on a fucking tractor?!" I asked.

Warren then pointed to the lorry in the shed. "It won't win any races, but it'll get you to the airport."

"I don't know Warren; this could be dodgy."

"It's your shout. If you want to do this, then I'll help. I'm afraid I can't get involved in taking your money back because that's your beef and I only have your side of the story, but if you want me to be your getaway driver, then I will be."

"Okay, bro, thanks, I appreciate that. Let me think about it."

Now the stakes had just become very high. If I were to go through with this, I would have to venture into Billy's den, find the money and take it before he caught me.

And if he did catch me I had absolutely no doubts about it, he would kill me.

Chapter 75
Same Day

I continued to work in the afternoon, but my mind was elsewhere. If I tried to take back the money and Billy found me, then he'd kill me, if I got the money and headed back to London and the Russians find out, they would also kill me. And if Ashlee doesn't want to see me it will, in any event, be a wasted trip.

If I do take back my money and wanted to return here, I wouldn't be able to because Billy would kill me as soon as I rolled up the gravel driveway. Fucking hell, Isaiah, I wish you hadn't sent that postcard!

I was doing that shaking my head thing again. I was the boy's father though so if he was in trouble, and if for whatever reason, I found out in years to come, that I could have done something to prevent it, then the pain that would ensue would surely be worse than the loss of my own life.

I realised that this wasn't about me anymore. It was about my little lad back in London, my son whom I had abandoned.

It was time to act and for the first time in my life, I needed to perform a selfless deed. It would return to London and risk my life for a little man who needed his dad.

At the end of the working day, I walked back to the room with Warren.

"Fuck it; I'm going to do it, Warren."

"When?"

"Tomorrow; mid-morning. He tends to go out then. He walks into town most days and gets his gear and bottles of water. That's when I'll go in. If I get the money and you drop me off at the airport, I'll have a chance of catching a flight home. There's bound to be one going to a UK airport somewhere."

"Are you sure about this?"

"Whichever way I think about this, the needle always ends up pointing in the same direction."

"You know you won't be able to return here, don't you?"

"Yes, I had worked that out."

He placed his hand on my shoulder. "You're making the right choice, son. I hope it works out for you."

Suddenly I felt isolated. I was facing terrible danger, and I was facing it alone. A solitary figure; very anxious and more than a little scared.

Once I had returned to the room, I started to pack my clothes. My anxiousness turned to sadness to be leaving, but then back into fear.

What if there was no money left, or what if he had stashed it somewhere else and I couldn't find it, then what do I do? This would be a terrible outcome; he could catch me and chase me out of here and then I would have to leave with no money. What then?

"Warren, I've just thought of something."

"What's that?"

"What if I go to the den to steal back my money and -."

He quickly interrupted, "What if, what if, what if! Look, you believe that your son is in danger. You have a plan to go home and help him, but as with any plan, there will be flaws in it. Sometimes we have to stick with it and make it work. That's what you will have to do now."

"That's shut me up then," I said half joking.

"Just make sure you take your passport," he said before he continued to read his book about steam engines.

I went down for dinner, and while I sat there eating I looked at the knife I was holding. Bollocks to it; this was leaving the dining room with me. I wasn't going to turn up to a knife fight with just my passport in my hand. I finished dinner then slipped it in my pocket.

I returned to my room where I finished packing away my stuff before laying on my bed.

I should have died that day out in the field, the day Isaiah came to save me. I was finished; I had nothing left. This was my second chance, and he had instructed me what to do. I was going to do this, and if it didn't work out, then I'd lost nothing because, since that day, every day had been one that I probably wasn't entitled to.

Now was the time to show some bollocks. I decided that if I had to, I was going to kill Billy. I took the knife out of my pocket. It wasn't very sharp, but it would do that bastard some severe damage if I stabbed him with it.

And if I stabbed him, I would stab him again and again. I'd finish the job. Who would miss that horrible bastard, anyway?

I lay there all night mulling this over eventually getting up to do my work out. I used the shower for the last time. Warren and I then sat and had a chat about the plan. We agreed that at 10.30am I was to go to the den, he would then drive the lorry around to the front of the building while keeping the engine running. Provided I had found the money and got out uninjured, I would meet him out at the front, and we'd set off into the distance before Billy knew what had gone on.

At least that's what the plan was.

Chapter 76
Wednesday 14th October 2015.

Warren had gone off to the shed. I hung around in the room until just after 10am. I was dry mouthed and nervous as hell because whichever way I played this one out, I was sure that this morning would end in violence between Billy and me.

I collected my things and went to leave. As I opened the door, I turned and took one last look at the room, a place of mixed memories. But somewhere that will hold a special place in my heart as it was here that I met Isaiah. I closed the door and departed. I made my way to the shed where I deposited my things into the lorry before saying goodbye to my friend, Marcos. I thanked him for all of his help and support. I was going to miss him.

I then turned to Warren and blew my cheeks out. There would be no going back now.

"Okay, bro. I'm going in to get my money."

He nodded, "I'll be at the front ready to go."

"Nice one, look, I shouldn't be any more than five minutes so if I'm not out in ten will you come and find me?"

I pictured myself seriously injured, lying on the floor, screaming for help.

He looked at his watch. "Ten minutes it is. Good luck."

As I made my way to the den, in the distance I could hear the engine of the lorry rev up.

As I approached the entrance I recognised that scraping the rickety front door along the ground would ensure that if Billy were there, he would be alerted to me entering. I slowly opened it keeping the scraping sound to the lowest level I could. If he was out of his head on drugs, I could make my way in, take back my money, assuming there was any left, and leave without him even noticing.

As I crept in my eyes adjusted to the dark. I was wildly looking left and right, and as I did, I slowly took the knife out of my pocket. I was braced to attack him if I had to.

I could see that the lamp was on, the bare loose wires continuing to hang precariously out of the plug socket. As always, it's dim, low wattage bulb barely offering more than a twinkle. As I approached, I could see that both mattresses were unoccupied.

There appeared to be no sign of him.

Perhaps, as I had predicted, he was in the village. As I very slowly advanced towards the abhorrent mattress that had been my bed for six weeks, I could see a stash of notes on it. Fuck me he's been storing my money out in the open on my old bed! I then realised that next to the cash was a bag full of drugs, coke, tablets, heroin baggies and syringes, all neatly laid out. What was going on? I walked up to the mattress and knelt down. There must have been five grand in notes on the pile.

"Take the fucker," his voice came from my left, as he appeared out of the darkness.

"What?"

"Take it. Take it all. The money, the gear, take the fucking lot."

As he walked towards me, I stood up and showed him my knife. He looked at it and laughed.

"I don't want any trouble, bro. I just want my money back." I said.

"I told you, it's yours. Take it."

"As simple as that?"

"As simple as that. Are you going back to London?"

"I have to."

"The money will come in handy then."

"What are you going to do?" I asked.

"What choice have I got?"

"You don't need to live like this. Get your shit together, go back home, see your mum."

"My fate is out of my hands," he said, grimacing. "Nothing good comes from me. It's what I am."

"Are you going to be alright?"

"I'm a loner, amigo, always have been. But I'll be fine."

"I'm sorry, bro."

"Why?" he asked.

"Because I feel like I have used you."

"Everyone does, just some more than others. You know I thought I had taken you down."

"You nearly did."

He then slowly walked up to me, I braced myself. He stopped short and stared at me.

"And yet even now, I look into the eye of a man who could return to me at any time," he whispered.

"I won't."

"Really?"

"I burnt my fingers in here. It won't happen again."

"Let's see." he said.

I picked the money up and stuffed it in my pocket. I paused, preparing myself, waiting for him to attack me. I was certain it was going to happen.

"Go on then," I said.

"Go on then what?"

"I know you're going to come for it. Do it now."

"Been there, done that. Do me a favour, will you? Take the gear as well. It'll be no fun using that stuff without you here."

"I can't. Why don't you dump it?"

He laughed. "We both know that won't happen."

I looked at him one last time, "So long, Billy."

I pulled a handful of notes out of my pocket and threw them on to his mattress.

"I'll hang on to that. If you ever come back to see me then the first bag of skag is on me," he said.

I looked and smiled at him.

I then turned and walked out the den for the last time. Yes, he could have lurched at me and plunged a knife into my back, but I knew he wouldn't. For a brief moment we shared a modicum of warmth, and I felt that we had made our peace with one another, but most importantly, I had turned my back on him for the final time.

I walked around to the front of the house where the ever-reliable Warren was waiting in the lorry, engine running. I opened the passenger door and jumped in.

"Is everything okay?" he asked.

I nodded.

As the lorry slowly drove down the driveway, my journey back to London had started.

Part III

'The Past is never where you think you left it.'
Katherine Anne Porter.

Chapter 77
Thursday 15th October 2015

The skin of Joe Devonshire was shed at Alicante airport when I was standing at immigration, and I flipped my passport opened. It was time to remember who I was and what I was now about.

Boleyn Bates arrived in London and headed to Kings Cross. I had decided to grab a bed and breakfast for the evening before making tomorrow's precarious trip back into the East End to see Ashlee.

I had to assume that as soon as the Russians got whiff of me being back, they would hunt me down. This was a certainty. However, during the flight I had made a bold decision; despite being certain that they had killed Devo, I needed to hear his fate from someone that knew for sure and to do this I was going to risk everything by making a trip to the Three Bells.

I needed closure.

I had made another decision; if Ashlee were to let me into the life of Jermain, then I would find a base somewhere outside of London and come and meet her and my boy in places where there was no danger. While there was air in my lungs, I was determined to be part of that boy's life. It was the right and only thing to do.

I also had the police to think about. Would my passport alert them to my re-entering the UK? Would I be immediately detained at passport control and then charged?

The answer was no.

I sailed through passport control with no more than a customary nod from the official and made my way to Heathrow's underground station. Within a couple of hours I lay on the bed of the less than salubrious surroundings of my forty quid a night bed and breakfast shaking my head again. Right now, my immediate future seemed as uncertain as when Isaiah had carried me from the field. I just couldn't see which way this would play out.

I acknowledged that in front of me were a series of hurdles that I needed to get over and should even one of them trip me up, then the consequences would undoubtedly be grave.

I decided to pay the landlady a further forty quid for another night's stay. I somehow didn't see me back at home tonight with Mum on the settee chit-chatting about the day's episode of Bargain Hunt.

If only.

I cautiously left the bed and breakfast utterly and understandably paranoid. I departed at just after nine thirty and envisaged arriving at Ashlee's about an hour later. I made my way to the underground with my head fuzzy with the possible outcomes that could unfold. I imagined approaching the front door and hearing my boy playing, causing chaos with his favourite toys. As I walked to the station, I stared at anyone who seemed to stare at me. I could trust no one. It was as if the world was on the look-out for me. I had to assume a hefty reward was still out on my head and anyone could have me on their radar.

As I got on the train, I smiled at the thought that I was probably going to be united with my son while also feeling a little ashamed that this was to be our first meeting.

I exited the station, and the butterflies started. Just how was this going to play out? I walked down her street towards her house and stopped shy of the small front garden. I had never met her parents; the reality was Ashlee was too embarrassed to introduce them to me as I was jobless. What a sad indictment of my existence and one I had never appreciated at the time.

There was no doubt that my trip to Spain had changed me and changed me for the better. I had finally stopped thinking like a selfish kid.

I took a big gulp; it was time to knock on the door.

Within a few seconds, I could see a figure walking down the hallway. My palms were sweating, and my mouth was dry. A lady in her late forties answered the door. I spoke before she could.

"Oh, hello, sorry to bother you, I was wondering whether Ashlee was in?"

"Ashlee? No, I'm sorry she doesn't live here anymore."

I couldn't hide my disappointment. "Oh, I was hoping to see her. Do you know where she lives?"

"Yes, I do. I'm her mum. Can I ask who you are?"

"I'm a friend of hers from a few years ago."

"I can let her know you called around if you like?"

"If you could, that would be great. Shall I give you my mobile phone number?"

"Yes, okay, come in, I'll find something to write it down with."

I stepped into the hall and waited for her to return. I took out my 'pay as you go' mobile I had purchased the other day and tried to find my number. Before she returned I realised I was going to have to give her my name and that she would then know who I was. I needed to take the bull by the horns. As she returned, I got straight to the point.

"Look, I know you will have heard about me. I'm Boleyn Bates, Ashlee's ex-boyfriend."

She just looked at me slightly surprised.

"I'm sorry about the way things turned out. I was never horrible to your daughter. I just got things badly wrong."

"She's been trying to get in touch with you."

"Has she?"

"She's heard all sorts of stories about you being in trouble. Are you in trouble?" she asked.

"I'd like to tell you that I wasn't. I'd like to tell you a lot of things that would make my situation appear to be okay, but I can't, you see. I'm tired now, and I'm through with lying. I can't do it anymore."

"Is it serious trouble?"

I suddenly became emotional, "I don't know if I'm going to make it. Look, I'm sorry I have to ask this question. I saw Ashlee some time ago walking down the street pushing a pram. Is that my baby?"

"Yes, it's yours. Ashlee has felt terrible guilt about not being truthful to you. Her dad and I have been urging her to get in touch with you. Not for her sake, but for the baby."

I could feel myself welling up now. "I've been so stupid, I'm so sorry."

A tear rolled down my face.

She put her arm around me. "It's okay. We can make this right now."

"Is there a chance for me here? I need to know where I stand."

"Of course there is, Ashlee wants to work things out. But you're going to need to sort out whatever trouble you are in otherwise, you could be back to square one."

"Yes, I know. Will you give her my number and ask her to call me please?"

"Of course I will." She then wrote it down. "She's got her own place now, just the two of them. It's nearby. I would tell you where, but I think it's best that I let her contact you."

"Yes, you're right. Thank you so much," I said humbly.

I turned, opened the front door and left.

There was nothing else to say.

As I walked from the house I could not hide a smile. Jermain was my son and it appeared that Ashlee would let me be part of his life.

All I needed to do now was to stay alive and keep out of prison.

I planned to kill a few hours then at around four o'clock I would make my pilgrimage back to the Three Bells and hide myself away somewhere outside awaiting the arrival of the one person that I knew could provide me with the answers to the questions I had.

I would await the arrival of the Brigadier.

Chapter 78
Same Day

I decided to get out of the East End and headed into central London. I purchased a baseball cap and a pair of sunglasses for when I ventured to the Three Bells later to see the Brigadier.

It felt a little strange having a mobile phone again. I had grown used to not having one. I had weaned myself off my addiction of always having it on my person 24/7. I also currently only had one telephone number in my phone; Ashlee's.

Her Mum had told me that she was trying to get into contact with me. Was that regarding the urgent matter that Isaiah referred to? Maybe something had happened to our boy, and her Mum and Dad had told her that it was only right that I should know?

I sat in a café just staring at the phone, willing her to ring. I was feeling more and more nervous, and I wondered whether this anxiousness would ever leave me while I was in London.

How would the Brigadier be with me and what would he tell me? What was a good case scenario and what was bad? Could Devo still be alive? There was little chance. Murray would have got a message to me at the commune via the driver who had dropped me off. And where was Murray? A huge jigsaw puzzle was being thrown out in front of me.

When was I going to be able to go back and see Mum? I had to assume that the Russians had the place under surveillance and it was unlikely that they had lost interest just yet. I hope they hadn't called around to see her because they wouldn't have believed her when she said she didn't know where I was. Oh no, the possibility that they had hurt her crossed my mind. Please, God no! I couldn't bear that.

The Brigadier would usually finish work and head to the Three Bells at around five o'clock; it was as regular as clockwork. That's what he did. I didn't dare walk into the place. Instead, I would hang around in the little park just opposite. If he was early and I missed him, he'd soon come wandering out at some point for a fag. I was of course assuming that he was alright. Murray would have needed to convince the Russians that I was on the job with Devo before the Brigadier was deemed safe. What if he hadn't, and they had found the Brigadier at the pub hiding? If this were the case, then the big man would be dead.

I could finish up with nothing and no one; Murray, Mum, the Brigadier, Devo - all gone and then receive no contact from Ashlee. This was the worst case scenario, but a real possibility.

The time had come; I got back on the tube and returned to the East End. As I exited the underground, I put on my baseball cap and sunglasses. I headed to the pub and as it came into view I crossed over and diverted into the little park opposite. I checked the area out for seven foot, psychopathic Russians, but thankfully it was clear. I took a seat from where I could see the entrance. I checked my phone. 16.04pm. He could arrive at any time but make no mistake about it; assuming he was still alive, he would be at the pub.

I'd been there about an hour when I caught sight of a geezer strolling down the road, paper in his hand, fag in his mouth. I checked the time 16.59pm. You little beauty! I quickly walked out of the park with the intention of heading him off at the door. I obviously didn't want him spotting me from twenty yards, and then announcing to the world that I was back in town at the top his voice.

I took off my sunglasses, and as he walked up to the door, I approached from the other side and put my arm across it preventing him from going in. He turned and looked at me.

"Hello, stranger!" I said.

"Fucking hell it's Boleyn Bates!" he replied in a hushed voice and with a surprised smile.

I then asked him the all-important question "Am I safe to go in here, or not?"

"No," he bluntly replied.

Chapter 79
Same Day

We walked quickly to a quiet backstreet pub, the Black Boy, an establishment known to be an old boys boozer.

"No one will see us in here," he said.

As I followed him in, I felt disconsolate. Given his response, the heat was obviously still on.

The Brigadier got us both a lager, and we sat in a quiet corner. Once he placed it in front of me, I took it into my hand and for a second just looked at it.

"You alright?" he asked.

"I haven't had one of these since I left here."

"I thought as much. You've lost a shit load of weight."

I took a long swig and braced myself for the next few minutes of listening to the Brigadier.

"Okay, bro, give it to me, what's gone down?"

The Brigadier shook his head. "I won't lie to you Bo; it got fucking ugly. But there is light at the end of the tunnel."

"Devo?" I asked. He shook his head. "Did they find him?"

"They'd peppered him old son, six bullets, I'm sorry."

My very worst fears had been realised. Even though I knew it was going to be the case, I wobbled and took another big swig of my lager.

"The Old Bill found his body about two days after you left. That was the start of it. It killed Murray. I mean, it hurt us all, but you know what he was like with you boys."

He sat and looked at me for a moment, "Are you okay, old son?"

"Did he get a good send-off? " I asked.

"The best; the very best. Murray laid on a great spread, and we had a proper good old-fashioned knees-up. There wasn't one member of the immediate royal family who wasn't toasted."

"He would have liked that," I said with a smile.

"There wasn't a dry eye in the pub, old son."

"What's the deal with Murray?" I asked.

"After the funeral he started to go downhill. He was drinking heavily, and acting loose; I mean really fucking loose. We were all worried about him. You'd go into the pub, and you'd never know what sort of mood he was going to be in. So, you'll know that just after you went into hiding, Murray let it out that it was you who did the robbery with Devo. Now those Russians were all over the manor looking for you; they would keep coming into the pub offering more and more money to people for any info anyone had. It was getting out of hand."

"Did they call around Mum's house?"

"They did, but don't worry she was alright. I think when they turned up she was that fucking pissed that they believed her when she said she had no idea where you were."

One bit of relief.

"Anyway, one night the Russians came in, you know that big fucking horrible cunt with the scar on his boat race with his fucking posse, and Murray, who was four-fifths pissed, and been on it all day started gobbing off to them."

"Really?"

"He was shitfaced and was telling them to fuck off and that he knew where you were and how he'd never tell them a thing. We were like, fucking hell Murray, they'll beat that information out of you, what have you gone and done!"

"Shit, what happened then?" I asked.

"Sure enough, a few nights later they went after him alright, they bundled him into the back of the car and drove him off to some old factory somewhere. By the sounds of it, they had him hanging off a chain and were kicking the shit out of him. But listen to this; it only turns out that Murray had gone to the Old Bill after Devo was found and told them he'd take them to the Russians."

"What?!"

"No shit. The Old Bill had been tracking him for days. When the Russians snatched him and took him to the factory that was it, in they went, the whole fucking SWAT team. There were bullets everywhere, apparently. It was a total fucking bloodbath. Seven Russians were killed, the others were nicked and all on remand. They've matched the DNA of two of them to Devo's murder, so they're fucked."

"Is Murray's okay?"

"He's got a few bruises, a cracked rib and a black eye at the time, but otherwise he's fine. He fucked off afterwards to his brothers up north before one of the Russians popped him. Only maybe he shouldn't have bothered."

"Why's that?"

"With that many men down the vultures started to circle. Within a week, the Albanians had moved in on their turf. The Russians couldn't do anything because they were out of manpower, so retreated to fucking Siberia, or wherever they came from."

"So, it's over?"

"Yes, Murray is due to call me at the end of the month and then hopefully he'll be returning home. I hope so because that temporary landlady is doing my fucking head in."

"Christ, I thought he was dead."

"And here's the best bit, when he went to the Old Bill with his plan to shop the Russians' he told them it was him that did the robbery with Devo. But he only agreed to get involved with the sting operation if they dropped the charges."

"You're fucking joking?!"

"No shit. I'm not sure they believed him, but with you gone, it was a good way to close the fucking case."

Murray, you fucking superhero! He had once again pulled the stops out for me.

"So why are we drinking here and not the Three Bells then?" I asked.

"There's just one loose end, old mate, just one solitary thing that continues to bother me," he said pensively.

"Go on."

"The shopkeeper that got killed in the job that you and Dev pulled; it was not only the uncle of the top Russian but also the big geezer. Now the top boy bought it in the shootout, so you don't have to worry about him, but the big fella has got a right hard on for you and wants to find you real bad."

"What happened to him during the shootout?"

"He wasn't there, for some reason. Days afterwards when the Albanians moved in and the Russians fucked off, he stayed around still trying to find out where you were. He wouldn't let it go."

I gulped, "Fucking hell! Is he still here?"

"No one has seen him for over a week. The word around the campfire is the Albanians took an objection to him hanging around their manor and gave him forty-eight hours to ship out."

"Do you reckon he's gone?"

"Honestly, yes, it's just that I don't know where and for how long or whether he will be back. I think you need to keep your eyes peeled and keep your head down, old mate, because if that geezer pops up again around here, I suspect it won't be to take you and your mum out for steak and chips."

"Okay. But he's one man on his own. Maybe he's lost interest and fucked off after he had his shirt tugged by the Albanians?"

"Yes, probably," he paused, "no, you're right."

He was holding back on something.

"Come on; there's more isn't there?"

"About a week ago Julie, the temporary landlady at The Three Bells, said she went upstairs during a shift, and he was there, bold as fucking brass, going through Murray's things."

"Looking for what?"

"Fuck knows. She shouted out, and he left. But she swears he was carrying something out with him, a book or a folder or something."

"A book?"

"I think so; I don't know. I need to speak to Murray about it when he rings. But, listen, when you left here, what happened?"

"I got a flight out to Spain, and some geezer met me at the airport and took me to this commune in the countryside."

"Did Murray sort out the lift?"

"Yes, why?"

"Murray had all his contacts from over the years in an address book; now he always kept it in a drawer. When Julie told me the story that's the only thing I could think of that the big geezer would have any use for. So I checked, and it's disappeared."

"Yes, I saw it once. It was full of business cards, scraps of papers, all sorts of shit. How would he work out what was what? He didn't know what he was looking for, did he?"

"I don't know, Bo. Murray could have even taken the book with him. Anyway, fuck him! That big cunt will be back in Russian now hanging out the back of a whore and getting tanked up on vodka. But you keep your eyes open though old son, you know what I mean?"

Chapter 80
Friday 16th October 2015

I was lying on my bed reading when my phone started ringing. Startled, I fumbled around, nearly knocking it off the bedside table.

"Hello?"

"Bo, it's Ashlee."

"Oh, hi babes, are you alright?" I felt decidedly awkward.

"Fine, but more importantly, how are you?"

"I think it's going to be okay, babe. It's not been good, but it might have sorted itself out."

"That's good news. We've been worrying about you."

"I know it's not been a good time. Anyway, can I come round to see you? I've heard from your Mum, and I know the score with the baby."

"I'm sorry about what's happened, Bo."

"I'm through with finger pointing and blaming one another. There are no hard feelings or anything. I just want to make this right."

"So do I."

"He is alright, isn't he?"

"Yes of course, why?"

"I've just had this odd feeling. Can we meet up? I can be over in an hour."

"Okay, come over to my Mum and Dad's."

I got showered and ready. Emotionally I was all over the place. I was excited to be seeing my son, sad about Devo, but glad that most of the issues relating to the robbery had been settled.

'Your son needs you urgently.' This still confused me. What did Isaiah mean? Had he met Ashlee?

Once again, I made my way over to Ashlee's parents. I was mindful that the big Russian might appear at any time, but if a seven-foot fella had not been spotted for over a week then maybe he had disappeared back to Russia, especially as the new Albanian mob had made him feel unwelcome.

I arrived at her house and rang the bell. She answered and was looking beautiful. I could not hide my smile.

"Hey babe," I noticed she was acting sheepish.

"Hi, Bo, bloody hell, you look like you've lost weight."

"Yes, I've been on a diet. Well, a kind of diet."

Fucking hell, if only she knew the truth.

"My Mum's taken him to the park so we could have a chat."

"Okay, will I get to see him?"

"Yes of course. She'll be back soon, come on let's go through to the lounge."

We walked through and sat down.

"I don't know where to start, Bo."

"Why don't we start from today?" I said.

"Would you do that, would you forgive me for telling you such a lie?"

"I've been living a lie babe. I'm not sure what that would make me if I didn't forgive you."

"If you could I would really appreciate it."

"Clean slate works for me. Today is about moving on, it's about the future, and I think you'll find me a different fella to the one you knew."

We then sat and talked. She explained that she had met someone whom she had seen for a few weeks. He too had a child. I won't deny that I was a little disappointed, but this wasn't about Ashlee and I getting back together, that would never happen, and I knew that. This was about my relationship with my boy.

I didn't go into details about what had happened to me, beyond that I had been in serious trouble. I told her about my time in Spain in terms of the last few weeks working with Warren in the garage. This wasn't the time to dig up the dirt. That was between me and my friend from Ghana. I had decided never to talk to anyone about what had happened in those dark weeks, ever again.

During our discussion, Ashlee explained that she was happy for me to see the child pretty much whenever I wanted. This was a great relief to me. I had been presented with an opportunity to make this right, and I wasn't going to blow this chance.

I made no pledges to her, no commitments and no wild predictions about the future. Isaiah had taught me to be mindful of my weaknesses and the daily battle that I would have to control them.

I gave her five hundred pounds, and I was pleased that she was both surprised and grateful. She told me exactly what she was going to buy him and this finally made me feel part of the story. As we talked, the discussion became ever friendly and relaxed. We were two people who had experienced much and maybe had changed just a little.

"I must ask you a slightly odd question," I asked.

"What's that?"

"At any time in the past week have you come into contact with a big black fella that you didn't know?"

She looked puzzled, "No, why?"

"Long story and I thought as much, don't worry!"

The door opened, and I could hear Ashlee's Mum bringing in my son. Ashlee got up and went to greet them.

Kumasi - I could now see what you were up to! I smiled. If he was here now and I put it to him that my son didn't need to see me urgently, he would say otherwise. He would argue that the boy needed his father and that was urgent enough.

And as ever, he would be right.

Ashlee walked back into the lounge holding my son.

"Look who this is, this is your daddy."

I stood up and took him from her. I held him tight, my emotions wobbling, yet again. Ashlee's Mum then walked in and stood smiling at me with my boy.

"Hello, there little fella! How are you then?"

He just started to play with the string from my hoodie.

"It was all worth it in the end when I look at him," said Ashlee.

"What do you mean?"

"When I went into labour, there were complications, and I nearly didn't make it."

"Really?"

"It wasn't nice."

"Blimey."

A pang of guilt struck me, because, even though she had decided not to tell me that she was keeping the baby, it was still mine and I should have been there.

"The weird thing, when I was in trouble during labour, I called out your name, Bo."

"I'm sorry, babe, I should have been there next to you."

"It wasn't your fault."

"Of course it was. It's all been my fault. It comes down to me."

We just sat there for a few moments in silence. Maybe this was a time to reflect on how we had both got it so badly wrong.

"Hey babe, I've got a confession to make, don't worry though, it's nothing bad."

"What's that?"

"When I knew I had a son, I needed to be able to identify with him, so I made a name up for him. I called him Jermain."

"Jermain!" she said laughing.

"He was one of my favourite West Ham players."

"Well, strangely we didn't call him Jermain!"

"No, I thought not."

"Daddy, I'd like you to meet William."

Chapter 81
Same Day

The lights on the driveway of the *Casa de las Almas Perdidas* had just been switched on as the last of the daylight started to fade quickly.

A brand new silver Mercedes drove along the gravel and slowly approached the entrance door. As the car's engine was switched off, the driver's door opened and out walked the big Russian. He casually closed the door of the car and walked to the boot of the vehicle. As he opened it he pushed the body of the driver who had picked Boleyn Bates up from the airport away from the bag that he was lying on. He unzipped the bag and took out a handgun, which he slipped into the back of his trousers, concealing it with his suit jacket. He closed the boot and slowly walked into the entrance.

As he approached the makeshift reception, he was greeted by Tira.

"Good evening, can I help you?"

"I understand that you have someone called Boleyn Bates staying here?"

"No sir, you're mistaken, we don't have a guest of that name."

"Yes, you do. Now tell me where he is?"

"I can assure you; we don't, sir. Now would you like a room for the evening?"

"He may be using a false name." He opened his wallet and pulled out a picture. "He looks like this."

"Yes, he was staying here but -"

"But he has gone now," interrupted a man who had approached the Russian from behind. The Russian turned and stared at him aggressively. "And who are you?"

"I am Boleyn's former roommate, Warren."

"Can you tell me where he is? I need to speak to him urgently."

"He had befriended a couple of bad men while he was here. They were gangsters who took him under their wing. I tried to talk him out of it, but he seemed to think they could protect him against his enemies."

"Where did they go?"

"I'm not sure, but this fella might be able to tell you though."

Isaiah then approached, "they returned to Ghana, to a city called Kumasi. You could go there to try to find him my friend but I wouldn't recommend that. I suspect in a place like that, a man like you wouldn't last long."

The Russian was disappointed. His trail was going cold. "Maybe not," he snarled.

"I think I have an address for him somewhere in my room; we agreed to stay in touch. It'll be the address of one of the gang leaders though. I can get it for you if you like?" Isaiah said with just a hint of a cheeky smile on his face.

The Russian just stood there snarling. "No, forget it," he eventually spat out.

He then turned and walked out.

"Boleyn Bates – was that Joe's real name?" Tira asked.

"He was hiding from someone and I guess we have just met who it was," replied Isaiah.

"A few months ago I got a letter addressed to Boleyn Bates. As I didn't know it was Joe I never gave it to him," said Tira.

"Have you still got it?" Isaiah asked.

"I'll have a look."

After several minutes Tira reappeared from the back office with the letter and handed it to Isaiah.

"How will you get it to him?" She asked.

Isaiah smiled, "Don't worry, whatever is in the letter I'll make sure he finds out."

Chapter 82
Thursday 15th October 2015

"Yes, I saw it once. It was full of business cards, scraps of papers, all sorts of shit. How would he work out what was what? He didn't know what he was looking for, did he?"

"I don't know, Bo. Murray could have even taken the book with him. Anyway, fuck him! That big cunt will be back in Russian now hanging out the back of a whore and getting tanked up on vodka. But you keep your eyes open though old son, you know what I mean?"

"Oh don't worry, bro, I fucking intend to. Fancy another pint?"

"It goes without saying, old son. Oh hang on, while I remember did you ever get a letter from Murray when you were in Spain?"

"No. When did he send it?"

"I sent it, airmail, the day after Murray led the police to the Russians."

"What did it say?"

"No idea, but he was insistent you got it. He had to contact his mate in Spain who drove you to get the address."

I was intrigued.

"Perhaps he was going to tell me it was safe to come home?"

"I'm not sure. He was in a funny state of mind and talking like he was going away for a long-time. Looking back I think he thought he was going to get killed that night. Actually, I'm convinced of it. The letter was like something he needed to get off his chest. When he handed it to me he practically made me promise that I'd send it. He said that it was something he should have told you years ago."

"Blimey, what do you reckon it was?"

"Fuck knows. Still, he's coming back in a few weeks so he'll no doubt tell you himself."

Chapter 83
Same Day

I sat there with my son, William, on my knee.

"Mum and I love the name, but some people pull faces when I tell them," said Ashlee.

"I love the name as well," I said, as I looked at his little face, "it's perfect."

I unzipped my jacket, "I've bought him a present."

I pulled out Devo's West Ham scarf.

"It used to be my brothers. I want this little lad to have it. He can wear it when I take him to his first game. I'd rather you keep it here, though."

I was still talking as a person who hadn't escaped danger. Maybe I hadn't yet, but I hoped so, as I now had a reason sitting on my knee in front of me to get through this. Unlike me, William was not going to be without a father. I would assume the responsibility and step-up to the mark. This little fella was going be proud of his dad.

William started to lightly pull at the threads at the end of the scarf.

"There you go; he's a West Ham fan already," I said.

"He might want to support Manchester United, "Ashlee said, teasingly.

"He had better not!"

Ashlee's Mum walked in with mugs of coffee for us.

"Come on then, Bo; tell us, what do you think of the name William?"

Ashlee jumped in, "He loves it, Mum."

"Yes, I love it," I confirmed.

"So do I, but you know, this is the East End. William somehow seems a little too regal."

"Well, I doubt 'William' will stick once he starts school, they'll soon shorten that. I mean Boleyn lasted about five minutes." I said.

"Will is becoming popular at the moment; I like that name," said Ashlee.

"Yeah, I like Will," I added.

"There you go then, Will it is. That's what we'll call him." Ashlee said.

"The problem is, it'll probably go the other way, and they'll end up calling him Bill," said Ashlee's Mum.

I looked at my son. He doesn't look like a 'Bill,' I thought. But then again, who does.

I stopped dead in my tracks.

Something was wrong.

I looked at my boy. Bill, Bill, Bill, It won't be Bill though, will it?

I froze as I had suddenly seen it all so clearly.

It had hit my like a freight train; I swallowed hard.

My mind zipped back to Isaiah talking to me in our room.

"What would you do if someone gave you an opportunity to peer into your future, would you take it?"

I went cold.

I remembered him taking his shirt off and me seeing the bullet wounds, then the Brigadier telling me about Devo. 'They'd peppered him, son; six bullets. I'm sorry.' Then I recalled counting Isaiah's wounds when he first removed his shirt in front of me; four, five, six.

I recollected seeing 'Ashlee' for the first time on her name badge at work and then 'Elesha' etched into the wood, even the letters of their names were the same. One name an anagram of the other, one the mother of my son, the other a secret messenger.

Ashlee's announcement that she would call the boy Will, and the time Elesha and I were on the bench and I was looking at her tattoos relating to the person that was causing her so much torment; 'Will I let you down'.

The future, neatly laid out in front of me.

My imagination flashed to Ashlee screaming out my name in the hospital bed, then to Elesha and me on the bench during our final conversation, 'I'll cry out for you, and you won't be there.'

The signs, the signs that had all been orchestrated by Isaiah. He was behind it all.

When Billy had sent me to the safe to get the money for the drugs, I recalled seeing Isaiah.

'Remember, Bo, not too close.' At that time he didn't know that my name was Bo. Shit, I hadn't noticed it, but why would I? People had called me that name for twenty-two years.

Then I recollected what was to be our most pivotal exchange. I recalled Isaiah sitting next to my bed.

"I stopped being a dick and realised that life was worth something."

"I wish I was you, Kumasi."

"Trust me; you have my spirit in you, you've just got to find it."

I turned to Ashlee and then to her Mum; I was in a state of shock. I had been visited by someone, and he had changed the course of my life, and more importantly the life of my son.

'A boy without a father, it's like a boat without a rudder. He's the most important person a young man needs when he's growing up. He's his guide, his mentor and his conscience. What's worse is fatherless parenting seems to get passed down to the next generation, and so it continues. The cycle needs to stop. I wish, on just one occasion, I could do that.'

"I think I know what he'll get called at school," I said. I then turned and gazed into the eyes of my son.

"It will be Billy."

Chapter 84
Same Day

He was lying on his miserable mattress with a syringe hanging out of his arm. He was as high as a kite, passed out and floating in his dreamy world.

Raindrops started to enter the den from the roof, and as they did, the loose wires, hanging out the socket, began to fizz, again.

Only this time the crackle resulted in the spark of a flame which ignited the scraps of paper that were littered on the floor, quickly leading to the mattress catching fire.

Eventually, the smoke would engulf the den starving him of oxygen. He would remain oblivious to this, and his semi-conscious state would morph into lifelessness.

By the time the smoke that billowed out of the building was spotted, and the local fire brigade arrived, he would have been incinerated.

As no one knew that anyone lived in these outbuildings, there would not be a search for bodies.

Chapter 85

Several weeks later, a heavily built black man was scooping the charred remains up with a spade and dumping them into a skip. Suddenly he stopped and took from his pocket the letter that had been addressed to Boleyn Bates.

He had never opened it.

He didn't need to.

He flung the letter into the skip where he would eventually cover it with cremated debris.

The midday sun would be pounding down on him, and he would be sweating profusely, but despite the discomfort of his working conditions, he wouldn't be able to conceal his smile, for his work was complete.

The End

Printed in Great Britain
by Amazon